SANCTUARY

SANCTUARY

A HISTORICAL NOVEL ABOUT THE HUGUENOTS,
FORGIVENESS, AND GOD'S LOVE

Book One of the
FAITH OF OUR FATHERS
Series

Molly Noble Bull

Tsaba House
Reedley, California

All scripture quotations, unless otherwise noted, are taken from the King James Version of the Bible.

Cover and text design by Bookwrights Design
Author photo by Andrea Lundgren
Senior Editor, Jodie Nazaroff

Published by
Tsaba House
2252 12th Street, Reedley, California 93654
Visit our website at: www.TsabaHouse.com

First Edition: 2007
Printed in the United States of America

Library of Congress Cataloging in Publication Data

Bull, Molly Noble.
  Sanctuary / Molly Noble Bull. — 1st ed.
     p. cm. — (The faith of our fathers series ; bk. 1)
  ISBN 978-1-933853-50-5 (pbk. : alk. paper)
  1. Huguenots—Fiction. 2. France—Fiction. I. Title.
  PS3503.U5425S36 2007
  813'.54—dc22
                                        2007024082

Faith of Our Fathers

The Huguenots were French Protestants. Most eventually became followers of John Calvin. Though they suffered severe persecution, they continued to worship God in a manner not approved by the official religion of France, and many Huguenots fled France in the sixteenth and seventeenth centuries for religious reasons. Others remained and practiced their religion in secret.

The civil and religious rights of Huguenots in France were partially restored with the Promulgation of the Edict of Toleration in November 1787. However, Sanctuary begins in 1740, and these new rights didn't apply to the characters in the novel.

The author of Sanctuary, Molly Noble Bull, found a copy of an old hymn, "Faith of Our Fathers" by Frederick W. Faber, in a yellowed music book used in public schools in America in the nineteen forties. The modern generation might be surprised to learn that hymns were openly played and sung in public school music classes when their grandparents were children. The words of the hymn told of bravery, martyrdom and faith under fire, helping to motivate Molly to write Sanctuary and two other novels on the intolerance and persecution of the church in days gone by.

Frederick W. Faber (1814-1863) wrote the words to "Faith of Our Fathers" in 1849, but the music, first called "St. Catherine," was written in England by composer Henri Frederick Hemy in

1864. Ten years later, James Walton adapted the text of "Faith of Our Fathers" to the hymn tune, St Catherine, and composed the refrain.

FAITH OF OUR FATHERS

Verse One

Faith of our fathers! Living still
In spite of dungeon fire and sword:
O how our hearts beat high with joy
When-e'er we hear that glorious word

REFRAIN

Faith of our fathers! Holy faith!
We will be true to thee till death!

Dedication

To my husband, Charlie Bull, my family—Bret, Burt, Bren, Jana, Linda, Bethanny, Dillard, Hailey, and Bryson and to my writer friends—Kathryn, Tamela, Sara, Barbara, and Jill.

But to God give the Glory.

He that dwelleth in the secret place of the Most High
shall abide under the shadow of the Almighty.

Psalms 91:1

Acknowledgements and a Note From the Author

I want to thank members of American Christian Fiction Writers, the Prophecy Loop, Loveknot and the Love Inspired loop for all their help and friendships. A special thanks goes to Kathryn King Brocato, Tamela Hancock Murray, Jill Elizabeth Nelson, Barbara Warren, Pam Schwagerl, and the entire Tsaba House staff, for all their help and tender loving care.

Sanctuary is Book One in the Faith of Our Fathers series, three historical novels about the Huguenots. Book One begins in France and ends in Luss, Scotland.

The French Huguenots were a group of people in search of Freedom of Religion and a safe place to live, and the characters in *Sanctuary* trace some of the same routes my ancestors took after they left France. One set of ancestors spent a generation or two in Scotland and finally settled in the United States.

Book Two begins in Luss, Scotland. And yes, Luss is a real place. Come dream with me as these characters play out the spiritual journey of their lives. And learn a little history along the way.

Love and Blessings,
Molly Noble Bull
www.mollynoblebull.com

Prologue

D'Hannis, Alsace
1729

Death to Jews, she read. *Death to all Huguenots!*

Eight-year-old Rachel Levin felt her ire bubbling up from deep inside. Merely glancing at the sign nailed to the side of a building up ahead disturbed her. Actually reading the words printed on it in black letters made her want to shout in protest. But Papa would be angry if she did.

The wind suddenly picked up, causing her long blue dress to gather in a tangle of wool material around her ankles. Briefly, she lifted her skirt and let it drop. Most of the wrinkles disappeared. She shifted the gray sack filled with the items she'd bought at the store from her right arm to her left.

The odor of fresh bread and cheeses mingled with the delicate scent of grapes coming from the wine fields on the hills nearby. She continued down the street as if nothing unusual had happened. Contrary to her internal thoughts, her controlled response to distress was something she'd learned almost before she could walk. It had been handed down from father to child for generations.

Her Jewish ancestors had left country after country, searching for a place to live where they would be safe. They had been taunted and persecuted. She battled her secret fear of the unknown almost daily, but like those who had gone before her, she had no intentions of giving up or letting others know the way she really felt.

Jew. Death. Was there somewhere in the world where Rachel and her parents could live in peace? If such a place existed and she ever found it, she would stay there forever.

Rachel turned the corner and saw a boy about her age. He'd taunted her several times, and now he stood in her path just ahead. She sucked in her breath.

"All beasts are the same," her father had said. "Whether animal or the human kind, never run from a beast. Never show fear or look them in the eyes. Stand your ground, always, and continue on."

Hands on his hips, the boy wore a tan cap, dark trousers and a dark shirt. Rachel could turn around and avoid a confrontation.

I will not walk away.

Beyond the boy, she could see the little white house she shared with her parents with its green shutters and window boxes crammed with flowers. If she could grow wings and fly there, she would.

"Your kind is not wanted here," the boy shouted in French.

Her heart pounded.

Learning new languages had always been easy for Rachel. Besides her native tongue, German, she'd learned a little French from her father, enough to play with her friend, Marie. And enough to understand the boy's words as well as his harsh tone of voice. But she couldn't make a proper reply in French if she'd wanted to.

Something hard lodged in her throat. Rachel swallowed. If only she could know what would happen when she reached the boy. But Papa and Mama would expect her to continue on.

She looked slightly above his head and kept moving forward.

Her breath caught. She'd almost reached him—so close she saw that dark brown strands of hair had slipped out from under his cap. His eyes reminded her of black cinders found among the ashes that remained after a wood-burning fire in the hearth had died. If she didn't turn now, she would run right into him.

She took in a deep breath of air. One more step and they would bump heads.

He stepped to one side at the last instant. Then he spat on her cheek as she walked by.

"Take a bath in that, you dirty little Jewess. It is more than your kind deserves."

The disgusting liquid rolled down her cheek—all the way to her heart. She felt the wet remains when it landed on the shoulder of her new blue dress. Her jaw firmed again, and a wave of revulsion swept over her. She wanted to turn around and spit back, yet she kept walking down the path as if nothing important had occurred.

Rachel reached the stone steps leading to the front porch in the same even gait she had started out with when she left the store. As soon as she went inside the house, she put down the sack and turned to the bowl and pitcher by the front door. She felt like crying as she washed her face, but no tears came. Her well of sorrows dried up long ago. Only bad dreams remained.

"Come up stairs, Rachel," Mama said in German, "I want to talk to you."

"I am coming, Mama." She washed her face again.

She must never tell Mama what happened on the path today. It would make her cry, and her mother had cried too much of late.

Papa made his living making and selling barrels—as well as being a scholar, a teacher, and a historian. Besides French, he'd taught her a little English and Hebrew. In return, he expected her to be strong, work hard, and help Mama in any way she could.

Rachel took the cloth from the hook by the door and patted her face dry. Still, she felt dirty, as if a layer of filth stuck to her skin. She put the cloth back on the hook and turned toward the stairs. If only she could change out of the contaminated blue dress before going in to speak to Mama. No time for that now.

How many times had she heard Mama compliment her in front of Papa?

"Rachel is a sweet and gentle child, Amos," Mama would say, "and she cheers me up when I am low. Sometimes, she makes me laugh out loud."

And Papa would say to Mama, "I am proud of our daughter, too. Rachel is a good and brave girl and always does what is expected of her."

But she was neither sweet and gentle nor good and brave. She was Rachel, a girl trying to find a safe place where she could just be.

For now, she wouldn't think about the boy or what he said or did to her. She must be strong—for Papa. Mama was ill. She must think only of Mama when she went up to see her, and she must smile. That way, Mama would never guess what happened on the road today.

One

Benoit, France
Eleven years later

"You do as you wish, Louis," Pierre Dupre said to his brother. "But after the long walk from Paris, I want to stop and rest before going home. Mama and Henri will want to hear all about our journey, and I would like to get some sleep before I start telling our little brother tales of our adventures."

"Could it be that my big brother is tired?" Louis asked with a twinkle in his eye.

"Yes." Pierre yawned. "I admit it." He stretched his tired muscles and yawned again.

Louis threw back his head and laughed. "Sleep if you want. I intend to pay Rachel's parents a visit before going home. I plan to ask their permission to marry her."

"Is it not a bit late to be making such a request? We sail in two weeks and you said you would marry Rachel aboard ship, yet you barely know her parents. They might resent the fact that you failed to step forward with your proposal sooner."

"I will ask their forgiveness for the delay, of course. And I will also encourage them to sail to England with us. I fear Rachel will refuse to go at the last minute if we leave her mother and father behind."

"Rachel is strong-willed and unpredictable," Pierre said. "And she is always jumping to conclusions. However, she is also a good and faithful daughter. Were I wearing your shoes, Louis, I would have fears as well."

15

They stood in front of the small stone cottage where Rachel and her parents lived. They hadn't slept much since heading home. On the previous night, they seldom stopped to rest. Pierre doubted that Rachel's parents would welcome his brother into their home after they discovered why he came, and he had no desire to hear her mother and father scold Louis for his tardiness.

Pierre noticed a large tree surrounded by bushes a short distance away. "I will wait for you under that tree. It will be cool and shady there."

"As you wish." Louis smiled. "And sleep well, brother. I will not be long."

Pierre watched Louis walk up to the front door of the cottage and knock. He found a grassy spot under the tree. With his brown jacket as a pillow, he stretched out and went to sleep.

Pierre awoke to the rumble of horses' hooves and men shouting. He crawled on his belly to a bushy area near the edge of the tall grass. A young captain in the king's army kicked down the door of Rachel's house. Soldiers swarmed inside.

He'd defended his younger brother for as long as he could remember and often fought his battles for him. But he saw at least thirty armed men and he with no weapons. Pierre wanted to hang his head in shame because he couldn't do anything to help.

"Please, we are innocent!" he heard Louis shout out from inside the house.

Shattered, Pierre covered his mouth with his hands to keep from calling out in anger and despair.

"No!" he heard Rachel's mother say. "Have mercy! Please!"

Tears filled the corners of his eyes as Pierre heard more shouting, screams, and then silence.

"No. No!"

"Take the trunk outside!" the captain shouted to his men.

As they dragged a trunk out the front door of the house, the captain stood on the lawn outside. Sunlight glinted on the metal buckle of his jacket. The shiny object mesmerized a shocked Pierre as the other soldiers brought out furniture, clothes, and other items.

A thin soldier came out wearing a gray dress that must have belonged to Rachel's mother. He paraded around in it, swinging his hips and making distasteful gestures. Laughter echoed all around the soldier in the dress. Pierre fought nausea.

The captain opened the trunk, spilling its contents on the ground. Letters and papers blew here and there. The captain picked up a candlestick. The metal caught the afternoon sun, sparkling brighter than the buckle. From a distance Pierre couldn't tell for sure, but thought it might have been made of gold.

The expensive-looking object would hold half a dozen candles or more. He'd never seen a design quite like it.

The captain waved the candlestick in the air for all to see. "This is a Menorah and can only belong to a Jew. It proves the people who lived in that house were Jews!"

The rest of the men gathered around the captain, looking at the candlestick. When they tried to touch it, the captain jerked it out of their reach.

"Two Huguenots from this village conspired against the government of France. We only found one. We must find the other man and the rest of the Jews and kill them." The captain raised the Menorah in the air as though it were a kind of battle flag. "I shall not rest until the deed is done! Now, gather up all the papers and anything else you think I might want later."

As the soldiers began doing as they were told, the captain leaned over and picked up something from the ground. Pierre thought it looked about the size and shape of a small wooden frame. The captain pulled a white cloth from his pocket, wiped off the object, gazed at it for a long moment and tucked it inside his jacket.

"Burn this house to the ground," the captain demanded, "as a warning to all Jews and Huguenots!"

⚜

Rachel Levin stood in the center of the elderly baker's little shop surrounded by pleasing odors—cinnamon and sweet smelling pastries. Yet, her thoughts tasted only of the excitement her future marriage to Louis Dupre would bring. Louis and his brother,

Pierre, farmed a small piece of land in Benoit, but when they sailed to England and on to Scotland, they were sure to become much more prosperous and farm even more land.

She glanced at a display of dark bread on a table nearby. She would need to hurry or she would be late for her meeting with Louis. After almost two weeks, she would see him within the hour, and she'd been counting the minutes until that moment came.

Rachel grabbed a loaf of bread, put it in her wicker basket and handed the baker two small coins. "For the bread," she said in French.

He nodded, and a smile turned up the edges of his wrinkled mouth.

Rachel pulled the drawstring, closing the leather sack. The sack of coins jingled when she dropped it in the basket with the bread. She placed the hood of her cape over her tan cap and opened the shop's entry door.

"Au revoir, Monsieur."

"Good day to you, too, Mademoiselle," the elderly gentleman replied. "Come again soon."

The baker had been kind to her. However, he knew her as Rachel Zimmer, an immigrant who spoke French with a German accent, and probably assumed she was a Christian. Would he befriend her if he knew her as Rachel Levin, a Jew?

She disliked hiding her true identity and nationality because she felt it betrayed her people. But for reasons of safety, it had been necessary.

Rachel went outside and looked up and down the street. There had been reports of trouble brewing in a village nearby. Who could say but that trouble would come to Beniot as well? A single young woman of nineteen years couldn't be too careful this day-and-age.

A slender young man with an olive complexion came out of a shop two doors down.

"Louis?"

He turned and hurried away.

"Louis!" She ran after him. "Wait!"

He never looked back.

Why hadn't he acknowledged her presence? Her heart contracted. Had his love for her died since last they met?

As she watched, he raced down the cobblestone street, and it would be impossible to catch up with him. Maybe he hadn't heard her call his name. Besides, he looked too tall to be Louis.

How strange that she hadn't noticed sooner. The young man was Pierre, Louis's older brother. But why hadn't Pierre stopped or glanced back? He appeared to be in such a hurry. Why?

An old man and woman in black clothing hobbled into the butcher shop across from where she stood. Rachel started walking in the same direction that Pierre took. The narrow street curved to the left, and she caught a glimpse of the Catholic Church on the corner. She'd worked at the church helping the nuns clean the sanctuary since she arrived in Benoit a year ago.

When a personal disaster for her father caused her family to leave Alsace, they'd hoped to hide among the Huguenots, and she'd felt fortunate to find work in France. One day on her way home from the church, she met Pierre. Later, she also met his brother, Louis.

My Louis.

Meeting him had changed her life forever, bringing true happiness into her world for the first time. However, those good feelings disappeared each time she recalled how she'd deceived Louis by not telling him about her Jewish heritage. He would break their engagement if he knew.

Louis thought she'd told her parents of their love for each other weeks ago, and he'd wanted to ask them for her hand in marriage. But she'd insisted that he wait a little longer before making his request to her parents—then a little longer—and longer.

With a heavy heart she realized that she'd deceived her parents as well. They didn't know she attended a Protestant church now, much less that she planned to marry a French Huguenot, and guilt played on her mind for not telling them everything from the beginning.

Rachel and Louis had already paid their fees to cover the cost of their passage to England and were to be married aboard ship. Yet Mama and Papa knew nothing of this and barely knew Louis.

She would tell Mama and Papa everything. Today for certain. She'd put it off long enough.

Visions of her wedding put a smile in her heart. But when she considered actually telling her parents what she'd done and what she planned to do, a thick coil of worry choked her like a hangman's rope, squeezing out her last bit of joy.

Her parents might never speak to her again after they learned that she'd been attending a Christian church. But it was a chance she would have to take.

A line of brown fieldstone houses with red tile roofs lined both sides of the road. They looked like her house, as did most of the other structures in Benoit. Yet, according to her intended, Louis Dupre, some of the ordinary looking buildings held mysteries—tunnels and hidden rooms.

Gray smoke spiraled upward in the distance. Madame La Tou lived next door to her family's home, and the woman burned trash almost every day. Maybe she...

Rachel scrutinized the flames. The blaze seemed larger than usual.

No. Her throat tightened. *It cannot be our house.*

Rachel thought of another fire—the one in Alsace—where she grew up. Her ancestors left Holland, settled in Germany for a while, and her parents had moved to Alsace before she was born.

In the Alsatian village of D'Hannis, she'd seen a fire much like this one. Four innocent people lost their lives that day. But surely a fire like that would never destroy her home. Rachel and her parents had already experienced enough tragedies to last a lifetime.

Madame La Tou probably set that old shed behind her house on fire. She'd been saying she would do it.

Yes, that is what must have happened.

She tried to convince her mind that her assumptions were true. Still, she worried.

Louis had been in Paris on some sort of secret mission, and he had told her to meet him at a new location. Though she wanted to see him, Rachel felt torn between her desire to spend time with Louis and the fact that she might be needed at home.

"When you come to meet me," he'd said before he left, "make sure you are not being followed."

She looked around. The streets of the village were unusually quiet for four o'clock in the afternoon. She turned left at the corner.

Rachel would be meeting Louis at what he called the Safe House. Though she had strolled by the stone building many times, she'd never been inside.

Was she being followed? She cast a glance behind her. The street looked empty. Only French Huguenots knew about the Safe House. Ahead, she saw a door.

Two-story buildings lined both sides of the shadowy street. The iron latch on the door felt cold when her hand touched it. The heavy door creaked open.

The rank odor of rotting fruit and other garbage flooded her senses. Her eyes stung. She blinked and went inside.

At first, the hallway seemed dark; haunting. As she moved along, her eyes became accustomed to her new surroundings, and everything looked lighter. She could see the door at the end of the long hallway.

Third door to the right, Louis had said. She continued on toward her destination.

Something with quick little legs raced across her right foot. She tensed, praying it wasn't a rat. In the dim light, she saw a gray mouse scamper ahead of her. It found a hole and disappeared.

Louis had said to knock on the third door. When she reached it, she stopped.

Pushing her cape back around her shoulders, Rachel pulled off her cap and unbraided the tight bun at the back of her neck. Her mother would be shocked if she knew. She put the cap back on and tied it under her chin. Still, her long hair fell in waves below her head covering, swinging around her waist—exactly as Louis liked it.

Satisfied that she looked her best, she knocked three times, waited, and knocked again.

"Who is there?" a man asked.

"A friend of Monsieur Chabor."

"What is your name?"

"Rachel Zimmer. I am on the list."

"Wait, please."

In a few moments, the door opened. A middle-aged man holding a book stood in the doorway, blocking her passage.

He had slicked-back gray hair, one squinty brown eye, and a black patch over the other. A missing tooth in front added to his frightening appearance.

"Have you paid your fee, Mademoiselle?"

"We—we paid three weeks ago."

"We? Who are we?"

"Louis Dupre. I am to be his wife."

He looked down at the book. "Louis Dupre." His eyes narrowed. "Very well, you may come in."

They were in another hallway. He pointed to a door at the end. "Go in there. And may God go with you."

She forced a smile. "Same to you, Monsieur."

This time she didn't knock before opening the door. Rachel paused to untie her cap. She pushed back a stray curl and stepped inside.

The dimly-lit room appeared to be filled with people; men and women of all ages, as well as infants and children. Some sat on wooden benches. Others squatted or rested on the rock floor. She searched for a familiar face but saw none.

A young woman sat on a bench near the door, holding a baby. She'd been looking down at the child, but when she turned and glanced toward the door, her eyes connected with Rachel's. Putting the baby on her left shoulder, she stood and patted the child's back.

"Forgive me for staring," the woman said. "But you have such beautiful auburn hair; so long, thick, and wavy. And green eyes. We seldom see women who look like you here in Beniot."

Rachel smiled. "Thank you. Your dark hair is pretty, too."

The woman nodded. "May I help you, Sister in Christ?"

"Yes. I am looking for Louis Dupre."

The woman's face paled. "Louis Dupre? I am afraid he—he is not here." She bit her lower lip, and her gaze darted away.

A shiver shot down Rachel's spine. The woman's dark eyes had taken on a sad expression, and her smile had disappeared. Had Louis been delayed? Had he been in an accident?

"As I said," the woman continued, "Monsieur Louis Dupre is not here but his older brother is. Shall I take you to Pierre Dupre?"

"Yes. Please do."

Rachel followed the young mother to the far end of the big room. Pierre sat on the floor by an old wooden door painted dark red—like old blood. He looked down at his feet as if his thoughts were far away. Maybe he hadn't noticed when she came in.

"Pierre. Good to see you."

He stood, eyes downcast. "It is good to see you, too."

"I saw you on the street near the bakery earlier," Rachel said. "But when I called out, you continued on. You should have stopped."

"Forgive me. I was leaving an important meeting and in a hurry to get here. I neither saw nor heard you."

"You are forgiven."

After gazing at her for a moment, he looked away as if he didn't want to meet her eyes.

Her pulse raced. "Where is Louis?"

Pierre hesitated.

Her heart pulled into a hard knot. Something had happened. She knew it. Why was he keeping things from her?

He glanced her way again. "Louis is—he is gone."

"Gone? Where? By now he would have returned from Paris. And he promised to meet me here. We were to talk to Pastor Picon about our marriage ceremony on the ship."

"Yes, I know."

Pierre motioned for her to come closer and grew silent. Rachel didn't have to ask. Something was wrong.

She swallowed the lump of dread rising in her throat. "What happened?" Her voice was barely above a whisper.

"Dear, sweet Rachel, our Louis has gone—to be with the Lord."

"To be with… What are you saying?"

Pierre looked away as if he didn't want to answer.

"Pierre," she exclaimed, "tell me the truth. What has happened?"

"Soldiers," he said wearily. "They were searching for two young men suspected of conspiring against the French government. I managed to get away before anyone saw me. But Louis . . ."

"They—killed my Louis. . . ." Rachel covered her eyes with both hands, but no tears came. Her chest tightened, and her heart compressed again.

After what seemed like a long time, she uncovered her eyes and looked up at him. "What is the matter with me? I cannot even cry."

Pierre embraced her. "The weeping will come soon enough."

She could scarcely breathe. Her head swam. She pushed away from Pierre and glared up at him. "You are lying," she shrieked. Rachel slammed her fists against his chest, pushing him away. "Why are you telling me this? It is untrue. You know it is."

Pierre sighed heavily and stared at the ground, his own pain evident in his face.

"Louis," she whispered as realization dawned on her. "My Louis is—is gone."

"Yes." Pierre's dark eyes told of extreme grief. "But I am here. I will always be here for you."

I care nothing for you, Pierre. A wave of bitterness engulfed her. *I want Louis.*

The fact that Louis had gone to be with God gave her no comfort. Rachel needed him here—at her side. She wanted to see his handsome face, hear his whispered words of endearment. Her eyes burned with unshed tears.

"You look pale," Pierre said. "Why not sit down for a minute?"

He spread a blanket on the floor and held his hand out to her. She stared at it for a moment because it wasn't the hand she desperately wanted. At last, she allowed him to help her sit down.

Rachel had no right to be angry with Pierre. He must be hurting, too. He had lost his brother. But she couldn't muster any sympathy for him. Not today. Her own pain went too deep.

"Would you care for a cup of water?" Pierre asked.

Rachel shook her head because she couldn't speak. The wailing inside cut so deep her chest hurt. She studied her hands and noticed that they were shaking. Would this nightmare ever end?

Louis couldn't really be dead. This must be some kind of terrible mistake. She would find him—prove to Pierre and his family that Louis was alive.

Yes. That is just what I shall do.

She started to rise. Her knees felt weak. The world began to spin around and around.

As if coming from a far away place, Rachel heard the voice of the young woman with the baby. "Can I be of help?"

Everything went black.

Two

Rachel sat on the wool blanket, too grieved to speak or move. People she barely knew stood around gawking. She faced them, and they looked away, averting their eyes from her tragedy.

She pushed her long hair back off her face, remembering that she'd loosed it for her intended. Her breath caught in her throat.

Louis. My beloved, come back to me.

Rachel pulled a loose thread from the blanket and wrapped it around her forefinger. She had no memory of sitting down on the blanket or how long she'd been at the Safe House. She glanced at Pierre and saw her grief reflected in his eyes.

She wanted to go home. Her parents would comfort her now despite all her lies and half-truths. She started to get up.

"Where are you going?" Pierre asked.

"Home."

"Please stay," he said.

"I cannot. My parents are expecting me."

"You are too weak to walk home, and I cannot escort you. I must stay here in case I am needed. But someone should be with you. You suffered a great loss. "

"Yes, I did. But I am perfectly capable of walking home alone."

"I need you here, Rachel—with me."

His soothing tone of voice and compassionate nature lifted her spirits. All at once she realized how much he reminded her of Louis.

None of this was Pierre's fault. He'd been kind and gentle and had only wanted to help. She didn't know when her anger toward him disappeared, but it had. Still, she needed the comfort of her own house—longed to fling herself into her mother's arms and cry for hours.

"I appreciate all your help, Pierre. But I must go home now."

Pierre looked uncomfortable. He opened his mouth to speak but stopped when his dark haired mother and his younger brother, ten-year-old Henri, came in the main door and started toward them. Rachel tried to swallow her pain and produce a smile. She couldn't. At the least, she should offer them sympathy. But how could she do it in her grieved state?

As they came closer, Rachel could see that their eyes looked red from crying. She got up from the blanket. Stretching out her arms, she embraced Madame Dupre and felt the woman's shoulders tremble. Rachel opened her mouth to express her sympathy. No words came.

"Oh, my little Rachel," Madame Dupre said with deep emotion. "Our hearts cry out for your loss."

Henri didn't say anything, but he patted Rachel's shoulder.

Her heart swelled with love for Louis' family. Until now, she'd never shown her love for them. How could she accept their compassion when she had given them so little in return?

"Please accept my sympathy for your loss as well," Rachel finally said to Pierre's mother.

Madame Dupre hugged her again, weeping openly. To Rachel, it almost seemed that Pierre's mother and little brother considered her loss worse than theirs.

"We are going home now," Madame Dupre said to Pierre. "Will you and Rachel be leaving with us?"

"No," Pierre said. "I must talk to someone first."

"We shall see you later then." The older woman turned to Rachel and hugged her again. "And may the Lord bless you, my dear."

Rachel noticed that someone had opened the red door and that people were going through it. As she looked on, Henri and his mother exited through that door as well. Rachel sat back down on the blanket spread over the rock floor.

She kept hoping Louis would suddenly appear—prove he hadn't died. While knowing that outcome seemed unlikely, she didn't want to believe that he wouldn't return someday, and she wanted that someday to be now.

Her marriage to Louis aboard the ship, the ocean voyage to England, their plans for the future, and all their dreams were gone forever. She longed to share her grief with her mother.

Mama hardly knew Louis. Still, she would be upset when she heard of his death. Mama hadn't been well for years, but she'd always had a compassionate nature. Rachel would wait until she felt a little stronger, and she would go home.

❧

Pierre saw Pastor Picon when he came in and wanted to speak to him at once. He needed advice on the best way to comfort Rachel. This might be his only opportunity. But his pastor appeared to be engaged in a conversation with another man. When the other man walked away, Pierre got up and started toward him.

He'd almost reached the elderly gentleman when the minister made eye contact. With arms outstretched, Pastor Picon embraced Pierre warmly. They stood there in the center of the room as a father and son might, and Pierre felt his body drawing strength from the gray-haired minister's comforting arms.

"Pierre. I regretted hearing about the untimely death of your brother. I have already expressed my condolences to your mother and little brother. How is Louis' young lady doing?"

"She will recover. In time."

"Poor girl." The pastor shook his head. "Her tragic situation is almost too much to bear. I was about to go over to express my sympathy."

"Have you heard any word from the elders since I told them what happened today?"

The minister shook his head. "Like you, I am still waiting to hear."

Rene, the man who had been guarding the main door, raced into the room—obviously upset. A group of men gathered around him.

"Excuse me, Pastor." Pierre hurried over to see what news Rene might have with Pastor Picon right behind him.

"What is wrong?" Pierre asked.

"I just learned from one of the elders that soldiers are searching houses at the far end of village and could be here at any moment," Rene said. "After what happened to Louis Dupre, we must take action. Thus, there has been a change in plans. We must leave for the ship immediately."

"My mother and little brother were not told of this," Pierre explained, "and they have already left."

And I can never leave without them.

"They know by now," Rene assured him. "Your mother and little brother would have been told the news as soon as they stepped outside. Small boats are loading now."

"How can we leave on a different ship?" Pastor Picon asked. "We paid for a voyage to England in two weeks and have no money to pay again. Besides, how can we be sure there will be room for us?"

"Have you forgotten that the ship-owner is our friend?" Rene asked. "We can trust him. Besides, we are only a handful. He said he would make room for us on any ship he owns and would apply fees we already paid for passage on any of his ships. By now, he would have been told about the meeting earlier today and be making arrangements. That is all I can tell you now."

Pierre tried to swallow something hard that had lodged in his throat. *I must warn Rachel.*

He turned back toward her. But how would he convince her to leave now that Louis was gone?

Pastor Picon touched his arm. "As a result of this new information, I will not have time to speak with the young lady now. I will speak to her on the ship."

Pierre nodded. "Yes, on the ship will be satisfactory."

He motioned for Rachel to get to her feet. "It is time to go, Mademoiselle." He patted her arm. "I know how you must feel and you need to rest; unfortunately, it is not safe to stay here any longer."

❧

Rachel had watched the men gathering in the middle of the room, talking fast and looking agitated. The news must have been bad. Pierre's grim expression confirmed it. Rachel got up and took a step toward the door she entered earlier.

"Not that door—the other one. I will explain more later on." He picked up her basket with the bread and the sack of money in it and gestured toward the red door. "We will leave through there."

Rachel crossed her arms over her chest. "I refuse to go out through the red door. It is for Huguenots. I want to leave the way I came in."

Pierre shook his head. "It could be dangerous to leave the way we came."

She felt as if she was dying inside. Yet his quick smile encouraged her.

"Come on, Rachel. The red door is for all of us."

She glanced up at him.

"Trust me to do what is best," he added.

A strand of Pierre's dark, curly hair fell across his forehead. His black eyes gleamed with warmth and compassion. Some thought the brothers were twins, but Pierre was taller and two years older. He looked so much like Louis, Rachel couldn't bear to be near him. At the same time, he made her feel safe.

"All right, Pierre. I'll go with you."

"Good."

A large, oak armoire stood against the back wall of the second room beside a big canopy bed. The double doors to the armoire had been opened. People were squeezing through a secret door at the back of it.

Rachel wiped away a tear as she noticed Pierre's sad facial expression. Did he expect her to follow them?

"Quickly," he insisted, "go in, now. The time is short. I will be right behind you."

"But I—"

"Trust me and go."

First he wanted her to go through a strange-looking door. Now he wanted her to climb through some sort of secret opening. It all seemed more than odd, but rather than argue, Rachel did as he requested. Nothing mattered now that Louis had left his earthly home.

"It is very dark inside," Pierre warned. "There is a platform just ahead and steps going down. Five steps exactly. There is also a railing to your right. Hold on to the railing as you descend the stairs."

She nodded.

Rachel found herself in a dark tunnel. Some people carried candles. Pierre didn't. The cave reminded her of a tomb and smelled like dead animals. She'd heard there were secret rooms and tunnels all over this part of France and that the Huguenots did much of their traveling from house to house that way. Until now, she'd never seen such a dismal place.

"Where are you taking me?" she asked.

"To the ship."

"The ship? No!"

Her hopes of a future with Louis had been shattered. How could she sail now? Without Louis at her side, there would be no joy—no point in dreaming. And her parents; she couldn't leave them.

She stopped and turned back.

"What do you think you are doing?" Pierre asked. "You cannot stop now. You are blocking the way for those behind us."

Rachel pressed her body as close to the stone wall as she could, motioning for the others to go on by. Pierre sidled up beside her. The air seemed thin, somehow, making it difficult for her to catch a breath, and the interior of the excavation felt cold and damp. She heard no sound except the rise and fall of her own breathing.

"We cannot talk here," he whispered. "We must keep moving. The door has already been closed and locked from the inside."

"But the ship was not scheduled to leave for two weeks."

"Those plans have been changed, Mademoiselle."

Mademoiselle. Why did the rules of society dictate that she could be known as Rachel in private but must be called Mademoiselle in front of others? Somehow, it seemed dishonest.

"I will explain everything later," he added. "We have to continue on."

She wanted to protest but felt too drained to argue. "Very well."

Someone brushed her shoulder as they walked along. She flinched.

"Pardon me, Mademoiselle," she heard a woman say. "I did not mean to bump you. But it is difficult to see in here."

"All is well." Rachel pressed her arms close to her sides. "I am unhurt."

They walked in silence, but Rachel's mind raced—wondering—longing for answers. How had Louis died? She hoped his death came quickly and that he hadn't suffered.

She'd thought traveling with Louis to a new life would be thrilling. Now, she had no desire for adventure or a trip by boat. She wanted her parents and she couldn't, no, she *wouldn't* leave without them.

Perhaps she had waited too long to convince them to board the ship, but she had to try. She knew they dreamed of living in Jerusalem someday, but England had to be better than where they lived now.

Louis had relatives in Scotland, and he'd said that their final destination was the village of Luss. Her parents would be safe there. However, if they refused to leave France, she would stay with them. She would tell Pierre of her intentions as soon as they reached the end of the tunnel.

The group of Huguenots continued down the tangle of dark passages. Rachel put her hands against the rock walls for support, feeling her way through the maze. They took sharp turns, climbed inclines and waded through cold pools of shallow water.

Rachel's ancestors had left country after country, seeking a safe place to live. They had been taunted and persecuted, exactly like the Huguenots.

After she began attending church services with Louis, she had feared for her life on two counts. A Jew by birth, her connection to the Reformed Church made her appear to be a Christian, and some would call her a Huguenot, as they did Louis. *Louis.*

Moisture gathered in the edges of her eyes. To keep from crying, she tensed and bit her lower lip.

I will not weep in front of others. Not again.

Though she still didn't know how Louis died, she remembered how he lived and that he'd always said that Christians should forgive others.

Louis had been young, strong, and had never been sick a day in his life that she knew of, and yet he died. What if someone killed him? How could she forgive his murderer? How could she forgive anyone who intentionally harmed others?

Rachel planned to demand that Pierre tell her how Louis died as soon as they left this dark place. Then she would go home. She wanted to be around her own kind instead of these church people.

She hadn't minded attending church services with Louis and enjoyed the beautiful hymns they sang. However, she never intended to become a religious fanatic like some in his faith. And what of this Jesus the Huguenots talked about daily? Could he really be the Jewish Messiah as they claimed?

She shivered, trying not to think of Louis. Her shoes, stockings, and the hem of her brown dress were soaked. Her shoulders shook as she tried to focus on the candle lights flickering in the near darkness; anything to get her mind off Louis. However, she trembled almost as much from what might lie ahead as from the cold and dampness of the cave. Obviously, they were in some kind of danger.

The tunnel took another sharp turn. Sunlight reflecting off a body of water streamed through the door ahead.

Rachel released a deep sigh. The glow coming from the doorway, together with the light from the candles, made it possible for her to see where they were headed. A flash of blue water reminded her of the beach and the waiting ship.

"It is time to blow out the candles," someone said.

Darkness washed over her physically and emotionally. Rachel took another step and stumbled. Pierre grabbed her waist from behind to steady her.

"The tunnel slopes downward from here on," he said softly. "Be careful. You will be all right."

"Thank you, Pierre."

She wanted to weep, to cry out because of her loss. No time for that. Pressing one hand against the wall, she measured her steps carefully. At least, she would soon leave this dreadful place and could go on home.

Rachel paused at the doorway. A middle-aged man from Louis's church stood just outside, smiling and pointing toward the sea.

"She already knows," Pierre said.

The man stepped to one side.

"Go on, Mademoiselle," Pierre urged. "It will be all right. I assure you."

She stepped into the damp chill of late afternoon, squinting toward the water. A cold wind had whipped up since she left the bakery shop. Her skirts billowed around her ankles. She moved forward slowly like a small child walking barefoot on sharp rocks. When she glanced back, she noticed that Pierre still trailed her, holding her wicker basket.

Beneath the fading red blush of a dying sun, rowboats lined the shoreline; their noses pointing toward the seaport town of La Rochelle. Rachel stopped for a closer look. Pierre bumped into her.

"I beg your pardon." Pierre put his hands on her shoulders from behind, and she felt the soft bump of the basket against her back. "What is wrong now?" he asked.

"What do I already know? And what are the boats for?"

"The boats will take us to the ship. Remember, I told you our plans had been changed."

"Your plans, perhaps! I am not leaving."

Pierre turned her to face him. "What do you mean?"

"I refuse to go on that ship. I shall stay here with my parents—unless I can convince them to go with us."

"That is impossible. There—there is no time. Besides, I have yet to tell you everything."

"Pierre, as I mentioned before, you have been very kind." She forced calmness into her tone. "Thank you for it. But I must go home, now. My parents will be worried that I have taken so long in returning home. Au revoir." She turned and started to walk away.

"No, wait!"

"I cannot."

Rachel raced down the beach in the direction of her house. She needed time to grieve and would feel safer under her father's roof.

She sensed Pierre's presence behind her. He grabbed her arm, jerking her back, holding her.

Rachel struggled. "Let me go!"

"I cannot." Pierre put both arms around her and held her close.

She felt his breath on her neck. "Why?" She twisted around, glaring at him. "What reason could you possibly have for not letting me go home?"

"The soldiers, they—"

"What about the soldiers?"

"They…" His voice cracked.

Rachel didn't care to hear more. She wanted to run away from Pierre and the evil things he had told her today. Yet the tender urgency in his tone made her squelch the thought.

"We must go now, Rachel. It could be dangerous to tarry too long."

Rachel glanced at the bay. She wanted Pierre to leave her alone. Why didn't he? His kindness could not be more obvious, but his handsome face and gentle words only served to remind her of her loss.

Numbly, she sat down on a beached log and watched the afternoon sun drop lower in the western sky. A line of boats bobbed in the water. Most were loaded with people. Some had left the shore.

Pierre sat down beside her. "This is a difficult time for both of us, but we must board that ship."

A child raced toward them, waving both hands and shouting. Rachel leaned forward, unable to identify the boy or hear what he said. The wind blew his words away.

A moment later, Pierre said, "That looks like Henri coming."

Pierre's little brother stopped in front of them, panting. "Pierre! Mademoiselle! Mama told me to remind you that our boat is leaving. If you fail to sail with Mama and me, that leaves only one boat. And it is very small. Please, you must come now or we will leave without you."

"I plan to stay." Rachel crossed her arms over her chest. "You go with your mother and little brother, Pierre."

"You misunderstood, Mademoiselle Rachel," Henri put in. "It is not safe to—"

"Stay here any longer? I know that, Henri," she said. "Still, I am not boarding that ship. I need to be with my parents now."

The child's brown eyes suddenly looked enormous. "But your parents are—"

"Run along, Henri." Pierre's voice had an impatient snap. "We will catch up with you at the ship."

"Hurry!" a man shouted from the last of the larger boats. "We are leaving!"

"Go on, Henri," Pierre insisted, "and take care of Mama. I will catch up with you before the ship sails. And remember, until you see me again, you are the man of the family."

The child faltered. Then he hugged Pierre around the neck. "Goodbye, brother, God speed."

"Goodbye, little one. I will see you soon." Pierre gave Henri a gentle pat on the back. "Now, go!"

Rachel watched the boy race away. A fog had blown in rather suddenly, swallowing the larger boat in one gulp.

"I can take care of myself, Pierre." Rachel got to her feet. "You should have gone with them."

"No. As my late brother's betrothed, you are my responsibility now."

She shook her head, emotionally exhausted. "I appreciate your kindness, but you do not need to feel responsible for me. I want my family. They will take care of me until…"

Her words tailed off. She couldn't depend on her parents any longer. She was an adult. She must learn to take care of herself.

"Dear, sweet Rachel, you cannot—" His voice broke, and he embraced her again. "I cannot let you go."

She tried to wiggle out of his arms. "Why not?"

Tears brimmed at the edges of his eyes. "You have no home." He squeezed her to him. "Everything inside your house burned."

"Burned?" She thought of the fire she'd seen earlier. Rachel gasped. "My parents!" She jerked away from him. "I must go to them!"

"They are gone, Rachel, just like Louis."

Her jaw hung limp as she peered at him. "No! No, no, no."

Tenderness emanated from his dark eyes as grief and hopelessness washed over her. She collapsed against him, buried her head on his shoulder and wept.

After several minutes, she lifted her head and wiped her face with her hands. "Why, Pierre? Why did this happen? I do not understand."

"I told you. The authorities learned that Louis and I went to Paris and attended a meeting with other Huguenots. The king's soldiers must have followed us to Benoit. Shortly before we arrived in the village, I told Louis that I heard hoof beats in the distance and that we should take cover as soon as possible. He refused to listen, insisting that we stop at your house before going to ours. I think the soldiers killed your parents because they were with Louis."

She trembled in his arms. "I should never have left the house today. I should have been there when my family needed me the most."

He patted the back of her head. "You would not have been of any help to them, Rachel. They were probably glad you were away from the house. If you had been. . . ."

He didn't need to finish the sentence. If she had been in the house, she would have been killed, too.

Fresh tears welled in her eyes. If only she could have warned them. They never knew they were in danger. She should have told them about Louis, about their engagement, about everything. She pressed her fist against her mouth to muffle a sob. If only she could have said goodbye.

Pierre didn't know Rachel and her family were Jews. Nobody did. Nobody else ever would if she had anything to say about it.

She looked up at Pierre again. He looked so unhappy, so grieved. She wasn't the only one suffering. Pierre and his family had lost Louis, too. Under other circumstances, she would do all she could to comfort him, but not today. Her losses overwhelmed her. Taking on Pierre's pain would be more than she could bear.

"Tell me what happened," she said. "I have to know how they died."

He hesitated. "Very well." Pierre glanced down—avoiding eye contact. "As I told you, soon after we arrived from Paris, Louis stopped by your house to see if he could persuade your parents to go on the ship with us. I waited for Louis in the bushes outside your house while he went inside.

"We had learned some new information while in Paris. And though your parents were Catholics, they would have been in danger once you left on the ship, and they needed to leave France with us."

"And then?"

"Some men rode up. Soldiers. Thirty or more in all."

Her face must have revealed the pain she'd tried so hard to hide because he reached down and brushed her hair from her face. Though a simple gesture, it touched her heart.

"Please, Rachel, let us not talk of this now."

"No, now! I have to hear everything."

He released a deep sigh. "The men surrounded your house, and they—" He pressed her head against his chest. "They stormed inside and killed everyone. If only I had carried some kind of weapon, but I—" Pierre cleared his throat. "I hid in the bushes while they burned your house to the ground."

"And—and nobody escaped?"

"Nobody."

Rachel's breath caught. Pain like sharp knives sliced her, scraping her very soul. Memories of her father and his sayings filled her mind.

"Jews never give up, Rachel," Papa had said over and over. "We press on, always."

Rachel lifted her head. "I will go with you now. I have nothing left here."

Pierre grabbed her hand. "We must hurry. Come."

They raced down the beach to the small boat. Pierre untied the rope attached to the wooden dock, snatched one of the oars and handed it to Rachel. As he reached for the other one, he hesitated, studying the bottom of the boat.

A break in the fog caused light to reflect off a pool of water on the craft's wooden bottom, and moisture seeped in from a small hole near the center of the boat. About an inch of water already covered the boat's bottom. It appeared to be filling fast.

"Can you fix it?" Rachel asked.

"I think so."

Rachel thought she heard something. Voices carried by the breeze. Pierre glanced toward a line of trees. Rachel stiffened.

"What is it, Pierre? What do you see?"

"Someone is coming." He seized her arm. "It could be the soldiers. We must hurry!"

"What about the boat?"

"There is no time to fix it now. Run!"

They fled down the beach in the same direction the boats took earlier. Looking back, Rachel couldn't see their pursuers. That didn't mean they weren't being hunted.

Three

At dusk, Pierre listened to the roar of waves splashing against the shore and tasted a salty breeze. The Bay of Biscay flowed into the ocean. No doubt the ship had sailed hours ago. To tarry could be dangerous. The sea was a blanket of whitecaps. He glanced at Rachel, strolling beside him near the water's edge.

He couldn't see her facial expression in the semi-darkness, but with her head down as if her damp and tattered leather shoes fascinated her, he sensed her grief. Her shoulders drooped. She seemed lost in thought, and her long auburn hair blew in the wind below her cap.

If only he knew of something that would lighten her burden. She'd lost the three most important people in her world and had nowhere to go, and she would never be safe in France.

Pierre tried to look away. Yet he couldn't stop gazing at the outline of her heart-shaped face—remembering the long, dark lashes that framed her large, emerald eyes. He liked the way her nose turned up on the end, and her smooth ivory skin. The dimple in her chin seemed to punctuate her strength, determination, and yes, bravery.

She is my dead brother's fiancée. He tensed. *God forbid. What kind of a man am I?*

Louis could always make her smile; laugh. Now all Pierre saw in Rachel's face was devastation as thick as the mist rolling in from the sea.

He should have told Rachel about her parents when he reported what happened to Louis. If he had the opportunity to say it all again, he would have disclosed everything in one breath. But he couldn't, not then. She'd looked so lost, so sad.

He needed to stop dwelling on the fact that Rachel had fit perfectly in his arms when he held her back at the Safe House. Guilt flooded him along with still more thoughts of her. Under such disastrous circumstances, his musings seemed especially distasteful.

If he'd been able to save Louis, she wouldn't have to suffer in this way. Yet at a time when his brother's needs cried the loudest, he'd been unable to do anything to help. He felt the edges of his mouth turn down and forced a smile by sheer willpower.

Rachel would be in mourning for a long time, as would he. He wanted—needed to pray that all disturbing thoughts would disappear from his mind.

Pierre and Louis had always been close. He would never have done anything to come between his brother and Rachel, then or now. Her memories of Louis should be protected and cherished, always.

But Pierre met her first.

Nevertheless, when he realized that Rachel and Louis were in love, he stepped back. Only God knew how he truly felt about her.

They had both suffered because of his brother's death, but Rachel's grief seemed almost overpowering. She'd lost her parents, too.

Her quick steps had looked purposeful when they first left the village. When no soldiers caught up with them, her pace slowed. Now, she dragged her feet.

He should tell Rachel about the ship. But she looked so torn and exhausted. He would tell her later.

Pierre turned and looked behind them to see if they were being followed, but he neither saw nor heard a thing. The village was at least three miles back.

"You look tired," he said. "Let us stop now to rest?"

"No, I am all right. I think we should continue on." Rachel took another step and hesitated.

Pierre held up her wicker basket. "Supper time." Pulling out a loaf of bread, he broke it in half and led her to a rise nearby. "This is for you."

Rachel sat down on the mound of earth and took the bread from his hands. "I—I am not hungry, Pierre."

"Try to eat a little." He sat down beside her. "It will help preserve your strength for the journey ahead."

"You sound like my—my mo-th-er."

Her lips quivered. He put his arm around her and felt her shoulders shake as she wept. At last, she sniffed and wiped her eyes with the back of her hand.

"Seeing me like this," she said, "it would be hard to believe that I once cheered up my parents and made them laugh."

"You will make people laugh again, Rachel."

"Will I? I doubt that, but I will try to eat." She took a bite of the bread.

"Please, wait." He forced a smile. "We have not blessed our food yet."

"Oh, yes, of course."

Pierre bowed his head and assumed Rachel did, too.

He thanked the Lord in the Name of Jesus for providing for their needs and for making it possible for Rachel to have bread and a sack of money inside her basket. Before ending his prayer, he gave thanks to God for hiding them in the secret place of the Most High. Then he sat and watched her as they ate.

She picked at her food, a small bite here, another there. He prayed her strength would hold until he got her to safety.

"What is the secret place?" Rachel looked away as if she really didn't care to hear an answer.

"The Bible says that he who lives in the secret place of the Most High shall abide under the shadow of the Almighty."

"But what does that mean?"

"I think it means that all those who truly love God and accept Jesus as the Sacrifice—the payment for their sins—can live in the secret place of peace and safety, regardless of the storms going on around them."

"Surely, you cannot think we are in that place now."

"Yes, I do."

"How can you say such a thing after—" The muscles around her mouth looked tense, and moisture filled her green eyes. She wiped away her tears. "After all that happened today."

"What I said about the secret place came from the Bible, Rachel, not from me."

"I had almost forgotten. You have been studying the Scriptures with your pastor."

He nodded. "We studied the Bible shortly before I left for the city."

"What news did you hear while in Paris?" she asked. "It must have been important. I saw the way you raced out as I was leaving the baker's shop. Had you just left the meeting?"

"Yes. And the news from Paris disturbed all of us."

He didn't want to say more, not now.

Dark clouds blocked out the moon. He could no longer see her face and prayed that what he'd already mentioned hadn't upset her too much.

"I smell rain," he said. "We should start off again before we are caught in a downpour."

He rose and offered to help her to her feet. She took the hand he offered and got up as well.

The night looked darker than ever. Were it not for the sound of waves lapping against the bank, he might not have known their location. Pierre hoped the moon remained behind the clouds until they reached the church. If soldiers were still out there, the darkness would make it difficult for them to be seen.

"What did you mean when you said the news from Paris disturbed everybody at that meeting?" she asked. "What news?"

"In Paris, we heard that the King ordered his soldiers to arrest a Huguenot minister and some of his followers not far from Benoit. They were declared enemies of the crown for religious reasons. Apparently, the minister said something in one of his sermons that reached the authorities in Paris. The soldiers claimed that the Huguenots resisted arrest. Two were killed. The women and children in the group were terrified. I knew that pastor and doubt they resisted. Some think the revocation of The Edict of Nantes has returned to haunt us."

"What is The Edict of Nantes?"

"The Edict of Nantes gave Huguenots some protection from persecution, but the law was revoked a long, long time ago. Huguenots still talk about it. Members of the Reformed Church have never felt secure in France because its kings wanted all French citizens to join the French Church. For a while, the French court pretended to protect Huguenots. But after the Edict of Nantes was revoked, Huguenots were no longer safe. Many fled the country."

"Why did your family stay here?" Rachel asked. "They should have left."

"My ancestors were not members of the Reformed Church. They were Catholics. Therefore, they were not in danger. There would have been no reason for them to leave. Like me, many members of the Reformed Church have ancestors who worshipped at the French Church. But now, our church leaders think it is time to leave."

"What happened to Huguenots who stayed after the Edict of Nantes was revoked?"

"I was told that some were killed or put in prison. Their children were taken from them and raised by nuns acceptable to the King."

"And you think this is happening again?"

"Who knows? But it is possible, I suppose. As I mentioned, there was an incident recently in a nearby village. We—I mean, I heard more details in Paris. After reporting this news to the elders, they voted to leave the country instead of waiting two weeks as we had planned. It would not be worth the risk of being captured, and we intended to sail anyway."

"Maybe we should walk faster." Rachel increased her pace.

Pierre caught up with her in one stride. He still hadn't told her about the ship and would put off telling her a while longer. How many tragedies could a person accept in one day?

He blinked as if that simple act would erase the horrible images rolling around in his head. He kept seeing what happened to Louis and her parents; hearing their cries for mercy. He pictured the captain waving the golden candlestick in the air and calling it a Menorah.

Was Rachel a Jewess? If so, why had she and her parents pretended to be Christians? He thought he knew. The lie had been a kind of covering, a means of protection from persecution. He knew all about hiding from one's enemies—all Huguenots did. He'd heard about Jews all his life, but until now, he'd never known one.

Pierre had thought that most Jews would never set foot in a Christian church much less pretend to be a Christian. Perhaps Rachel's family had never practiced their religion. Some Jews didn't, he'd been told.

A sudden splash of cold water brought Pierre out of his memories. He hadn't been paying attention. Wet feet and ankles told that he'd stepped away from the beach and into icy ocean water.

"Oh, that is cold," Pierre said.

"What happened?"

"I stepped into the bay, that is what happened." Embarrassed, he waded back to shore.

Rachel's hand found his in the darkness, guiding him to the bank.

"Thank you," he said.

"Are you all right?"

"Yes." He laughed. "I must have been dreaming while awake, or either went walking in my sleep. My mother said I did that all the time as a child."

Instead of laughing at his stab at humor as he'd hoped, she grew silent.

"I worry about what the soldiers might do if they catch up with us," she said at last. "Are you afraid?"

"I am concerned but not afraid."

"How can you not be afraid, Pierre, after all we have been through?"

"Because I know God is with us, and I trust Him to protect us. Still, we must keep a watchful eye, always."

Rachel looked off into the bay as the moon came out from behind the clouds. As she turned back to Peirre, she found him watching her.

"When will we reach La Rochelle?" she asked.

"We are close. But there is something I must tell you—something I should have told you before." He hesitated. "The ship would have moved out under the cover of darkness and be on the open sea by now."

"Surely, you cannot mean we missed the ship."

"I am afraid so."

The muscles in her face tensed, and a wave of anger engulfed her. Pierre should have told her this as soon as they left Benoit. Why hadn't he? Why did he let her race down the beach until she could run no longer? And why had he allowed her to hope when there was no hope?

Pierre would say they were running from the soldiers. But what soldiers? If they existed at all, where were they?

She put her hands on her hips. "If the ship has already gone, why are we going to La Rochelle?" she asked with a trace of sarcasm. "Would you mind telling me that?"

"I know a Catholic priest by the name of Father La Faye who serves a church not far from La Rochelle, and he will help us."

"A Catholic priest?" She sensed that a hint of bitterness had mixed with her anger and sarcasm. "Really, Pierre, have you forgotten that I worked for a Catholic priest in Benoit?"

"He is not like the priest in Benoit. He will help us."

"How?"

"Father La Faye was a childhood friend of my late father. He has an uncle who is a high official in the French court. His uncle is also very close to the King himself. It is true that some in France hate Father La Faye, but as long as his uncle lives, Father La Faye and those under his protection will be safe."

"But if he is a priest, how can we trust him?"

"Not all Catholics are beasts like the King of France, Rachel. Father La Faye is kind, gentle, and loving. As I said, he will help us, as will the nuns serving under him."

Rachel bit her lower lip, waiting to see if he would say more. The moon went behind a cloud again, and he still hadn't opened his mouth.

"Father La Faye knows I am not of the Catholic religion,"

Pierre explained at last, "and he will assume you share my faith. To him, it will not matter. He will protect us in any case. But he will expect us to pretend to be Catholics while we are staying under his roof.

"Spies are everywhere. One can never tell who might be listening when words are spoken, even in private. Have I made the situation clear to you, Rachel?"

So much had occurred in such a short length of time. Now he wanted her to lie, and that bothered her. She needed to think, but there didn't appear to be time for reflection.

"Yes," she said after the long pause. "I know exactly what you are asking of me."

She'd pretended to be a religious person to please Louis. Yet the Levin family, her family, had been riddled with deaths in the name of religion for generations. After hearing what the priest in Benoit had to say about Jews and Huguenots, she would have a hard time trusting any Catholic.

Was Father La Faye any different? Pierre appeared to think so. Rachel would wait and see.

The clouds parted. The moon came out again, lighting a little of the countryside. Rachel gazed at Pierre.

He looked dashing even in shabby brown pants cut in the style of days gone by. He wore a tan doublet with long sleeves, and a tan leather vest. The vest had been tied with leather strings that crisscrossed down the front. His brown hat looked older than he was. Still, regardless of their lack of wealth and fashion, Rachel considered Louis and Pierre to be the handsomest men in France. And for some unknown reason, Pierre made her feel safe.

In the distance, a light shined from a lantern at the top of a strange looking building. It had a wide base with a high, tower-like structure beside it. The long neck of the tower stretched toward the stars. The large rock building stood on a rise near the water's edge. Even in semi-darkness, she could make out the tile roof.

"What is that building ahead?" she asked.

"Saint Joseph's. Father La Faye is the priest there. Some call the church The Sanctuary."

"Why is a tower next to the church?"

"Everybody asks the same question. You see, Father built a tower beside his church with a big lamp on top of it so lost boats and lost souls can find their way home."

She slanted her head to the side. "What a nice thought."

"Yes, it is."

She hesitated before moving on to consider what she'd just heard. *A man who would do all the good things the priest has done cannot be truly evil.*

"As you know, we—" She swallowed. "I have not lived in Benoit long. I have never been this far from the village. Are we in the town of La Rochelle?"

"No. It is still a few miles further on."

A damp breeze moaned around the corner of the church building by the time they reached the heavy double doors. Cold air bit Rachel's hands and face and whipped her clothes. She shivered and wrapped her arms around her chest.

Pierre handed Rachel her basket and grabbed the metal knocker, pounding it against the door. He waited and knocked again.

A small shutter at the top of the door opened. "Who goes there?" a man said in a gruff voice.

"Pierre Dupre, son of Andre, and I have a friend with me. We have come in peace to see Father La Faye."

"Wait." The wooden window closed.

Pierre shifted his weight from one leg to the other. A few minutes later, the shutter opened. A face appeared.

"Good evening, Father," Pierre said. "It is good to see you. It has been a long time."

"So it *is* you." The priest chuckled, and the double doors opened. "Come in, Pierre."

A heavy-set priest in a dark robe smiled at them. His belly looked as round as his bald head. Father La Faye stepped forward and stretched out his arms, embracing Pierre warmly. The two men separated, and the priest squinted at Rachel.

"And who is she, my son?"

Rachel held her breath, waiting to hear how Pierre would introduce her.

"This is Rachel Zimmer." Pierre glanced at her and smiled. "A friend of my family."

Father La Faye nodded. "Therefore, she is also my friend. What brings you here?"

"Trouble is brewing in Benoit," Pierre said. "A house was burned to the ground."

"So it has started again." The priest shook his head. "Welcome. Come in."

Father La Faye motioned Rachel and Pierre inside. Standing between them on the dark oak floor, he gestured toward a long hall and draped an arm over the shoulder of each of them.

Rachel flinched. In the dim light, she glanced at the wide, thick-fingered hand now resting on her shoulder. As they moved down the hallway, she remembered what she had heard about Catholics. Father La Faye seemed kind, but the fact that he was Pierre's friend would never be enough for her.

She needed something to focus on. A line of doors to their left caught her attention. The doors opened onto the wide hallway. Heavy double doors that had been left open welcomed worshippers to a chapel off to their right. The scent of incense encouraged her to look inside. Candles flickered against the dark stone walls of the sanctuary, and nuns in black robes prayed on their knees near the altar.

"Wait here," Father La Faye said. "I will return."

The priest went into the sanctuary and whispered something to one of the nuns. She got up and followed Father La Faye up the aisle.

Father La Faye gestured toward the elderly nun. Her dark eyes shined with what Rachel deemed gentleness, making her wrinkled face seem younger somehow.

"This is our Mother Superior," the priest said with a smile.

The nun returned his smile, and her yellowed teeth contrasted with the white collar of her black habit. Though her sweet expression told of a kind heart, Rachel also saw power and authority in the erect, almost stiff, way she moved.

"This is Monsieur Dupre, the son of a very old friend." The priest sent a nod to Pierre. "And this is Mademoiselle Zimmer.

Please take the Mademoiselle upstairs and find her a place to sleep."

"Of course, Father." The nun curtsied before the priest. She turned to Rachel. "Welcome, Mademoiselle."

"Thank you." Rachel glanced at Pierre.

He looked as if he had something he wanted to say to her but didn't speak. If only he would. She felt uncomfortable with these strangers and was a little unsure of what to do with hands that wouldn't be still.

"Thank you, Father La Faye," she said at last. "You are very kind." Rachel went down on one knee and bobbed up in imitation of the nun.

The nun took a lighted candle from a holder on the wall. "Come now, Mademoiselle, and follow me."

The tap of their shoes on the dark wooden stairs sent a haunting chill up Rachel's spine as they made their way to the door at the end of another long hall. Mother Superior opened the door and nodded for her to go in first.

"You will sleep in here, Mademoiselle."

Exhausted from a day and night filled with pain and heartache, Rachel forced a smile. The one small candle did little to brighten a room engulfed in shadows. Still, the nuns had seemed kind, and to show her appreciation, she hoped to project an interest in her surroundings.

"The room is very nice indeed."

From the doorway, it looked neat and clean. Dark furniture and unpainted wooden walls contrasted the metal cross that hung from the ceiling over the sleeping area. A spread encased the bed like a blue cloak, and plain blue curtains covered the windows.

"Ordinarily, this is our quiet time here at Saint Joseph's." The nun placed the candle on a table beside the only chair in the room. "But because you are Father's guest, I am allowed to talk to you for a while, if you like."

Rachel set her basket on the table. She'd made a mental list of questions she wanted answered, but until she knew the nun well enough to think she could be trusted, she wouldn't mention them.

The nun bent down to start a fire in the hearth. "You are fortunate to be staying in a room with a fireplace, Mademoiselle. I will have someone bring supper up to you later."

"Thank you. But I wish for nothing."

"I will send a tray anyway, in case you change your mind. I will also have a pitcher of water sent for washing. The room across the hall contains a bowl for use at night and in bad weather. During the day, you will be expected to relieve yourself in the small building behind the church which is provided for that purpose."

Rachel nodded. "I understand."

When the fire blazed, the older woman opened the armoire near the bed. Several black dresses hung from hooks inside, as well as a long white gown. Other dark items waited on a shelf above the hooks.

"These are the clothes you are to wear while you are here, Mademoiselle, and they should fit your small frame well, I think. You will dress as a young woman who has not yet taken her vows. And of course the white dress and cap are for sleeping."

Obviously, the nun knew she was not a novice and had no intentions of taking vows. Yet she agreed to help her.

Rachel appreciated all that had been done for her. She also felt slightly ashamed of her lack of trust in the nun earlier, but not enough to change her original opinions of those she'd met so far. She would wait to see what the morning brought.

"You are most helpful, Sister. I am grateful."

"Please, call me Mother."

Mother? Rachel stiffened. The nun couldn't know she'd just lost hers and that she could never call any other woman by that name.

"Leave the clothes you wore here by the door. Someone will pick them up and wash them. You will hear a bell before daylight in the morning, Mademoiselle. Dress quickly and come downstairs. We will expect you to attend all worship services with the other sisters while you are here and join us when we break the fast."

"Will Monsieur Dupre be breaking the fast with us?"

"No, he will be eating with Father in the tower. All the men live near the tower, making sure a light is always burning there. Perhaps you noticed it when you arrived."

Rachel nodded. "Yes, I did."

She started to ask when she would be seeing Pierre again but changed her mind. It might be best to keep quiet and hold her questions close to her heart. The less they knew about her the less information they could pass on to others.

The nun paused as if waiting for Rachel to say more. "If you have no more questions, I will leave now."

"Good night." Rachel curtsied again. "You have been most helpful and kind."

"Good night. Until the morrow."

"Until the morrow."

Rachel closed the door and sat down in the chair beside the candle. Her shoes pinched her toes, and the bottoms of her feet burned from all the walking she'd done that day. She removed her shoes and heard them hit the wooden planked floor. *Plop. Plop.* The rest of her body ached, too, but she wouldn't think about that now.

A picture of Pierre's handsome face appeared in her mind. If only she'd asked him more questions about this place and what would be expected of her when she had the chance. She'd thought she would be with him at supper. Now, she had no idea when she would see him again. If she managed to speak to him, she doubted they would have the opportunity to talk privately.

Rachel leaned back in her chair, and memories of all that had occurred since she left the baker's little shop hammered her brain. She blinked back tears. Along with everything else, exhaustion overwhelmed her.

Oh, Louis. Why did you leave me?

She finally fell asleep in her chair.

Some time later, a knock at her door jerked her out of a sound sleep. Rachel tensed, wondering who could be at her door. "Who is it?"

"I have brought your supper, Mademoiselle."

Her apprehensions partly vanished on hearing the sound of a woman's voice. She got up and made her way to the door. Her bare feet on the cold floor sent shivers through her. Rachel opened the door a crack and peered out. A nun in a black robe stood in the hallway holding a tray. She had soft brown eyes, and Rachel thought she looked younger than the elderly nun she had met earlier.

"I am Sister Mary."

"I am Mademoiselle Zimmer. Please, come in."

The nun swept across the room, placing the tray on the little table with the lighted candle on it. "I will return with your bowl and pitcher." She hurried out the door and closed it.

Rachel sat down. A cup of milk and a steaming bowl of porridge centered the wooden tray. She reached for the spoon. Perhaps she would eat a little after all. As Pierre had said, she should keep up her strength.

She'd attended Christian worship services with Louis for months but had never been what Pierre would call a true believer. Pierre had prayed before they ate the bread. But she didn't know how to pray.

Rachel had never learned any of the prayers that most Jews recited, much less Christian prayers. Her family had never practiced their religion. Maybe her parents were afraid their Jewish heritage would be discovered, and they would be persecuted.

She'd barely finished eating when Sister Mary returned with the pitcher. "I have brought you two cloths for washing and drying. If you need anything during the night, please pull the cord by the door. It rings the bell outside, and the sound of it will be heard by the sister in the room next to yours. She will come to your aid quickly."

"Thank you, Sister Mary. You have all been kind to me."

"Here, we treat others as we would like to be treated."

"That is what Jesus said to do."

"Yes, I know." The nun pulled a white paper from the pocket of her black dress. "Oh, I almost forgot. Here is a letter for you from Monsieur Dupre." She handed Rachel the note.

"Thank you, once again," Rachel said.

The nun smiled. "My pleasure is serving others. But now I must go. Sleep well, Mademoiselle."

"The same to you, Sister."

The door closed. Rachel opened her letter.

Dear Mademoiselle,

I hope you will sleep well and find everything to your liking here. Father La Faye says it might not be safe to travel now. Soldiers are guarding all the roads. We could be staying here for many days—perhaps months. But never forget the Lord is with us wherever we go and whatever we do. Someday we will find a place where freedom lives. We must pray that day will come soon.

Your humble servant,
Pierre Dupre

Rachel read the letter again, committing it to memory. Then she put it to the candle. When a flame started, she threw the letter in the fireplace, watching until it burned to a pile of gray ashes.

Like the letter, her heart was ashes. Yet the burning continued. Would the pain ever stop? She bit her lower lip as moisture trailed down from her eyes, and she tasted the salt of her tears.

"The weeping will come soon enough," Pierre had said.

The truth of his words took hold. Rachel folded her arms on the table, laid her head down, and cried. Her time of mourning had arrived.

Four

Early on Sunday morning, Rachel pulled one of the dresses from the armoire. She smoothed the fabric, wondering who had last worn it. The material felt rough to her bare skin, and the black color blended with her sorrowful mood. She wound her hair in a tight bun and covered it with a dark veil.

Rachel folded the clothes she'd worn on the previous day, placed them by the door and went downstairs to break the fast. The nuns from Benoit attended a church service each morning. She would probably be expected to do the same. If only Pierre would be seated in the pew beside her. She wouldn't feel as lonely with him at her side.

Downstairs and standing in the doorway of the large and poorly lighted dining room, she saw about a dozen nuns inside the room. All eyes appeared to be focused on her, and she felt more alone than ever. Her insides churned as she studied the rock walls to keep from staring back at the nuns. The walls were devoid of paint or adornments except for a huge, stained-glass window. An image of Jesus with young children all around him was shining through the colored glass.

Once, she had dreamed of having children; of being a mother. Rachel swallowed. Now Louis was gone, and all her dreams went with him.

The chairs were of dark wood, like the three crude tables. Two of the tables looked fairly large. A long table filled with food stood at one end of the room. Though Rachel had no desire to eat, she took her turn in line and scooped up a serving of porridge, dark-colored bread, and a bit of boiled fish.

Mother Superior sat with two other nuns at the table near the door. Sister Mary and several middle-aged nuns occupied the other large table. Sister Mary motioned to Rachel from across the room. Rachel smiled and started toward them.

When she reached the table, she pulled out a chair and sat down beside Sister Mary. Rachel dipped her spoon into the porridge bowl and lifted the spoon to her lips.

The warm, whitish mixture tasted flat without salt or other spices. However, she managed to swallow the mouthful and send Sister Mary a quick smile.

A young monk hurried into the room and handed a small sheet of paper to Mother Superior. Rachel watched the elderly nun read the message. A somber expression appeared on the woman's face. Mother Superior stood and nodded to the priest. The nuns, seated at Rachel's table, looked at each other.

"Sisters," Mother Superior said calmly. "Soldiers have almost reached the door of the church. We must prepare our hearts for whatever comes."

Not more soldiers. Rachel felt as if an invisible knife had stabbed her.

Memories of what Pierre said had happened to Louis and her parents destroyed what remained of her fragile composure. She needed Pierre. However, she doubted she would be able to find him. The church's huge size would make it difficult to know where to look. Unable to eat more, she put her spoon in her porridge bowl and looked around for a way out.

The nuns rose in haste. Rachel got up, too, and stood behind her chair as she saw the sisters doing, wondering if these were the soldiers who killed her loved ones and if now they had come for her.

Had she put these innocent women in danger?

"Carry your plates to the kitchen," Mother Superior continued. "Then go directly to the church sanctuary for prayer as if nothing unusual is about to happen."

Rachel followed Sister Mary outside to the kitchen house. Determined to mimic the nuns, she scraped the contents of her plate into a large wooden barrel and placed her plate and eating utensils on a table near the fireplace. Bowing her head, she folded her hands and fell into line behind Sister Mary.

At last, they reached the worship area of the compound. A huge golden crucifix hung over the carved, wooden altar. Candles and stained-glass windows edged the north and south walls of the sanctuary, producing a haunting glow that Rachel might have found restful under different circumstances.

She knelt among the sisters and tried to imitate their pious concentration on prayer. Shouts sounded outside the open doorway.

Rachel gasped. Had the soldiers come to arrest her? Kill her?

"I am looking for a Huguenot and a nest of Jews," a man said in a loud voice. "All are enemies of the crown. I plan to search this church and want to talk to those nuns."

"You cannot go in there, Monsieur," Father La Faye insisted. "The sisters are in prayer."

"I will go where I please, Father."

Heavy footfalls broke the silence of the quiet sanctuary. Soldiers stormed down the center aisle. Rachel kept her eyes straight ahead.

"Get up!" a soldier shouted. "All of you. Come out into the hallway, and be quick about it."

Rachel rose when the other sisters did. Her heart pounding, she endeavored to appear as if she belonged there. At least twenty years younger than the other nuns and the only woman dressed as a novice, the soldiers were sure to notice her.

"I want to talk to the pretty little nun on the end," one of them demanded. "What is her name?"

"She is new here and only a novice, Captain Vallae," Mother Superior replied coldly. "She has no Christian name yet."

Rachel lifted her chin. "My name is Magdalena Poyer."

The captain laughed.

Why had she said what she did? The name, Magdalena Poyer, meant nothing to her.

Taking off his black hat, he bowed as if he thought Rachel was royalty. The other soldiers echoed his laughter.

Her boldness must have surprised him. But she still didn't know where the name Magdalena Poyer came from. Maybe she read the name in a book somewhere. In any case, the lie had fallen from her lips easily; too easily, perhaps.

Tall and thin with a dark complexion, the young captain had broad shoulders. The shape of his black eyes reminded her of the almonds she chanced to eat once when they lived in Alsace, and the scar above his right eye gave his handsome face a hint of danger that she might have found attractive if he hadn't been a part of the French army.

He watched her with what some in Alsace had called the "evil eye." As a child in Alsace, the young boy who spat on her that day had evil eyes, and there had been others. But until now, she had never known anyone with the ability to grab and hold her attention in such a commanding way. A shudder crept down her.

"You speak French with an accent, Mademoiselle," he said. "Why is that so?"

"I lived for many years in Alsace."

"Ah, Alsace. Do you speak the German language?"

"Yes, Monsieur."

"Where did you live when you were in Alsace?" he asked in German.

"The small village of D'Hannis."

"I have heard of it." He turned to Father La Faye. "I find the Mademoiselle charming," the captain said in French. "I wish to speak with her privately."

"That is impossible," Father La Faye snapped. "She is under the protection of the church."

"I make the rules here."

The captain grabbed Rachel's arm, jerking her out of the line of nuns. Her dark head covering fell to the floor.

The captain smiled. "A redhead, are you? That pleases me very much."

He pulled the combs from her bun. Her auburn hair fell loose in deep waves around her shoulders. A contemptuous grin continued to turn up the edges of his mouth, and his dark eyes gleamed with something cold and frightening.

"I like that even better," he said. "Perhaps I will take you for myself. Yes, that is exactly what I will do."

Rachel wanted to melt into the floor under her feet. But Papa would have said that she should never let her enemies know she was afraid.

Despite her pounding heart, she glared up at the captain as if his humiliating words hadn't upset her. Out of the corner of her eye, she saw a movement among the clergy.

Pierre stepped forward, wearing the robes of a monk. Until that instant, she hadn't known he stood with the priests and monks, and Pierre could be in danger, too.

"The mademoiselle is the sister of a high government official," Pierre announced boldly. "Though I am not at liberty to reveal his name at this time, if she is harmed in any way, I am sure His Majesty's assistant will be very angry with you, Captain."

The captain grimaced, glaring at Pierre. He ran his hand across his mouth like a child wiping away a bad taste. "I will investigate to see if what you say is true, Monsieur. If it is, you will be spared. But if it is not true, you will be arrested as an enemy of the crown."

❧

Rachel stood in the hallway with the other nuns for over an hour, barely moving. She'd learned the name of the leader of the soldiers, Captain Jean Vallae. Captain Vallae and his men had searched every inch of Saint Joseph's Church. Pierre also waited in the hall with the other priests, but Rachel dared not glance in his direction for fear of drawing more attention to herself and to him.

One of the soldiers came into the hallway holding a bundle of clothes—the ones Rachel and Pierre had worn when they first arrived.

"Mon Capitaine, I found these on a shelf upstairs." The soldier handed the clothes to the captain.

The captain's dark eyes burned with deadly zeal. "How did the clothes of peasants get here?"

"We collect garments for the poor," the priest said in a calm tone. "Those belonged to a man and his wife. They left those here after we gave them new clothes. If possible, we will repair them and give them to other needy people."

"We are here in search of enemies of the King." The Captain lifted one dark eyebrow. "May I remind you to be careful what you say? Now, where are these peasants and where do they live?"

"I have no idea who they are or where they live." Father La Faye shrugged. "People come and go here all the time."

"What did they look like? Were they young or old?"

"Old, I think. Maybe not."

"I am weary of your games, Father. I want answers."

"They could have been any age. Hard work does that to the poor. The man was of average height. The woman was shorter. As I said, their names were never given. We never request them because names are not important here."

The captain's dark eyes narrowed. "We will search for them in La Rochelle as soon as we leave here. Now, where do you keep these clothes you give to the poor?"

"Alas." Father La Faye shrugged once more and shook his head. "We have already given away all we had. We must gather more before we can help the poor again."

The muscles in the captain jaw tightened as he turned to his men. "Prepare to take our leave."

The soldiers stood at attention in two lines against the walls of the wide hallway. The captain adjusted his hat as if he expected it to fly off his head as soon as he stepped outside. He turned to Father La Faye.

"I will return in a few days after I find out who is lying and who is telling the truth, Father." He glanced back at his men. "Turn about! Go forth!"

The soldiers marched toward the entry door. When Rachel could no longer see them, she took a deep breath and released it.

She'd squeezed her hands together for so long her fingers had turned white. Slowly, a sense of relief filled her. Yet the name *Vallae* kept running through her mind.

I have heard that name before.

If only she could recall when and where. Now two names puzzled her; Captain Jean Vallae *and* Magdalena Poyer.

❦

Captain Jean Vallae lined up his men in front of the church before moving on, hoping one of them would provide him with the information he needed.

"Do any of you know any of the priests or nuns here?"

Head held high and body like iron, a young foot soldier stepped forward. "I do, Mon Capitaine."

"What can you tell me?" the captain asked.

"My mother knew Sister Mary when they were both young girls and lived in houses that were side by side in Paris."

"Do you know the young nun, Magdalena Poyer?"

"No, sir."

"Very well. You may step back."

"Thank you, Mon Capitaine." Stiffly, the soldier stepped back in line as if only his legs were moveable.

The captain peered at the rest of his men. "Do any of you know the young nun or have heard about her?"

Nobody spoke.

"You are dismissed to your horses. Mount now and prepare to ride."

The captain stared at the door of the church for a moment, feeling like a fish caught in a net. It had been a long time since a young woman had so imprisoned his heart. She would not be easy to forget.

❦

Later that morning, Rachel left the chapel with Sister Mary. In the hallway, she studied the doors the captain went through when he left. She noticed the two narrow windows on the north wall that framed the entry doors; the window on the right in particular. Were the captain and his men waiting beyond the heavy doors or had they moved on?

A shower had grayed the sky outside soon after the captain left. Now a heavy rain pounded the roof and the windows, and water trailed down the panes like the tears Rachel had shed on the previous night.

She wondered if Captain Vallae ever wept over all the misery he forced on others. From what she had seen so far, she doubted it. She wanted to ask Sister Mary to tell her what she knew about the captain, but nuns here were not allowed to engage in conversation except under unusual circumstances.

Sister Mary grabbed her hand and gestured toward the library. Rachel nodded back at her and started walking. Until the nun touched her arm, she hadn't realized that she had stopped or that she'd been staring out the window.

They had almost reached the library where lessons on the Bible were taught. A plump little monk wearing a cook's white apron waddled toward them holding a sheet of writing paper.

"Sisters." His voice had a tinny ring to it, and he spoke louder than Father La Faye or any of the nuns. "Wait!" he ordered.

Rachel and Sister Mary stopped, but neither spoke.

"I have a message from Father La Faye." He handed the white sheet to Rachel. "This is for you."

Rachel took the letter in both hands. She almost said thank you and remembered that speaking wasn't allowed. She nodded and started to go down on one knee.

Sister Mary frowned as if to say "do not bow either." Rachel voided the bow and stood there a moment, wondering how she could learn the ways of the nuns when nobody was permitted to talk to her.

The monk turned and tottered back down the hall. Rachel stopped to read her letter while Sister Mary went into the library.

Father La Faye's note requested that Rachel and Pierre come to his office for a private meeting when the big bell above the door of the sanctuary rang ten times. She would barely have time to run up to her room and attend to her toiletry before it would be time to go.

As she climbed the stairs to the second floor, she thought about the captain. Did he plan to ravish her when he returned in a few days? The mere thought of such a thing made her shudder with pent-up anger.

Rachel longed for sound counsel. She thought Mother Superior and Sister Mary could be trusted. But how would she know for sure? Besides, they couldn't provide the advice she needed unless they were given permission to speak; and that seemed unlikely.

Was Father La Faye the person to give the guidance she needed? If so, would he protect her? And could she trust him? At least the priest didn't know of her Jewish background.

Rachel went to her room. She removed her head covering and washed her face and hands in the white bowl. She couldn't guess what the priest intended to discuss with them, but it must be important since he sent her a special note requesting that she and Pierre meet him in his office.

She pushed back a curl that had escaped the tight coil of her bun and put on her head covering. As an afterthought, she straightened the collar of her black dress.

Rachel strolled back down the hall toward the stairway, listening to the tap of her shoes on the wooden planks as she went. The squeak of a door caused her to stop and turn. A hand closed over her mouth, making it impossible for her to call out. Someone pulled her into one of the other bedrooms.

Five

"Sorry, Rachel," she heard Pierre say. "I never should have grabbed you and pulled you inside this room. But I must not be found in the nun's quarters. I wanted to talk to you and could not take the chance you might call out." He removed his hand from her mouth. "I have something important to discuss."

Weak with relief, Rachel turned to face him. "All right."

She wanted to scold him for scaring her out of her wits, but his smile held a hint of amusement. Smiling faces had always improved her outlook for the better, and at least now, she would have the chance to speak to him again.

"Now, what is so important that you saw fit to seize me unaware?" she asked.

"I regret that." A sober expression swept over his face. "But the captain who came to the church today is no stranger to me."

"You know him?"

"Not on a personal level. But I know the kind of man he is. The other monks told me that his full name is Captain Jean Vallae, and—and"

"And what, Pierre?"

"Captain Vallae is the one who ordered your house burned and your parents and Louis killed."

"No!"

Rachel's mind produced a swirl of pictures like paintings she'd seen in churches and on the walls of buildings. But these paintings were different; they showed soldiers killing Louis and her parents.

More pictures of murder and death appeared before her. Were her loved ones killed before the house was burned to the ground or were they locked inside with no way to escape? Louis would have done all he could to save them but with thirty soldiers under the captain's command, there was little he could have done.

Louis!

She balled her fists, and her heart cried out for revenge against this man; this captain.

I will never forgive Captain Vallae. Never.

Rachel swallowed, hoping the nasty taste in her mouth would go away. "Do you think the captain and his men tracked us to the church?"

Pierre shrugged. "I know little about French soldiers, but I think he is searching for me. They were looking for two Huguenots from Benoit who attended a secret meeting in Paris with other Huguenots. They only found one." He hesitated. "Rachel, are you all right?"

She sniffed, choking back a sob, and shook her head.

He reached out and hugged her as a brother might embrace a sister. "A lot has happened to us in a short period. I cannot blame you for being upset. I am furious, too, but we must believe things will soon get better." He released her slowly and stepped back. "I told Father La Faye that the captain killed Louis and that he is looking for me, but I never mentioned what happened to your parents. It might be best if we keep that information a secret between us. However, I wanted you to know what I have learned about this man before we talk to the priest."

"I am glad you told me, and glad the priest doesn't know what happened to Mama and Papa. As you said before we came here, it is best not to reveal too much to these people." She sent him a weak smile. "But next time you have something important to say, try tapping me lightly on the shoulder."

He laughed.

"And you agree not to mention my connection to what happened?" she asked.

"I do."

"Thank you, Pierre, for putting your own life in danger by defending me against the captain. Most men might not have."

"Thank you for standing firm in front of formidable enemies today," he said. "You are a brave and bold young woman."

"You are also bold and brave; and a loyal friend."

⚭

On the road to La Rochelle, Captain Vallae trotted his black horse into the shade of a large Chestnut tree and signaled for his men to gather around him. A damp wind cooled the countryside. Summer was slipping away, and soon the leaves on the trees would change to red-brown and gold. Like the trees, his thoughts kept changing. He tried to concentrate on his job, but his mind returned again and again to the lovely young nun he'd met at the church.

She'd looked like an auburn-haired angel— even in dark clothing. Her beauty outshone every other woman he'd known in his twenty six-years of life, including his new wife, Yvette.

His men sat on their horses at attention, waiting for his next command. So far, he'd been unable to keep his thoughts in line enough to give an order. But as a leader in the king's army, he knew that he must. Duty came before personal desires. At least he'd written a report.

Jean had been ordered to arrest two young Huguenots who attended an unauthorized meeting in Paris, and in part, he'd told in his report what happened at the cottage owned by the Jews. He'd merely added that those inside the cottage resisted arrest and that he had no choice but to kill them and burn down the house.

"Monsieur Pascal," Captain Jean Vallae shouted. "Come forward."

"At your service, sir." The young officer guided his horse closer to where the captain waited.

Jean Vallae reached in his breast pocket for the letter and felt something hard. He'd almost forgotten about the miniature portrait of the young Jewish woman he found before he set fire to the house. After a moment, he found the report and held it out to Monsieur Pascal.

"Ride to the Office of Records in Paris, give this letter to Monsieur Touchet and make haste. It will take time for him to form a reply, but I want you to wait until he does—no matter how long it takes. Is that clear? And report back to me as soon as you return."

"Yes, Mon Capitaine." He hesitated. "Anything else?"

"No, that will be all."

"Then I shall take my leave."

The young officer turned his horse around and galloped away.

Jean faced the rest of his men. "Restore your ranks and prepare to ride."

The captain loped his gelding to the head of the line. When his troops fell in behind him, he slowed his pace.

He'd found something exciting and quite unique in the eyes of the young Jewish girl in the portrait. He pulled out the painting and gazed down at it. Though quite small, the portrait appeared to have been painted by a true artist. The young girl's lovely face had been partly covered by a thick mass of long hair, and she reminded him of—of—

The nun, Magdalena Poyer.

Was it she? Could the Jewess and the nun be one and the same person? The possibility seemed unlikely and yet—

Wrath boiled inside at the mere thought that Magdalena might be a Jew. How could he care so much for a Jewess? Unthinkable. He must be mistaken. She couldn't be a Jew. His jaw firmed. He'd always hated Jews and Huguenots.

Jean put the portrait back in his pocket and dug in his heels. The gelding's easy trot became a gallop.

The young officer would return in a few days with a report from the Director of Records, and Jean would know the truth. If his suspicions proved correct, he would act without delay. He looked down at his reins.

If Magdalena is a Jew, she must be killed. He released a breath filled with his own frustration. *Pity, without a doubt, she is the loveliest creature I have ever seen.*

⚜

Rachel stood with Pierre in the hallway outside Father La Faye's study, trying not to think about her hatred for the captain. Pierre knocked at the door.

"Come in, children," the priest said.

Pierre opened the door for her and stepped back before she entered. Rachel saw book-laden shelves reaching from the floor to the high ceiling.

Father La Faye had been seated behind his massive oak desk, but he stood when they came into the large room. "Welcome."

Rachel felt Pierre's gaze at her back as she swept across the dark Persian rug. Three chairs with oak arms in the style of the French court had been arranged in a circular pattern in front of the desk. Anger blocked out everything else.

The priest gestured toward the sitting area. "Please, sit where you like."

As soon as Rachel and Pierre were seated, Father La Faye pulled his chair near theirs. "I suppose you are wondering why I called you here this morning."

"Yes, Father," Pierre said. "I wondered."

The priest leaned forward in his chair. "As you must know, Captain Vallae will discover that what Pierre told him is untrue. It is unlikely he will come back for several days, but the captain will return and do what he said he would do. To avoid a calamity, both of you must leave here immediately. I have already made the arrangements. You will sail tonight on a small fishing boat belonging to a friend of mine. Later, you will board a cargo ship bound for England."

Rachel tensed. *Cargo ship?*

She questioned the wisdom of his words. How could a young woman board a cargo ship? If the tales she'd heard were true, she would be ravished before she set foot on deck. Still, she agreed that they should leave the Sanctuary. The captain and his men were probably searching for them at that very hour.

She thought of the young captain of the soldiers. After what happened to those she loved, she wanted to hit back—get even for what he had done. Revenge wouldn't bring them back. However, she sensed that she would feel better when Captain Vallae got his just reward.

"The fishing boat is not a large one, Mademoiselle," the priest continued after a long pause. "But the boat owner is kind to those in need. You should be safe—at least for a while. However, there are a few things to be done before you sail. And it is important that you do exactly as I suggest if you hope to survive."

"Then of course we shall," Pierre said. "Please tell us what must be done."

"Within the hour, we will go into the sanctuary of the church here, and I will join the two of you in Holy Matrimony."

Holy Matrimony? Rachel almost jumped out of her chair. She couldn't believe he would suggest such a thing.

"As you know, today is Sunday," he went on, "and we seldom perform wedding ceremonies here on the Lord's Day, but it is not unheard of. I am sure the bishop will agree with my judgment in the matter when I write and tell him what I have done."

"You mean you want us to wed, Father?" she asked. "Now?"

He nodded. "It is necessary, Mademoiselle. It would be unseemly as well as dangerous for you to travel without a gentleman at your side to protect you day and night, and as a representative of the church, I cannot help you unless you agree to become man and wife. Are you willing?"

"I am," Pierre shot back.

The priest turned to Rachel. "And you, Mademoiselle. Will you also agree?"

"Is there no other way?"

The priest shook his head. "None."

Though arranged marriages were commonplace, Rachel's heart cried out for the man she loved. Louis. Nevertheless, she knew she must do this. What other options did she have?

"What is your answer, Mademoiselle?" the priest asked again.

"I will do as you request, of course."

From the look of relief in his gray eyes, Rachel thought Father La Faye must be pleased.

"Your decision is wise, Mademoiselle. Mother Superior and Sister Mary will help you prepare for the ceremony." He smiled. "We happen to have fine wedding garments available here at the church for both a man and a woman. Garments we were able to hide from the soldiers, I might add. The clothes were made for a wealthy couple that had planned to marry here. However, the young woman changed her mind about marrying this man and returned to her family. They left their wedding garments here at the church, and you are free to wear them.

"The woman was small" the priest added, "like you, Mademoiselle. I think her dress will fit you perfectly. And the man was about your size, Pierre."

Rachel felt no joy at the prospect of marriage, especially at this time. Still in mourning, the black dress she wore now would make an adequate wedding gown. Although, she hated to refuse the priest's gift of fine clothes given in such good faith and kindness.

"Thank you, Father," Rachel said.

Another lump formed in her throat. Pierre didn't tell Father La Faye what happened to her parents and neither would she. It was probably best this way. If the priest had known about her trag-edies, he might have insisted they put off the wedding until her period of mourning came to an end. By then, it might be too late to escape safely.

"I know the two of you must flee France quickly," the priest said. "But in any case, you cannot leave until it is dark. A young woman's wedding day is always important, regardless of the circumstances.

"Some disapprove of laughter and light-hearted celebrations at weddings and such. However, I see things differently. We here at Saint Joseph's never miss an opportunity to praise and glorify the Lord.

"Besides, it would give me great pleasure to prepare a wed-ding feast for the son of my dear friend, Andre, who has gone to a better place. I think we can and should rejoice in the blessings of marriage, despite the perils going on around us. I hope you both agree with me."

Rachel didn't know how to reply. She had no wish to marry anyone but Louis, and the deaths left her numb to all emotions. She glanced at Pierre to see if she could guess what he might be thinking.

He caught her watching him and smiled.

She didn't feel like smiling. Rachel hoped for the opportunity to talk to Pierre privately before they took their vows, regardless of the fact that such a desire appeared unlikely. She would barely have time to change her clothes before the ceremony.

"I know this is not the wedding you hoped for," Pierre said to Rachel. "I am not the man of your dreams. But I will honor you with my life and protect you always."

What about love? Rachel knew she could never love any man but Louis. Could Pierre live his whole life without love?

Oh, Louis, I love you so.

She swallowed tears, and moisture filled her eyes. Pierre pulled a white cloth from the waistband of his monk's robe and handed it to her.

"Is she all right?" the priest asked Pierre.

"She will be. The Mademoiselle is upset because of the Captain's visit, I think, and because of the possible danger we are in."

The priest nodded. "Yes, I am sure that must be so."

Pierre and the priest continued with their conversation. Rachel's mind drifted, contemplating her future.

Soon the priest would join Pierre Dupre and Rachel Zimmer in holy—

She hesitated. *I am not Rachel Zimmer. I am Rachel Levin.*

Would the marriage be valid if she married under a false name? It was too late to explain things to Pierre. Besides, she had no desire to tell him that both her parents had been Jews.

Nobody in France knew. Even Louis never knew. In Alsace, others had looked down on her once they learned of her Jewish background. Pierre might think less of her as well. If only she knew the right thing to do.

Rachel and her parents had lived mostly in hiding in Alsace. After her father was falsely accused of a crime, the family rushed to leave the country before he could be arrested.

She remembered how isolated she had felt when she and her parents first arrived in Benoit. At least in Alsace, they had friends among the handful of Jews who lived there.

Marie, a little Jewish girl from Alsace, spoke French and helped Rachel improve her skills in that language. As a child, Marie had been her only playmate, but Marie and her family moved away years before Rachel's family did. Though she and Marie corresponded for a while, they had lost contact in recent years, and she missed her friend and thought about her often.

French words and phrases she learned from Marie had served Rachel well when she moved to Benoit where German was seldom heard. Her father spoke and taught the French language to foreigners in Alsace, but he knew nothing about the Catholic religion. By accepting employment at a French church in Beniot, Rachel made it possible for her parents to be accepted as members of the French Church.

The nuns at Saint Mary's had needed help with cooking and cleaning the church and hired Rachel for that purpose, and she'd felt fortunate to get the job. The family had needed the extra money, and if Rachel hoped to convince others in the community that she and her parents were Catholics, she had wanted to learn as much about the French church as possible.

Rachel had often cleaned and dusted in the hallway outside the priest's office while discussions were going on inside. Occasionally, the priest cracked his door enough that she heard prayers and conversations during confessions. Though risky, she had made sure that no one caught her listening.

After sitting near the back and watching what the others did during religious services a few times, she had felt comfortable enough with what she had learned to teach these rituals to her parents. She carefully taught them all the procedures before escorting them to their first church service. Jews in hostile lands were careful about everything.

She'd discovered that members of the French Church considered confessions to be a sacred trust and that the information given during a confession could never be revealed to anyone for any reason. Perhaps she should reveal her real name to Father La

Faye before taking her wedding vows. Otherwise, she would always wonder if their marriage was a real one.

"Father," she said. "I would like to talk to you privately before the ceremony. Is that possible?"

Rachel thought the priest looked surprised.

"Do you desire to make a confession?" he asked.

"Yes, Father, I do."

He glanced at Pierre. "Monsieur Dupre, would you be so kind as to leave us now so I can hear the Mademoiselle's confession?"

"Of course." Looking confused, Pierre got up and stood in front of his chair. He gazed at Rachel before starting for the door.

"Pierre," the priest said. "I would like for you to come back here after the Mademoiselle takes her leave. I have a few more details I want to go over with you before you sail tonight."

"I will stand outside and wait."

When Pierre left and the door had been tightly closed, the priest gestured toward a low bench with a chair behind it in one corner of the room. "You may kneel there if you like."

Rachel groaned but so softly the priest probably couldn't hear. Earlier, when she'd spent time on her knees, the bench had felt rough and hard. From the looks of it, this bench wouldn't be comfortable either.

Father La Faye sat down in the chair. "I am ready to hear your confession. Are you ready to give it, Mademoiselle?"

"I am." Rachel paused again, wondering what to say. Maybe she should throw caution from her and tell him what she had been thinking. "I am not a follower of the Catholic faith."

"I know that, Mademoiselle."

"You knew?"

"From the beginning. Why else would you have come here with Pierre? I have known his family for years, and they are all members of the Reformed Church."

For a moment, Rachel couldn't speak. She had pretended to be a Catholic for months. Yet logic must have revealed the truth to him. Did he also know she was a Jew?

"You need not follow the rules that Catholics use when giving your confession, Mademoiselle." He smiled. "Try to relax. We shall just talk. Is that acceptable to you?"

"Oh yes, sir." Rachel reached down and rubbed the top of her aching right knee.

"You need not kneel, Mademoiselle. It is not likely that anyone will see or hear you here. Instead, why not pull up a chair and sit down?" He turned his head at an angle and studied her for a moment. "Pierre said your name was Rachel Zimmer. Who is Magdalena Poyer?"

"I have no idea. That name just popped into my mind. Sometimes, when I am nervous, I say things without thinking." Rachel settled onto a chair and gazed up at the priest. "My name is not Rachel Zimmer either."

His forehead wrinkled. "What?"

Her words appeared to have taken him by surprise. He recovered quickly, gesturing for her to continue.

"My name is Rachel Levin, and I want to be married using my real name."

"Levin?"

He opened his mouth as if he planned to say something, but no sound came from his lips. She wished she knew where his thoughts had taken him.

I should never have told him my secret.

However, it was too late to take back her words.

He remained silent for a moment longer, perhaps digesting what she had said. Would the priest tell Pierre what he knew or simply turn her over to the soldiers to be killed?

If God existed and if he helped people as Louis and Pierre had said, she needed His help—now.

Six

"If I use your real name in the wedding ceremony," the priest said to Rachel, "your true identity will be revealed. Is that what you want?"

Hope filled her heart. Perhaps Father La Faye's intentions were to help, not harm, her after all.

"Would it be possible for you to whisper my name?"

"Yes." His deep chuckle ended in a grin. "I think that can be arranged."

"Please speak as softly as you can. If you do, I will be eternally grateful."

"It shall be as you requested." He paused. "But time is short. Have you more to discuss?"

"No, that is all I have to say now."

"Perhaps I should ring for Sister Mary." The priest rose from his chair, went to a cord hanging from the ceiling and pulled it three times. "She should arrive soon."

❧

In the kitchen house, Pierre lifted a cup of cool water to his lips and drank. When he finished, he placed the cup on a table and backtracked to the hallway outside the priest's office. He planned to wait there until Rachel left so he could go inside.

A little monk in a baker's apron stood in front of the door. He had chubby cheeks and a round belly, and with his ear against the door, he appeared to be listening to the conversation going on inside.

Pierre stepped out of sight, pressing his body against the stone wall. His purposes might be served best if the baker questioned whether or not he'd been caught. However, he intended to report this incident to Father La Faye as soon as possible.

After a long pause, he turned the corner again. The monk had disappeared.

Pierre watched as Rachel exited the priest's office. Her loosely fitting black garment swirled around her slender body as she shut the door.

He must tell her about the baker, but not now. There would be time for that later on.

"Did everything go as you hoped?" he asked.

"The priest is very kind—as you said."

A nun approached them from the opposite direction.

"That is Sister Mary," Rachel said. "She has come to take me to the place where I am to prepare for the ceremony."

He'd hoped for the opportunity to speak to Rachel privately. But that chance appeared lost to him now.

"Then I shall see you at the chapel."

A somber expression swept across her face. "Yes, at the chapel."

She misses my brother. Pierre released a deep sigh. *How I wish she cared for me.*

Pierre knocked on the door to the priest's office. As he waited to be invited inside, he watched Rachel hurry down the hall to meet the nun. Today they would become man and wife, but if things had been different, she would be preparing for her marriage to Louis.

⚜

Rachel followed Sister Mary to a room behind the main sanctuary. Nuns waited for their arrival. All eyes centered on Rachel, and every nun smiled when she came in.

"Helping you prepare for your wedding is a joy and a celebration to us," Mother Superior explained. "Am I not right, sisters?"

The rest of the nuns clapped their hands, some nodding and others beaming with a look of excitement in their eyes.

Mother Superior held up a gold gown. "Here is the dress you are to wear during the ceremony. It belongs to my niece, Lucy. We have kept it here all these months on the chance that Lucy will change her mind and marry the young man after all. But so far, she has not returned to claim her dress or wear it at her own wedding. Nor has the young man returned to claim his clothes."

Rachel studied the wedding garment the nun held; the gown that belonged to her niece, the rich young woman the priest had told them about. Lucy had cancelled her wedding at the last minute and gone back to her parents. Though Rachel still wondered, she might never know why Lucy rejected her future husband and went home, leaving her clothes behind.

She was tempted to cancel her wedding to Pierre and run away as Lucy had done. But where would she go? What would she do? Where would she hide?

The gold gown looked expensive and appeared to be fashioned in the latest style. But if things were normal, she would be wearing black and preparing for three funerals instead of putting on a silk wedding gown.

To Rachel, dressing in such fine clothes seemed wrong. Yet she might have appeared ungrateful if she hadn't pretended to be delighted with the ceremony and wedding feast planned by such a kind and compassionate man as Father La Faye. She would simply act as if she enjoyed the wedding celebration while focusing her mind elsewhere.

"Feel the material in this dress," Mother Superior said with excitement in her voice. "It is so lovely."

Though she had no interest in the garment, Rachel ran her fingers over the smooth softness of the fabric and the stiff pattern of French lace. "Yes, the dress is very beautiful."

"The ladies of the French court would be impressed with a garment as fine as this," Mother Superior went on.

Rachel felt fortunate to be wearing it. Still, she wished she could run away and hide.

Sister Mary held up the veil that matched the gown. White lace edged it, and the gold veil looked so frothy and delicate Rachel could see right through it.

"Hurry now, Mademoiselle. You must wash yourself so we can dress you for the ceremony."

Rachel removed all her clothes except her chemise. As she leaned over the white bowl filled with water, she lifted her long hair and rubbed her neck with a wet sponge. The gentle washing warmed her chilled skin and seemed to give her comfort regardless of her crushing grief.

When she finished bathing, Rachel put on a fresh chemise of the softest linen and a pair of white stockings. Sister Mary handed her a strange-looking garment.

"Wear this over your chemise," she said. "This bit of clothing will make your waist seem smaller than it already is. The stays that were sewn into it are made of whalebone, and I think you will like the way it will make you look and feel."

Like magic, the stays pulled her shoulders back, her chest up, and pinched in her slender waist. She'd never owned such a garment and felt like a princess in it.

"Now for your dress," Sister Mary said.

Despite all she'd been through, the soft stir of silk material put a brief smile on her lips.

The nuns pulled the gold gown over her head and shoulders, and yards of material rippled to the floor. The cloth's smoothness brushed her skin going down.

Mother Superior smiled. "Sister Mary will fix your hair." She handed a stick lined with horsehair to the younger nun. "Sister Mary is from Paris and knows what is in fashion."

Rachel started to sit down.

"No, you must not sit, Mademoiselle. It will wrinkle your pretty gown. Stand, please."

The nuns climbed on stools and began brushing out her hair with the strange-looking stick. At last they placed the veil like a crown on Rachel's head.

Mother Superior clapped her hands. "You look perfect, Mademoiselle, absolutely beautiful."

The other nuns gathered around her, hugging her and kissing her on both cheeks.

"Your groom will be pleased," Mother Superior assured her.

Groom. If his name was Louis, everything would be as it should be. Unfortunately, it was not.

She thought of her mother and father and how much she had loved them. They should be standing with her as she said her vows. But as Papa had always said, she must continue on.

Rachel put a smile on her face she truly didn't feel. "I suppose I am ready."

"Yes," Mother Superior said. "You most certainly are. Come." She nodded toward the door. "Your bridegroom waits."

As they walked by a window, Rachel glanced out. A flower garden dotted the green grass below, and she saw blooms in white, yellow, pink, and blue. Rachel would have liked to stand at the window a little longer, but the nuns urged her to move on.

All at once she remembered something she'd heard at the Reformed Church.

"Jesus is the bridegroom," Rachel said, "and He is coming soon, is he not?"

"Yes," Mother Superior said. "Jesus is coming soon."

Rachel had heard once that if God attended a wedding ceremony, all would go well with the couple. But she never prayed or truly believed in God as Pierre did.

Before Rachel went out the door to meet Pierre, Sister Mary handed her a bouquet of white flowers from the garden. A sweet odor floated up to her nostrils.

Rachel stared at the beautifully arranged bouquet. "Thank you."

Sister Mary gestured toward the door. "Hurry, now. It is time to go."

Her future husband stood at the altar, waiting. The priest had said Pierre would be wearing new clothes, but she hadn't expected such finery. Dressed like a prince or perhaps a king, he looked so handsome in black wool breeches and black shoes of the finest leather she couldn't stop staring.

His white doublet had full-length sleeves, and soft ruffles circled his neck and hung from his white collar. A black cape matched his breeches, covering his broad shoulders.

Father La Faye stood before them. Rachel's knees shook, wondering if the priest would keep his promise and whisper her name. He could still betray her in front of everyone and turn her over to the captain.

No, the priest is kind. He will never betray me—I hope.

A window made of colored glass provided a fitting backdrop for the service. In Rachel's opinion, the entire sanctuary of Saint Joseph's Church provided them with the perfect setting for a wedding. If only she loved her future groom, the days ahead would be flawless, but she did not; she could not.

Rachel blinked, trying to pretend that her beloved stood beside her instead of Pierre, and that her parents sat in a pew waiting to witness this solemn event. However, as hard as she tried, she couldn't make her wishes come true.

Glancing behind her, Rachel noticed that the nuns and a few young monks waited in pews near the front. Sister Mary smiled.

Rachel nodded to them. In spite of her grief and fear, she felt a sense of love and safety among these strangers. When she gazed up at Pierre, he winked at her and grinned. She felt encouraged, but knew the feeling wouldn't last.

Though she might never love him, she could think of no better friend than Pierre Dupre, and she intended to be a good wife to him. Rachel wanted to believe that her true identity wouldn't matter to Pierre, that he wouldn't mind learning that she was a Jew, but she couldn't take the chance by telling him the truth.

During the ceremony, Father La Faye whispered her full name, speaking so softly that Rachel doubted Pierre heard his words. Still, she gazed up at her future husband to see his reaction. Pierre merely smiled down at her as if nothing unusual had occurred. She uttered a thankful sigh.

A moment later, she repeated her vows in a voice that sounded almost as soft as the priest's whisper. Yet Rachel couldn't keep from glancing quickly at Pierre and then at those behind them to check their facial expressions. Nobody in the chapel seemed in the least surprised or shocked by what they had seen and heard.

Perhaps she would get through the wedding ceremony after all.

⚓

Captain Vallae engaged his men in the task of watering and grooming the horses while he went back to the Sanctuary for a second look, half hoping to see the young nun again. From a distance, he stared at the compound for half an hour, squinting and shading his eyes from the late afternoon sun. When he could think of no reason for tarrying any longer, he trotted his gelding back to the compound to join his men.

He reached the main road and stopped, gazing back for one last look at the Sanctuary. A peasant in a two wheeled cart drove his sway-backed horse right toward him.

Jean dug his heels into the sides of his mount in order to reach him quickly. The stranger appeared to be coming from the Sanctuary, and the captain hoped to question him.

"Good afternoon," Jean said as if he were speaking to a nobleman. "I am Captain Vallae. What might your name be, sir?"

"They call me Herder because I have a small flock of goats."

"I assume you came from the Sanctuary. Have you news from there you are willing to share with me?" Jean tossed a coin at the man.

The peasant caught the coin and put it in his pocket. The captain smiled.

"I daresay a fancy celebration is going on there now, sir," the peasant said. "Father La Faye sent word this morning, asking my wife to bake bread and sweet cakes. I delivered them."

"A celebration at the Sanctuary on Sunday is unusual, is it not?" Jean said. "Do you know the kind of celebration that might be going on?"

"I would not know formation like that, sir. I do know that a baby in the village was to be baptized soon, but the baby is sickly. Maybe they had him baptized today before the child got sicker."

"Yes." Jean nodded. "A child's baptism is a good reason for a celebration. Do you know a young nun at the Sanctuary by the name of Magdalena Poyer?"

"No. I know Sister Mary and Mother Superior but none of the others."

"You go there often, then?" Jean asked.

"I deliver bread and cakes when they are needed."

"I will be sending one of my men to talk with you—see what you can tell me about the doings at the Sanctuary. And you will get another coin each time you have something new to report."

The man smiled, displaying a mouthful of rotten, yellow teeth. He looked down at the coin in his hand. "For coins like this one, I will tell you and your men anything you wish to know."

⚚

A wedding luncheon of boiled fish, dark bread, butter, eggs, and sweet cakes followed the ceremony in Father La Faye's formal dining room. Rachel couldn't remember seeing a better meal spread before her, but she couldn't eat a bite. Neither sweet cakes nor the kind words spoken during the wedding feast would heal her broken heart. If she could manage to keep from crying until nightfall, she would weep on the boat while Pierre and the boatman slept.

When the meal ended, Pierre took her hand. "Father La Faye has given us permission to use his study for a private conversation, but we cannot talk long. We must hurry. Tonight we sail, and it will be impossible for us to talk privately then. But we have a few minutes alone now, and we can be thankful for that."

Rachel nodded. "Very well."

Pierre led her to the same chair in the priest's office that she sat in earlier and sat down beside her.

"Ma chere," he said tenderly. "There are still a few more things I must tell you—things Father La Faye failed to mention when you were in his office."

Rachel nodded, expecting the worst. She folded her hands on the skirt of her gold gown. "All right."

Pierre cleared his throat. "In order not be captured by the king's army, we must pretend to—

"We need not pretend to be married now, Pierre. We *are* married."

"That is not the kind of pretending I am talking about, Mademoiselle." He grinned. "I mean, Madame. We must pretend. You must pretend to be—to be a boy."

"A what?"

"You must pretend to be my younger brother. It is the only way. You must dress like a boy. And as my younger brother, you will sleep close to my side at night so I can protect you.

"We will both be safe on the little boat tonight because the fisherman who owns the boat is a Huguenot and one of us. I know him well. But we will encounter other men along the way to the ship and on board; sailors and ordinary men, some good and some bad. If evil men were to discover that you are a woman, you could be ravished. And there is more."

"More? What more could there be?"

He reached for a pair of scissors on the table by his chair. "I must cut off your beautiful auburn hair, ma petit chou."

"No!"

"I must. It is the only way to make sure these men will think you are a boy."

Dismay, mixed with regret, swept over her. Her hair had never been cut, and it fell in deep waves below her waist. She'd planned to keep wearing it long and flowing; forever.

Rachel lifted her chin. As Pierre's wife, she intended to do all that was required of her, even if that meant pretending to be his little brother. But when the scissors grew nearer, she shut her eyes.

Snip. She tensed. *Snip, snip, snip.*

Seven

On their wedding night, dressed in rags, Rachel and Pierre exited the back door of the church and crept silently down a narrow path toward the bay. She thought she heard someone following them, but if she looked back, she doubted she would see anyone on such a dark night.

A full moon hid behind a heavy covering of storm clouds, and the air smelled like rain. It might not be the perfect time for a trip by boat, but they dared not wait any longer. Pretending to be brothers, Rachel and Pierre headed toward the water's edge to meet a Huguenot named Rene LaToure.

Pierre had identified Rene as the man with the patch over his eye and the missing tooth that Rachel met at the entry door on the previous day. However, he doubted Rene would connect a boy to the young woman he saw at the safe house.

As they drew closer, she could barely make out the outline of a man standing in the water beside a small boat. "Is that Monsieur LaToure?" she whispered.

"Yes. I am sure of it."

Rachel hoped Pierre's assumptions proved to be right. It wouldn't be hard to be deceived on such a night. The entire coastline looked black now that the moon had drifted behind the clouds.

She felt Pierre's hand on hers. "God is with all those who truly seek Him." He squeezed her hand. "But from now on, I will call you Jacques. It is a suitable name for my little brother. Do you not agree?"

After all that had happened in such a short time, she wanted to pull away and bury her face in her hands.

"Do you not agree, dear one?" he asked again.

"Yes. Whatever you think is best."

Though still not convinced, she started walking toward the boat, and holding Pierre's hand did seem to give her strength.

He'd explained that they would sail to a small island off the coast of La Rochelle that Rene called Beraud, stay there for a few days while he taught them the art of net fishing, and continue up the coast. As fishermen, they would travel from island to island while moving slowly toward English waters.

"It is my hope that along the way, we shall be hired as sailors on a ship bound for England," Pierre had said.

Rachel shuddered at the thought.

Pierre helped her into the boat. "This is Jacques, my younger brother," Pierre said to Rene.

"I am glad to know you, Jacques," Rene replied.

She shook Rene's wet hand. *My name is Rachel.*

The boat moved from side to side as Pierre sat down behind her. She frowned briefly, worried that the little sailing craft might tip over.

"Do not be discouraged," Pierre whispered gently. "All is well."

She wondered if he knew how helpless she felt at that moment.

Rene handed Pierre an oar. "We must leave now, Monsieur, while the moon is behind the clouds. I want us to be far from here before the moon comes out again."

A soft breeze touched her face as Rachel looked toward the front and then the back of the boat, but she couldn't see an outline of the two men. All she heard were the sound of the waves and the splash of the oars as they broke the water.

Later, a swift wind came up. The moon moved out from behind the clouds. Rene sat at the front of the boat, rowing. She turned. Pierre manned the oars behind her as she expected.

The sea became choppy. Rachel gripped the sides of the small sailing craft as it swayed back and forth like a man who had consumed too much wine.

"The wind is a little stronger now," Rene said. "If it stays, we might be able to let the sails take over completely once we are further out from shore. But we must wait and see."

As they continued on through the steady up and down of salty waves, the wind increased. Rachel gripped the sides of the boat, and her stomach churned with every brush of the oars. She tried not to shiver from the dampness and the cold or dwell on her physical condition. Still, a million questions flashed across her mind, and she refused to complain about the nausea that began almost as soon as she climbed on the boat.

"Pierre," Rene said, "we can stop rowing now. Should we need to grab the oars again later on, I will let you know in plenty of time."

A mental picture of Rene flashed before her. She recalled how he had looked, standing in the doorway of the Safe House with the black patch over one eye and the missing front tooth. Pierre had insisted that the fisherman was a devout member of the Reformed Church and completely trustworthy. However, at the Safe House, Rene's appearance probably frightened small children and some adults.

"The King's men have ways of getting information from prisoners," Pierre had said, "and these ways can cause the strongest warrior to reveal information. The less Rene knows about us, the better for all concerned."

The wind slowly died to barely a whisper, and the full moon still darted in and out between dark clouds. The water looked as black as ever except during brief moments when moonlight cast silver shimmers on the sea. The men started rowing again. Rachel huddled at the bottom of the boat.

Rene chuckled softly. "Pierre. Does your brother think crouching down like that will keep the boat from being seen by others?"

"Jacques is tired," Pierre said. "It is past the time when he goes to bed."

"I thought Henri was your little brother's name."

"Jacques is my other brother."

"I didn't know you had two young brothers."

"Jacques is shy and doesn't go out much."

"I see," Rene replied. "Well, it is good that Jacques is able to rest now because it shall be a long night. As you must have noticed, the wind has died down. We might not be able to make it to the island as we hoped. The wind is not strong enough now."

"Where will we spend the night?" Pierre asked.

"On the deck of Little Flower; if we are lucky enough to find land where we can tie her up."

"Little what?" Pierre said.

"Little Flower. It is the name of my boat."

Pierre chuckled. "The name reminds me of a woman."

"It should. My late wife gave her that name."

Rachel had hoped to reach Rene's island, Beraud, and spend the night there; dry and clean inside his cabin. Apparently, that would not come to pass.

The boat slowed down. Rachel sat up to find out what happened. The moon came out enough to see the men anchor the little craft off a tiny island no bigger than a large sandbar.

"We are going to tie the boat to a nearby tree for the night," she heard Rene say. "Afterward, we will eat. I have food in a sack I brought along and heavy tent-cloth. We will cover with the tent material while we sleep."

"How good of you to remember those things," Pierre said.

"I spent many nights at sea after a day of fishing," Rene continued, "and I am always prepared for whatever happens. The tent-cloth will keep the bugs off us as well as the wind and rain."

The boat moved way to one side as the men got out. Holding tight to the sides, Rachel felt the splash of waves, lapping against the craft, and then the boat righted. Sleepy now, she crouched down again and closed her eyes.

A few minutes later the men climbed back into the boat, tipping the craft to one side again. Their cold, wet garments brushed against her, and Rachel shivered as large drops of water sprinkled the boat's small deck.

"Here is the sack with the food in it," Rene said. "We will eat now."

"I think we should give thanks to God for what we have and for keeping us from harm thus far," Pierre said.

"You are right, of course," Rene agreed.

"But first, I must wake up my little brother." Pierre gave Rachel's shoulder a good shake. "Wake up. It is time to eat our supper."

Rachel had been listening to their conversation, but she yawned and stretched as if she'd been sleeping. Louis would have said she was being deceptive. In trousers and pretending to be a boy, she had to admit that he would be right.

"Sit up now," Pierre instructed. "Rene has prepared a wonderful meal for us."

They prayed, and then they ate their meal. Rene told more of his plans for the next day, but Rachel barely listened. Exhausted, she went right to sleep.

❧

Rachel dreamed of a terrible man named Vallae and awoke during the night thinking of that name. She'd heard the name, Vallae, a long time ago when she was a child living in Alsace. She tried to go back to sleep but couldn't.

Not only did the name keep flashing though her mind, Pierre and Rene snored. With the three of them crammed together in the small boat, she could hardly breathe.

Then she remembered. How could she forget that day?

Rachel had just been spat upon by a nasty boy from Alsace who lived down the road from her. She couldn't remember his name, but she remembered how terrible he made her feel. All at once that dreadful day played out before her very eyes as if it was all happening again.

She'd climbed the stairs to the bedroom where her parents slept. Mama sat in her rocker by the big bed, her pale hands on the arms of her chair. She rocked slowly back and forth with practiced timing as if she'd been doing it for hours while waiting for Rachel to return from the store. Her dark hair had been pulled back in a bun under her white cap, and she wore a gray dress that matched the sadness in her pale blue eyes.

"There you are," her mother had said. "How was your day, child?"

"Good, Mama." She'd forced a smile. "Very good."

"And what did you learn?"

That gentile boys are mean, she remembered thinking.

"Speak up, Rachel. I asked you a question."

"I learned—I learned that people are different. Some are good and some are not."

"And?" A hint of a smile turned up the edges of her mother's mouth. "What else?"

"I wish to be good like my dear mother and father."

"Well, come closer and let me look at you."

Rachel stepped forward. Her mother smelled like rosewater.

Mama brushed back a long pigtail that had fallen across her shoulder. "There." Her mother gave Rachel a warm hug, and she hugged back. "Come and sit at my feet now. I am thankful that I can see at all, but my sight is not what it once was and I received a letter today." She handed Rachel a letter. "I want you to read it to me."

"Yes, Mama." Rachel sat cross-legged on the rag rug in front of her mother and opened the letter. "It is from Uncle Simon."

"Oh, Simon, my dear brother-in-law, far away in Switzerland." Her dreamy facial expression slowly melted into a frown. "Well, Rachel, read the letter, please."

Rachel opened the letter. "Dear Hadassah and Amos, I hope this post finds you and Rachel well in your location. I do wish I could see you more often, but the distance between us is too great.

"Something happened here recently that I must tell you about while I am still able to do so. If you fail to hear from me again, you will know that I was put in prison—or worse."

"Stop reading, Rachel," her mother demanded. "Your papa's eyes are better than mine. He will read the letter aloud tonight when he gets home from work."

Rachel had wanted to hear the rest of what her uncle had to say. It had sounded interesting. She handed the letter back with a sense of regret.

After supper that night, instead of going up to her room while Papa and Mama sat at the table talking, young Rachel hid in the space under the stairs with the little door opened a crack. Many candles on holders had been mounted on the wall to keep the stairs well lighted. Later, when Mama and Papa came into the main room near the stairs to read the letter in a better light, Rachel listened.

As Papa began reading, she saw his handsome face through the crack. He stood straight and tall, his dark eyes squinting to read the letter. His brown hair shone in the glow coming from the candle he held, and his reddish beard shimmered down from his chin.

Rachel opened the door a little wider and saw her mother. Mama sat in a chair beside Papa, looking up at him with love and admiration in her eyes.

"Something happened here recently that I must tell you about while I am still able to do so," Rachel heard her papa read aloud.

She swallowed, waiting to hear what he would read next.

"If you fail to hear from me again, you will know that I was put in prison—or worse," Papa went on. "I am sure my situation here in Switzerland is not much different than yours in Alsace. My store is doing well. My sales are better than ever before. Here is my dilemma.

"An elderly gentile man I know by the name of Monsieur Vallae became deeply in debt. He and his wife came to Switzerland from France, and he was about to be put in prison. The couple lives here, but their children and grandchildren remained in France. I pitied Monsieur Vallae because as a Jew, I have experienced similar fates. I offered to help, and I agreed to pay his debt for him to keep him out of prison. In exchange, he was to hand over a small piece of land near his house and put the land in my name.

"The land is not worth much. I really did not want it. But I bought it to keep the man out of prison.

"Now he has gone to the authorities stating that I cheated him out of his land, and that he would never have gone to prison but would have paid his debt in time. The authorities here always side with their own kind in disputes with Jewish merchants, and I have little hope of staying out of prison now. It is merely a matter of time. At least I have no wife and children that must suffer because of this.

"Please write me when you can. I will, of course, answer if I am able. Your Brother, Simon Levin."

Mama had started crying before Papa finished reading.

"Oh, Amos," Mama said between sobs, "poor Simon. What are we to do?"

"There, there."

Through the crack, Rachel saw her father lean down and take her mother tenderly in his arms. They talked in whispers for a while, and she could scarcely catch a word.

Then Papa said, "We cannot let evil doers such as these get us down, my dear. And we must teach our beautiful daughter, Rachel, to lift her head high. Make sure she knows who she is, Hadassah, and where we came from. Make her aware of the history of our people and how we came to settle in Alsace. It is my great hope that someday, we and our descendants shall live in safety."

Poor Uncle Simon, Rachel had thought.

Later, when she could no longer hear the thump of footsteps on the wooden stairs, she knew that her parents had gone up to bed. Rachel had remembered to remove her shoes before tiptoeing up the stairs to her room.

The boat bumped the shore. Rachel jerked, returning to the present.

An especially bright moon made it possible for her to see the rope still tied to a tree. She noticed that the rope had slacked and now floated like a leaf on the top of the water.

Pierre and Rene stopped snoring for a moment, and Pierre turned over on his side. The snoring started again—louder than ever. Perhaps nothing affected their sleep; not canon-fire, not thunder, or boats that hit beaches.

The name, Vallae, still haunted her. The man who caused her uncle so much grief had gone by that same name. It seemed unlikely that the French captain and the Frenchman from Switzerland were related. Yet in her mind, the two men were connected somehow. Of course, it could merely be the similarity of names, or was it the evil found in both of them that made them appear alike?

⁕

Captain Vallae strolled into the inn, carrying a stack of letters he got from the trunk owned by the Jews. He hadn't found the time to read them. Tonight he would. He nodded to the innkeeper behind the counter and climbed the stairs to the room he shared with his new wife.

Yvette stood inside the door, smiling. He'd thought she looked somewhat pretty on the day they wed, two weeks ago. What a change two weeks had made. Compared to the young nun, his bride's dark hair and eyes lacked luster, and her body looked flat and shapeless.

He kissed her lightly on the cheek. "I assume your day went well." Without waiting to hear a reply, he removed his jacket, tossed it on the bed and sat down in a chair in front of a small desk. "I have some reading to do before we go below stairs to eat our evening meal."

She grabbed his jacket. "Let me take your coat and hang it on the hook by the door for you."

The portrait of the young Jewish girl fell out and landed on the wooden floor. Thump. Yvette reached down and picked it up.

"What is this?" she asked.

Jean's eyes narrowed, reaching for the portrait. "Give me that!"

She jerked it out of his reach. "Who is she?"

"This is a portrait of a young woman I am investigating as part of my job, woman. Now, give it to me." He took it from her and placed it on the desk beside the stack of letters. "Never touch this portrait or these letters again. Understand?"

"Of course, I understand. How could I not when you raised your voice at me?" Her mouth turned down, and her dark eyes looked misty. "Do you still love me?"

"Please spare me your tears and words of woe. I have had a long day."

With a soft whimper, she sat down on the edge of the bed. The captain studied the portrait. The beautiful Catholic nun held a power over him in ways no other woman ever had. Apparently, the young girl in the portrait had similar abilities.

Jean reached for the stack of letters and surveyed the one at the top of the pile. *Alsace.* So the Jews came from Alsace, did they? How interesting.

He stiffened, and a curse blackened his brain. The nun claimed to have come from Alsace, and she spoke French with a German accent.

Eight

When Pierre awoke the next morning, Rachel's head was on his shoulder. He wondered if she'd slept in his arms all night, secretly hoping that she had. The priest had joined them in holy matrimony for life, and yet he had no notions of marital bliss—now or in the future. Their wedding had been a mere formality making it possible for them to travel together with the blessings of the church. Rachel still loved his brother, and that would never change. He must stop dreaming that it would—that it might. Pierre knew he would love Rachel forever and wanted to protect her. Would that be enough?

Rene had set out his nets before turning in the previous night. As Pierre lay there beside Rachel, Rene got up, stretched and pulled in his catch. Pierre got up, careful not to shake the boat and wake Rachel.

Rene grabbed a pan for cooking. "Come, Pierre. We will prepare our meal on the beach."

"What about Jacque?"

"Leave him. He would be of little help to us and probably needs the rest. We can wake him when the food is ready to eat."

Pierre followed Rene's lead and deserted the boat, wading to the shore. Seawater had caught in the cuffs of Pierre's brown trousers, and he had to shake it all out. Rene put a fish on a clean-looking rock and cut it down one side with a knife.

Pierre removed a sharp knife from a scabbard attached to his belt. "Let me help you."

"I would appreciate it." Rene glanced up from his work. "Are you a fisherman, Pierre?"

Pierre shook his head. "I like to put the bait on the hook and throw the line, but I am not a fisherman as you are."

Rene grinned. "You will be, soon enough." He pointed to a spot on the beach. "We will build our fire there. We need to gather dry leaves, sticks, and small logs for the fire. But stay away from the water's edge when gathering wood. The wood found there would be too damp to use in the fire."

Pierre nodded. "I know."

"I never intended to suggest that you would not know," Rene said. "Forgive me. I sometimes tell more than I need to in order to save time."

Pierre soon realized that Rene appeared to be something of an expert at everything he did—from fishing to fire building—and had a blaze going in minutes.

"Would you like for me to cook the fish?" Rene asked.

"Please do," Pierre said. "Since I know nothing about cooking, I shall leave you now and wake my—my brother. He will be hungry after the long night in the boat."

"There is a loaf of bread in a sack on the boat," Rene said. "Bring it with you when you and Jacques return to break the fast."

Rachel sat up as Pierre waded toward her.

"Rene is preparing a wonderful meal for us."

"I am sure I will enjoy it."

Pierre reached over and grabbed the sack with the bread in it. He helped her out of the boat.

She lowered her legs into the water. As she stood by the boat, she crossed her arms over her chest. "The water is c—cold."

"Yes," he said, "it is."

Rachel seemed chilled, all right. But what else did she feel? Was she tired? Depressed? Worried? Did she regret that they were married?

Pierre wanted those questions answered. How he longed to know Rachel well enough to identify those emotions in her movements and facial expressions. He hoped to learn her ways, her likes and dislikes, instead of merely guessing.

Perhaps she *was* worried. He knew that feeling well. Pierre hadn't wanted to stop for the night. The soldiers could have attacked them while they slept. He'd hoped to reach the island as soon as possible. Now it would be noon before they arrived at their destination. He squinted at the horizon.

"What were you thinking about just then?" she asked.

"The horizon. It is beautiful this morning."

"Yes. But that is not what you were thinking about. You were looking for something, perhaps a boat."

Could it be that Rachel wondered about his thoughts like he wondered about hers? Did she want to know him better? It seemed unlikely; she still cared for Louis. And yet, he hoped and prayed.

After eating a meal of fresh fish and dark bread, they started out again. The sea looked fairly calm that morning, and the rowing seemed faster and easier after the long rest.

Rene had said that they should reach Beraud in only a few hours.

On the previous night, Rachel had mentioned feeling sticky and dirty. He had felt the same, but didn't say so. Rene had assured him that his sister would provide them with a place to wash and change their clothes as soon as they reached the island, and Pierre knew Rachel would be pleased.

He thought of how fetching she had looked as she warmed her hands in front of the fire that Rene had made on the beach. The clothes of a young boy couldn't hide her beauty.

⸎

Pierre noticed that the noonday sun had warmed the air by the time he, Rachel, and Rene reached the shallow water near the island. He could see the beach ahead.

Rachel got out of the boat before they pulled it on shore. Pierre saw her shivering. By now, she would have noticed that the air had warmed some. The water hadn't and felt almost as cold as it had on the previous night.

Rachel took a step, slipped on the slick and muddy bottom and fell. Only her head remained above the water. She got up quickly. Round droplets of water streamed down her neck and shoulders.

Pierre got out of the boat to help. But before he could reach her, she turned and waded toward the shore.

The water came almost to her hips, and her wet clothes hugged her slender form. As she trudged forward, her short auburn curls came alive in the sunshine in shades of rust, gold, and copper. As he looked on, she pushed a stray curl behind her ear.

Pierre liked looking at her, but he didn't want other men to see her like that. He peered down at a jacket he'd dropped at the bottom of the boat. He would wrap it around Rachel as soon as they got to shore.

"Your little brother walks like a girl," he heard Rene say.

"She is just—I mean, he is tired."

Rene laughed. "So Jacques *is* a girl."

"Did I confirm that to be true?"

"Seeing her is proof enough. And it is not merely her walk but her voice, too. In fact, I judged Jacques to be a woman practically from the first moment she climbed on my boat. Now, I know for sure."

Rachel turned to face them. "I heard what you said." Hands on her hips, she glared at Rene. "I am Pierre's little brother."

"There is no point in pretending any longer, Rachel. Rene knows."

"I think I know you, Mademoiselle." Rene stared straight at Rachel. "But you look different now. Were you at the meeting place the day the ship sailed?"

Rachel didn't reply.

"She was at the meeting place that day," Pierre said for her. "And her name is Rachel Zimmer. She moved to Benoit a year ago from Alsace."

"Rachel Zimmer. You are the one with the long auburn hair. A man is not likely to forget a young lady like you."

"Pierre cut off my hair so I would look more like a boy. However, it did not suffice, did it? I still look like a girl."

"It *can* work," Rene insisted. "We merely have to teach you how to talk and walk like a boy."

Rachel nodded, and she turned back toward the beach. Pierre and Rene pulled ahead of her and dragged the heavy boat all the way to the tall grass. By the time Rachel joined them, several men, women and children had gathered around them.

Pierre wrapped his jacket around her shoulders while Rachel stood there shivering.

Rene pointed to Rachel. "I would like you to meet Mademoiselle Rachel Zimmer."

All eyes focused on her.

She blushed. Decent women didn't wear men's clothes, and everybody knew it.

Rene motioned toward a man and woman about his age at the edge of the crowd. Though shorter by several inches than Rene, the dark intense little man looked enough like the fisherman to be related. The short and plump woman at his side had a face as round as her fat little belly, and it occurred to Rachel that she must be with child.

"This is my brother, Felix, and his wife, Yvonne," Rene said. "The woman to the left of Yvonne is my sister, Suzette Debose."

Rachel nodded toward them and forced a smile. Suzette's grin made her feel welcome but only for a moment. She turned away from the crowd and gazed out at row after row of whitecaps rolling toward the shore.

They could see that she had dressed as a boy, and her garments stuck to her body like the clothes of a woman of the night. They must hate her. People always hated Jews.

I am so ashamed. If I could fall in a hole and bury my body in the sand, I would.

"Suzette," Rene said to the thin little woman with dark brown hair, "take this young lady to your house and give her dry and suitable clothes."

"I will be glad to."

"I think you will like my sister," Rene said to Rachel. "Suzette is friendly and known to be both gentle and kind."

"I am sure—" Rachel turned and flinched when she realized that Suzette had moved beside her. "I meant to say that I am sure I shall like your sister very much."

"Come." Suzette reached out and grabbed Rachel's hand. "I will take you to my house."

As they started to walk off, Rachel heard one of the children say, "That boy walks like a girl."

Rene laughed. "She *is* a girl, nephew."

Rachel felt her cheeks warm with a mixture of embarrassment and humiliation. Yet she forced a smile and allowed Rene's sister to lead her up the bank to the house on a nearby rise. As soon as she stepped inside, a fire in the hearth warmed her, and she smelled stew cooking. A pot hanging from a hook in the fireplace appeared to be the source of that pleasing odor.

She saw a table, four chairs, a shelf stacked with dishes and two narrow beds end to end along the back wall. A wooden screen covered one corner of the room and must serve as a dressing area. She also saw a door leading outside or to another room.

Suzette motioned toward one of the chairs. Rachel sat down.

"Why do you dress as you do?" Suzette asked.

Rachel didn't have an answer.

She'd intended to make everybody think she *was* a boy. Presumably, the deception didn't apply to these people, and not having to pretend would make life a little easier. She saw no reason not to answer Suzette's question now. In fact, she wanted to explain, lest Suzette think she enjoyed being the center of attention.

"Soldiers of the King are looking for us," Rachel explained. "My friend, Pierre, thought it would be best if I pretended to be his little brother."

"My son Anton was right. Boy's clothes will not convince anyone. According to the Bible, it is wrong for women to dress like men and for men to dress and act like women. But in your case, I suppose it is necessary. Tomorrow, Anton and the other boys will teach you how to walk and act like a boy." Her smile started in her eyes. "But for now, how would you like to wash yourself and put on clean clothes?"

"That sounds wonderful, but what kind of clothes?"

The older woman laughed. "Tomorrow is soon enough to dress like a man. But for the rest of the day, Mademoiselle, you shall wear one of the dresses I have here."

"Your brother said you were kind. Now I know you truly are."

Suzette went over to the other side of the room, pulled a clean but tattered green dress from a hook on the wall and handed it to Rachel. "Wear this dress with my best wishes. My daughter left it here when she married and moved away, and it should fit you perfectly."

"You cannot know how much I appreciate your kindness."

"As a woman, I think perhaps I can. You can dress on the other side of that wooden screen." She pointed to a metal tub on the floor near the fireplace. "I have water still warm from the fire for your bath."

"Thank you, Suzette."

"You are most welcome." She hesitated. "Is Pierre your intended?"

"My what?"

"Your intended husband." Suzette went over to the fireplace, grabbed a rag and pulled the kettle from the hook above the fire. "I am asking because I noticed how he kept looking at you when we were on the beach." She poured water from the kettle into the tub. "With the eyes of love," she added with a smile.

"Oh no, Pierre does not love me," Rachel said from the other side of the wooden screen. "Not at all; we are merely friends. He only married me because. . . ."

"Are you and Pierre married?"

Rachel hesitated. "Yes." She paused again. "Like you, Pierre and I have enemies who want to capture us or worse, and we needed to leave France in haste. A priest we know suggested that I dress as a young boy to keep dangerous men from bothering me while traveling. Journeys can be risky for a young woman alone. Being a priest, Father La Faye would not agree to help us escape unless we promised to become husband and wife."

Suzette smiled as if she knew something Rachel didn't and finished pouring water into the metal tub. "When did you marry?"

"Yesterday at the Sanctuary near La Rochelle."

"Yesterday?" Suzette put the kettle on a smooth rock by the hearth. "And on your wedding night the two of you slept in the boat with my brother?"

"Yes."

"Well, tonight you and Pierre shall sleep in my bed as a proper married couple should."

Bed? Rachel swallowed. *With Pierre? Not if I have anything to say about it.*

"Ours is a marriage in name only," she explained. "And not a real marriage at all."

"If you were married in a church by a pastor or a priest, it is a real marriage, Madame. You can be sure of that. And I will have the bedroom prepared when the two of you turn in for the night."

Nine

The breeze at sunset had a fishy odor as Rachel walked barefoot along the water's edge. The western sky glowed in shades of red and pink, and she felt the soft gush of wet sand between her toes and listened to the slap of waves against the shore. The clouds around the fleeing sun were edged in gold.

But only one cloud captured her attention. It looked soft and fluffy and was shaped like a bed; the bed inside Suzette's house.

In moments, it would be too dark to tarry by the sea any longer. Pierre waited for her in the bedroom Suzette had prepared for them, and she must meet him there regardless of her misgivings. She knew from past experience that worry-lines probably creased her forehead as she considered what lay ahead.

Her mother had said that a wife should always do exactly what her husband told her to do if she hoped to have a happy marriage, but Mama said nothing about the duties of a wife in the bedroom with her husband. What would Rachel say to him? What would he say? What would he do? Mama hadn't answered any of those questions.

She moved over to the wooden pier, sat down and wiped the sand from her feet with a cloth she used as a belt. A glance back at the cabin showed a weak light coming from the bedroom window, highlighting the guilt she felt at not returning sooner.

Rachel put on her sandals and looked up at the western sky. The sun had disappeared. Only a hint of red and pink remained.

Though early yet, Pierre had worked hard that day helping Rene and the other men chop wood and fix the roof of one of the huts. Perhaps by now, he would have fallen asleep. She started back to the cabin.

The instant she opened the bedroom door and stepped inside, she sniffed the too sweet scent of flowers. The strong odor of perfumed air tickled her nostrils. Rachel always sneezed after coming in contact with certain odors, an internal reaction she never fully understood. Pressing her forefinger under her nose, she waited, and then she sneezed.

The room looked dark except for a single lighted candle on a table near the bed. The glow surrounding the candle made it possible for her to see, but not much. She grew closer. The bed was empty. A large blue cloth covered it. Two wool blankets in shades of brown outlined the edges of the blue bed-cloth.

But where is Pierre? She'd expected him to be here.

The distant roar of the sea drifted in from a window, and she felt the chill of a brisk wind. Rachel hugged her shoulders, as she gazed around.

"Pierre?"

"I am here on a bench near the window," he said.

She saw the outline of a man in the far corner of the room under the window.

"Get the candle and sit with me," he said. "There is an extra chair. We can talk."

Rachel took the candlestick in both her hands and walked toward him. It seemed easier to move around now that her eyes had become accustomed to the dim light. But thoughts of the bed and what might happen there caused a shivery feeling to cover her like a cold blanket on an icy night.

Pierre sat on a wooden bench, and he motioned for her to take the only chair in the room. Rachel put the candle on the floor near the rock wall, where it would be out of the way. The chair creaked when she sat down.

She planned to tell him that she had no intentions of sharing his bed. All at once, she felt a blush coming. Though she'd been practicing that very speech all evening, she felt incapable of speaking her mind on such a delicate and very personal subject. Had it not been so late, she would have spent more time down at the beach, trying to come up with ways of expressing her feelings.

"Why are you trembling?" Pierre asked. "Are you cold or is it for another reason?"

She swallowed. "I do not suffer from the cold."

He nodded. "I think I see what you mean. Thank you for your honesty." He leaned forward on the bench. A moment later, he turned and looked at her. "You have no cause to worry, Rachel. I plan to sleep on this bench tonight. You can have the bed all to yourself, and nobody will be the wiser."

A sense of relief swept over her. "Thank you." She forced a smile. "But what about tomorrow night and all the nights to come?"

"I am your servant, Madame, and you have lost your parents and your intended husband. But even if you were not in mourning, I would honor you and your wishes. And I always will. I will sleep here on this bench as long as we are on the island, and nothing will change after we leave here unless you tell me otherwise."

I never will. She lifted her chin as if she thought it would confirm it.

Yet he looked so handsome seated there on the bench that she felt the urge to reach out to him; stroke his face or his dark, wavy hair.

Under the circumstances, that wouldn't be right. He could get a wrong impression, think that she cared more than she did or ever could.

Still, his lips looked soft and appealing by candlelight, and his brown eyes shone with warmth and tenderness. She'd never seen lashes on a man that were as long as his and she remembered how his muscled arms had handled the oars hour after hour, as if he'd rowed the ocean and battled waves forever. She knew those same arms would protect her, yet she still loved Louis. If only they weren't similar in so many ways.

Rachel took a deep breath and let it out slowly. What should she say or do now? Her mother had said that men don't always know how to talk to a woman and that a wife should keep the conversation going at all times.

"I understand that you and your family have an ultimate destination," she said. "First England and then Scotland. But why Scotland? What is the attraction there?"

"My mother had a favorite uncle who moved to Scotland almost twenty years ago. The uncle never married and recently died. He left his home in Luss, Scotland to my mother. We are losing everything we own here in France, but we have a home waiting for us there. It should not be surprising that we decided to settle in Scotland."

"No, not surprising at all." She glanced at the bed again. "I will give you one of the blankets. It will get cold later." Rachel studied the bed with its high bedposts and the blue quilt spread over the straw. "It is warm in here now. One blanket will be plenty for me."

"There is no need for you to do that. I will cover myself with my cape. I have done so many times on nights much colder than this."

"Very well." She gazed toward the wooden screen like the one she used as a dressing room earlier. "I will need to prepare for the night. Will you please turn away until I have gotten into bed?"

"Of course." He chuckled softly. "And forgive me for laughing. I am no more accustomed to our peculiar situation than you are."

She felt better. His nerves were as frazzled as hers.

Leaving the candle by her bed, she moved behind the screen and removed everything but her chemise. She hung her dress over the screen and climbed into bed, pulling the covers all the way up to her neck. The straw bedding under the covers poked her back in several places, but it felt more comfortable than sleeping on a hard bench, as Pierre had volunteered to do.

"You may turn back around now, if you like," she said.

She remembered how his face had looked at their wedding when he turned, and she saw it in profile. His nose had looked straight and strong, as did his chin. Surprised to realize that Pierre looked more handsome than Louis, she reminded herself that appearances meant nothing.

Rachel could never love Pierre as she'd loved his brother, but his friendship meant everything to her. Perhaps she should share her worries and misgiving with him while she had the opportunity.

"As we were hurrying to the boat last night," she said, "I thought I saw someone following us."

"I thought the same."

"Could it have been the captain, do you think?" she asked.

"No. If he were nearby, we would know it."

"Then who?"

"I saw one of Father La Faye's bakers—the short, fat, little monk—listening at the door when you and the priest were talking in his office."

Rachel felt her throat tighten. "Do you think he heard my confession?"

"He might have heard some of it but not all," Pierre said. "The baker was not at the door long enough. But if I were you, I would not think of this again. To worry will help no one."

However, she couldn't stop thinking about it. If the baker told the captain what he heard, they could all be in even more danger.

And Pierre would know I am a Jew.

She'd wanted to tell him about her Jewish heritage since the day of the fire. Somehow, she couldn't. Pierre could turn against her as so many had before him, and she couldn't—wouldn't let that happen.

❧

Five days later, the young officer returned from the Office of Records in Paris with the report. Captain Vallae sat at a table outside his tent, drinking a cup of tea when the post arrived. As soon as the young man left, he opened the letter and began reading.

Until they received his letter, the authorities in Paris knew nothing about any Jews in Benoit and had never heard of the name Magdalena Poyer. However, they promised to check again in order to make sure.

According to the letter, he was being reprimanded for burning down that house in Benoit and killing everybody inside. Jean had always thought he was the king's best officer. He couldn't believe his eyes.

So what if he said in his report that they resisted arrest when they hadn't. Every officer he knew wrote reports; reports that put them in a better light.

Jean threw his tin cup against the bell-pole. A metallic ding rang out. His eyes narrowed, and he glanced around. He didn't see anyone watching him, but someone reported what happened in Benoit to the authorities without his approval or knowledge. *How dare they?* He'd been betrayed.

Jean Vallae folded the paper and slipped it in his vest pocket. His hand brushed the portrait of the young Jewess. He frowned as anger and desire competed for control of his emotions.

The letter stated that though the king had no love for Jews or French Huguenots, he demanded complete control over their destinies. Apparently, the king disliked having others make important decisions on his behalf, even when justified. In the future, Jean would cover his tracks when making unauthorized decisions. He wouldn't risk a second scolding from the power-heads in Paris until he decided whether or not to stay in the military.

⚜

Using a pen and a sheet of paper that Suzette had given her, Rachel wrote a letter to Father La Faye and the nuns thanking them for all their help. It could be a long while before she would be able to send the letter, but when the time came, she would be ready.

For the next three days, Rachel along with Pierre listened as Rene taught them how to make and care for fishing nets, and he instructed them in the art of fishing and boating. Rene and his young nephew, Anton, also introduced Rachel to a new way of walking.

"Stop fluttering your hands about so," Rene suggested during the instructions. "Try keeping your arms to your sides unless you are doing something with them, like rowing a boat or chopping wood."

While Rene and Anton looked on, Rachel put her arms to her sides stiffly and moved forward.

Rene shook his head. "You look like a toy soldier. Show her what I mean," he said to his nephew. "Show her how to walk like a man with a purpose."

Anton nodded and did as he'd been told.

Rachel watched with her head slanted at an angle. She could see no difference between the way she walked and the way the men moved. Later, when she attempted to walk as she'd been told, the humor of her situation sank in, and she found it difficult not to laugh out loud. However, proper young women, even married ones, controlled their emotions in public. That rule had been forced upon her since early childhood.

She put her right foot forward, attempting to mimic their movements. She took a step and then another.

"Better," Rene said. "But keep walking. You will get it right if you keep practicing."

Rachel admired Rene, but she felt a weight had been lifted from her shoulders when a few days later he left for the mainland. Not only would she be spared lessons on fishing and boating, she wouldn't have to walk like a boy, and he'd promised to mail her letter.

⚜

Captain Jean Vallae had been seated at a table inside the tent he called his office for almost an hour. For the umpteenth time, he dipped a feather pen into a cup filled with ink in hopes of writing down his next plan of action, but he couldn't seem to come up with one.

According to the Herder he met outside the Sanctuary, the Huguenots had been having religious services in various homes in Benoit, and even some members of the French church knew about it. Jean meant to put a stop to it, regardless of his orders to the contrary.

Once, he'd loved the challenge of his job, but these new orders tied his hands, not to mention the letter of reprimand. Still he had to find the young Huguenot who escaped and Magdalena Poyer or whatever her name was. He would do anything to remove Magdalena and the young Jewish girl from his mind. They were all he thought about.

He put down his pen, walked to the door of the tent and pulled back the flap. A heavy mist covered the field where he and his men had camped. He couldn't see the other tents or the men who slept in them. He saw a mental image of a young woman, and she was not his wife.

Jean stepped out the door, reached up, and rang the bell to call his men. He waited and rang again.

A young soldier rushed up to him from one of the smaller tents. "Reporting for service, sir. What will you have me do?"

"Call all the men together and tell them to prepare to ride."

"You mean tonight, sir?"

"Yes, tonight. We will be riding into the village of Benoit. Huguenots live there, and we must discover who they are and where they live. I plan to round up all the men of the village for questioning."

"Anything else, sir?"

"I want to learn all I can about a handsome young Jewish woman with long hair, a young nun by the name of Magdalena Poyer, and a young man posing as a monk. I think the man is a Huguenot who attended an unauthorized meeting in Paris. As you know, we caught one of two outlaws on the day we burned down that house in Benoit. Now we must find the other man and the woman."

"Right away, sir."

Jean Vallae watched the young soldier disappear into the night. He grabbed his sword and dropped it into his scabbard.

Tonight we ride, regardless of the reprimand I might get for doing it.

Jean raced his gelding toward his destination with his men at full gallop behind him. Outside the village of Beniot, he instructed his men to stop and rest their horses. One of them had built a campfire, and tea warmed in a kettle there. He poured a cup of hot tea, drank a swallow of it, and stretched out in front of the fire with his head on a rolled blanket.

After a few minutes Jean snored loudly, pretending to be asleep, and he listened as his men talked among themselves. Previously, he'd gained important information in this way; information he might never have gotten in any other way.

"I think the captain could get into more trouble with the authorities in Paris if he raids the village again without written permission," Jean heard Soldier Duval say. "I heard that Captain Vallae was reprimanded for having those people in Beniot killed and burning down that house without an order to do it. If he ignores another command, we could soon have a new captain leading us."

"You might be right," Soldier Charbonneau said. "I admire the captain, but I think he has been acting strangely."

"Perhaps something is bothering him."

"Maybe he and his new wife are battling. All new husbands know about that." Duval laughed. "Is that not so?"

"Indeed." Charbonneau chuckled under his breath. "Pleasing a new wife is an impossible task."

Laughter rang out again.

The captain stiffened. He hadn't known that at least two of his men knew about the letter of reprimand, much less the problems in his marriage. Now all his men knew.

Jean had wondered how the authorities found out what really happened in Benoit. He'd glossed over the report, made the killings seem necessary, and he had assumed someone in Beniot turned him in. Now he thought one of his men had betrayed him, and for Jean, betrayal could only come from an enemy.

He liked knowing the identity of his enemies in order to monitor them and eventually get even with them. Instead of burning and killing the Huguenots left in Beniot as he wanted to do, for now, he would merely put a scare in them and send them a stern warning.

Jean thought about the raid in Benoit on the previous night as he went out the next morning to relieve himself. He'd almost reached the woods when an aid handed him a second letter from Paris. Jean skimmed the first two pages and sighed deeply.

No reprimands.

He sat on a bench outside his tent and read the letter again.

'It is likely that the Zimmer family came from Alsace and are Jews as you suggested,' he read. 'We have noted this for our records here in Paris, and I am writing to leaders in Alsace and elsewhere to see what they know. When a report arrives, we will have a copy sent to you. We still have no information on Magdalena Poyer.'

Useless. He tore the letter in half. *This document told nothing I did not already know.*

Jean decided to read one of the letters he found in the trunk again, the one that had interested him most. Perhaps some new insight might come from a second reading. He pulled it from his vest pocket and began reading.

It seemed ironic. Simon Levin, the Jewish merchant who cheated his grandfather out of lands in Switzerland, was related to the Jewish family whose house he burned down. Clearly, the Levin family got the punishment they deserved.

His grandfather had always said that the Jew who cheated his family had relatives in a small village in Alsace. But was the young Jewess in the portrait also the lovely young nun he saw at the church? He still didn't want to think so.

He needed proof.

Tomorrow he would go back to the church and confront that priest—even if he was related to a high government official. Then he would know the name of the Jewish girl as well as the identity of the beautiful nun.

Once and for all time.

⚬

The next morning, Captain Jean Vallae's men stood at attention in front of the church. He pounded on the door. Father La Faye opened the door and stepped back from it when the captain came inside.

A group of nuns stood in the hall in front of the church sanctuary.

"Move along," Mother Superior insisted, herding the nuns inside.

"Father La Faye," the captain said. "You are the person I came here to see."

"And for what reason might that be?" the priest asked in a gentle tone.

Jean reached in his vest pocket and pulled out the portrait of the young girl. "I came to find *her*." He handed the painting to Father La Faye. "Is she here?"

The priest studied the portrait carefully. "I have never seen this portrait before, Captain Vallae. Who is the young girl in the painting?"

"I think you know her." The captain smiled mockingly. "Is she not the young nun I saw the last time I was here?"

The priest shook his head. "The young nun you saw and the girl in the portrait look nothing alike; nothing at all."

"I disagree. Bring her out so I can judge for myself."

"Unfortunately, that is impossible."

"Why?" the captain demanded.

"She is no longer here."

"She must be here. Where else would she be?"

The priest shrugged.

"Your answer is not acceptable, Father. Bring out the girl and the young monk who spoke on her behalf as well. Do it at once. Or I will call in my men to search this building—inch by inch—including the nuns' quarters."

"If you do such a thing, you will be extremely sorry, Monsieur. As a priest, I must defend the nuns under my charge at all costs, and if you invade their privacy, I will have no choice but to report your actions to my uncle in Paris. I think you know who my uncle is and the connections he has."

"Stop hiding behind your uncle with me, Father. I have important friends as well. And I was ordered to find the young Huguenot, the nun, and the girl in the portrait—one way or another." The captain hesitated, waiting to see if the priest believed the lie he'd told. "So Father, will you do as I commanded, or will you ignore my orders?"

"I have nothing more to say on this matter, Captain, other than what I have already said. You must do what you were told to do. And I must do what I think the bishop would have me do."

The captain's hands became fists. His jaw turned to iron. He'd felt his anger boiling from the moment he stepped in the door of the church. Now it erupted deep within him, and he could feel it spilling out like molten rock. If he didn't control his emotions immediately he would strike the priest—or do something still more deadly. Not wise, considering the identity of the priest's uncle.

"I have my orders, and they will be carried out," Jean said. "My men will now search this structure as well as the out buildings. This will include the nun's quarters. I expect the nuns to answer all my questions to my satisfaction, and if they fail to do that, I will have my men examine them personally."

"No," the priest exclaimed. "You would not dare."

"Tell the nuns to cooperate. If they do, I will not have to use *other* means."

"My uncle will hear of this."

"It will be my word against yours. Besides, your uncle is in Rome."

"How did you know that?"

"I have my ways. Now, go in and tell the nuns what I said. It will sound better coming from you."

Ten

Well, it is done. Captain Jean Vallae dismounted, handing his reins to the groom that worked for the innkeeper.

At least now he knew the young nun and the monk weren't hiding in Saint Joseph's church. He would look for them and the young Jewess elsewhere—unless the two women were one and the same, as he tended to think.

He'd almost reached the front steps in front of the inn when he heard someone coming up behind him. He glanced back.

A short plump little monk stood a few feet away. "Captain Vallae."

His eyes narrowed. "Yes."

"My name is Brother Julian. May I speak to you for a moment?"

"If your aim is to make me feel guilty for making the nuns cry, you will be wasting your time, and mine."

"It is not about the nuns, Captain. I have information for you."

"Speak up, then." Eager to go inside and eat his supper, the captain held his riding quirt in his right hand and tapped its handle against his left palm. "I am meeting my wife inside, and I am late."

"This will not take long—for the right price, of course."

"Price?" Jean laughed. "A monk selling information? Has the church decayed to this?"

"The information has to do with the young nun you are looking for."

Jean paused to consider. Even a little news must be worth something.

"Very well, what is your price?"

"I am tired of being a monk. I want to work for you. For the information, I want you to hire me. That is my price."

"Hire you? A monk?" He gave a short laugh. "What possible need would I have for a monk? I have never believed in God."

"I am a cook at the Sanctuary, and a good one. I am also able at finding out information when others fail. In monk's clothes, I seem harmless. People talk to me—trust me—tell me things."

"Are you applying for the job of my confessor, sir?"

"You could do worse than have someone like me on your side."

"Let me hear the information you are selling. Afterward, I will decide about your future under my charge."

"Money first," the monk insisted. "Then I talk."

"Now you want money." The captain motioned toward the front door. "Come into the Inn. We can talk in there. I am sure we can come to an agreement. Besides, I am famished."

The monk followed the captain inside the inn and sat down across from him. Captain Vallae ordered mugs of ale for each of them.

"I shall drink while you talk." The captain handed the monk a silver coin. "But do hurry." Jean reached for his mug. "I arrived late getting here, and as I said, my wife is waiting."

Brother Julian had chubby fingers. Jean noticed them when the monk put the coin in a pouch attached to a belt around his ample waist. The monk also had an annoying speaking voice that reminded Jean of two tin cups banging together.

"What can you tell me about the young nun?" the captain asked. "Where is she?"

"The nuns seldom talk among themselves, Captain. However, I heard them talking today shortly after you left. The young nun you mentioned and a monk married on the very day you came to the Sanctuary the first time."

"Married?"

"Yes. I was busy in the kitchen on that day and didn't hear of it until now. The marriage was permitted because she had not taken her final vows. Nor had the monk taken his vows."

"How did they escape? I had assumed that ships on the high seas were being watched."

"I think she and the monk fled in a small boat; probably a fishing boat. Two people walked toward the bay after what I now know was a wedding ceremony, but it was a dark night, making it impossible to see much."

"Who might the owner of the boat be?" the captain asked.

"I have no answer at this hour. But if I worked for you, I would find out soon enough."

"How?"

"I am known and trusted by the fishers. They talk quickly when they have a jug of wine under their belts. As your hireling, I will find out the information you need."

The captain smiled mockingly. "Perhaps I do need a confessor as well as a cook, after all. If you will find out the information I desire, I will make you my priest. When can you have this new information for me?"

"It should not take long. A few days." The monk shrugged again. "Perhaps a week."

"Very well. I arrive here at the inn every night around this hour. When you have the information I want, come back here and we will talk again."

A week later, Jean still hadn't heard from the monk, but the young soldier he'd planted in Benoit had returned. Jean was eager to hear what the young man had to say.

"Did anyone report seeing the young women I am seeking?" the captain asked.

The soldier shook his head. "I am sorry, captain. No such report came in."

The next morning Captain Vallae paid a visit to his superiors in hopes of getting permission to chase after the missing nun and monk despite the lack of new information coming from Benoit. If his effort failed, he planned to take on the task anyway—with or without military orders to back up his decision. He'd inherited a great deal of money from his maternal grandparents and together with what he'd saved since joining the army, he'd accumulated enough wealth to make an extended trip to England possible.

As soon as he arrived at Station Headquarters in La Rochelle, a young aid escorted him down a long hall. His love of the army had evaporated along with his interest in his young wife, and he wanted to travel now. Still, he would need to display discipline and respect for authority if he wanted his request to be granted.

"The general's office is ahead," the aid said.

Jean nodded. "Thank you very much."

As a general in the king's army, his father–in–law had helped Jean get his commission. Now stationed at military headquarters in Paris, Yvette's father would hear what he said and did today soon enough.

He shrugged. *No matter.*

He felt fortunate that his father-in-law lived miles away. If he had been stationed in La Rochelle, Jean would probably be put in prison for wanting to leave the military and for deserting his daughter, Yvette.

The general in charge of the army in La Rochelle sat behind a large oak desk and frowned when Jean came in.

Shoulders back and head held high, Jean hoped to present a respectful pose. "I have reason to believe that two or possibly three citizens of Benoit are enemies of the crown. I wish to be assigned the job of tracking them down and arresting them as enemies of the state no matter where their paths might lead."

"I have received several negative reports on you in recent days and weeks, Captain Vallae," the general said. "One came from a priest. So, I must refuse your request." The general paused, sending Jean a hard look. "The ice you are standing on is very thin, captain. Need I say more?"

The general had said what Jean had expected. Somehow he felt relieved.

"Since my request to go in search of these criminals was denied, I have no choice but to resign my commission, sir," Jean said louder than he had intended.

Out of the corner of his eye, Jean noticed that instead of leaving the room as he had expected, the young aid stood in the doorway of the room's only exit. Apparently, his duties included protecting the general. Or maybe he wanted to hear as much of their conversation as possible for other reasons.

The general leaned forward in his chair. "Since I am sure you would never consider leaving the army, I assume you are joking."

Jean shook his head. "I am serious, sir. I assure you. "

The general's dark eyebrows appeared to grow together, and he sent Jean a hard look. "If you truly intend to do this, Captain Vallae, you must wait a week or so. This will give you the opportunity to reconsider. Besides, it will take time for us to find a replacement."

"Take all the time you like. But I am no longer a soldier—as of this instant."

The general's eyes opened all the way. "What?"

"I am resigning my commission as of now."

The general rose from his chair, shaking a finger at Jean. "You cannot do this."

"Oh yes, General, I can. And I have."

Jean turned and headed for the door. The aid stepped to one side, as Jean left the room in a hurry, running out the main entrance in case they followed him. He would be pursued, certainly. Perhaps he would need to relocate to another country immediately where his past, as well as his present, history was unknown.

His mind raced. The authorities would come after him. If not now, they would come as soon as his father-in-law learned all that he had done. He'd hire a few men and they would leave as soon as all the arrangements could be made. He would need to be careful though.

Desertion is the charge the army will bring against me.

Jean had one regret. In a fit of anger, he had told Father La Faye exactly what he planned to do. If possible, the priest would pass that information on to others, including the nun with long auburn hair and the young monk.

❧

Rene returned to the island after an absence of almost two weeks. Pierre could hardly wait to talk to him, to learn what he had discovered while he was away. Rene secured his boat at the end of the pier. Pierre strode toward him.

"May I help carry your supplies from the boat to your cabin?" Pierre asked.

Rene grinned. "Of course. Can you handle a rather large box? Or would you prefer my fishing gear?"

"I will take the box, if you please. I have smelled your fishing gear before."

Rene laughed as he reached down and grabbed the box. "Here."

As they headed for Rene's small hut, Pierre asked, "Did you deliver the letter Rachel wrote to Father La Faye and the nuns, thanking them for their kindnesses?"

"Yes," Rene said in a voice that had lost some of its excitement. "I delivered the post personally, and while there I learned a great deal from Father La Faye. But not good news, I am afraid." Rene paused before speaking. "I have a lot to tell you and the other men on the island. They know to come to my cabin after each of my trips, and they will be along shortly. I will tell all I have learned at one time."

From the look on his face, Rene had nothing but bad news to report; probably concerning Captain Vallae. If the captain was still chasing them, how could he tell Rachel?

When the other men on the island had joined Pierre in front of the cabin, Rene's expressive eyes darkened.

"There was another raid on the town of Benoit," he said.

A collective gasp echoed all around them.

"The second raid for that village," Rene added. "According to what I heard on the mainland, both were led by a Captain Vallae. At least most of our friends left on that ship."

Pierre had prayed that the ship carrying Huguenots from Benoit arrived safely in England, but he couldn't stop wondering about his mother and Henri. With no man to help them, how had they managed once they reached England? And were they on their way to Scotland now? As far as Pierre knew, there had been no news from the ship at all.

"Was anyone hurt during the raid?" Pierre asked.

Rene shook his head. "There were no casualties, but a lot of people were upset." Rene pulled a knife from his scabbard. "A monk is asking the other fishers questions about us in the villages. I think the monk must be working for someone higher up. At first, I thought he worked for the clergy, but Father La Faye thinks I am wrong."

His jaws like iron, Rene stuck the knife deep into the trunk of the tree and screwed it around several times. He reminded Pierre of a knight of old, lancing the heart of an enemy during a battle.

"Things could be worse." Rene pulled out his knife and put it back in the sheath attached to his leather belt.

"According to Father La Faye," he went on, "this Captain Vallae and his men marched into his church for the second time. The captain made demands, terrified the nuns, and threatened the priests.

"Later, he read a report that he claimed came from the authorities in Paris. The captain said it was a reply to a letter he wrote the authorities, and he read the report aloud in front of Father La Faye, the other priests, and the nuns—insisting that they stand there and listen. However, the captain wouldn't let Father La Faye actually read the document for himself. Father La Faye thinks the letter was a fake designed to force them to comply with the captain's wishes; that he made up part or all of it to frighten and confuse them."

Rene paused. "The priest said that Captain Vallae hauled in all the men in Beniot for questioning, whether Catholic or Huguenot, in regard to a fire in Benoit. He is especially interested in finding a young man who met with other Huguenots in Paris." He glanced at Pierre. "The captain is also looking for two young women. Women he claims are criminals. However, Father La Faye knows on good authority that those killed in the fire were law abiding citizens and innocent of any crimes. And he thinks the others are probably innocent, too."

"But we know nothing about these women," Felix said.

"Do you think the captain cares?" Rene shook his head. "Apparently, Captain Vallae told Father La Faye more than he planned to."

"And what might that be?" Pierre asked.

"He told the priest that he intends to give up his commission and go after these people on his own, but we have time. It will take a week or so for the army to find a replacement."

Pierre frowned. *This is my fault, all of it. I should never have taken Rachel to that church.*

Rene glanced at the ground and shook his head. "I have a friend on another island whose cousin is a soldier. The solider is an aid to the general in La Rochelle. Sometimes the cousin gives me information helpful to our cause. I will be sailing for that island tonight to see what I can learn. If the situation has worsened, we must abandon our homes here and go to our designated locations immediately instead of waiting until the replacement arrives."

"And where are these locations?" Pierre asked.

"They are different for each family. Everyone but you already knows where they are to go, if it ever comes to that."

"I am the Huguenot he is looking for. I am sorry for all the trouble Rachel and I have caused."

"You need not worry about that now," Rene replied. "Huguenots are always in trouble. Had it not been you and your wife that brought it to us, it would have been someone else. And if we are forced to leave the island, you and Rachel will be traveling with me."

Rene squatted and motioned for the men to come closer. He picked up a stick and made a mark in the dirt. "We are here." He made another mark. "Most of the soldiers are stationed there. It will take them half a day to reach us by boat."

"And if the captain and his men are no longer soldiers," Pierre said. "What then?"

Rene shrugged.

"Should we not tell the women to prepare?" Pierre asked.

"Our women are always prepared." Rene dropped the stick and got to his feet. "As I said, the captain will wait until his superiors find a replacement before coming after us. But Father La Faye thinks that once his replacement arrives, the captain is likely to chase after us until we are captured. No matter how long it takes."

"When is the replacement expected?" Felix asked.

"I cannot say." Rene shrugged again. "But we should have a few days of grace before he comes looking for us. Only the Lord can protect us."

"Amen," Pierre said. "It is time to pray."

When the prayer ended, the rest of the men walked back to their huts. Only Pierre and Rene remained.

"According to Father La Faye, Captain Vallae is obsessed with finding your wife, Pierre," Rene said. "Until the two of you are arrested, he will keep following you, no matter where that path leads. I assume that if you flee to a foreign country, he will still pursue you."

"I never heard of someone being followed into other lands," Pierre said. "I thought once we were away from French waters, we would be free of the captain and his men."

"Maybe not. Either Captain Vallae has convinced the authorities in Paris that it is important to capture the two of you as an example to others, or he will come after you on his own. He is a rich man and could well afford the cost involved. But the priest thinks the captain is chasing after you for another reason as well." He hesitated and glanced away. "Captain Vallae wants Madame Dupre at any cost."

Pierre nodded. "I think I knew that all along." He turned toward Suzette's cottage.

"No, wait," Rene said.

Pierre stopped and turned back around.

"What I have to say now," Rene continued, "is for your ears only."

❧

Late again, the captain climbed the stairs to the room at the inn he shared with his wife, smiling as he reached the first landing. He would see Yvette now, perhaps for the last time. She had mildly excited him once. Now she bored him.

He knew as soon as she opened the door that his wife had been crying. Yet she smiled through her tears.

"Jean, dear, you are home at last. I was worried."

"Sit down, Yvette," he demanded. "I want to talk to you."

"Yes, Jean." She sat down on the edge of the bed and gripped the bedpost. "What is it you want to say?"

"I have resigned my commission as captain of the soldiers."

"Resigned? Why?"

"I have hired a few men, and we will be leaving the country, perhaps for as long as a year. I hope to leave tomorrow."

"Tomorrow? I will certainly try to prepare for the trip as quickly as I can," she said. "But it might take a week or so merely to pack."

"You will not be going with me, I am afraid. I want you to go and stay with your parents in Paris."

"Stay with my parents? You are my husband, Jean. I wish to go with you."

"That is out of the question. I will have business to attend to. A woman would be in the way. I am sure you will enjoy a long visit with your parents in Paris."

Yvette got down on her knees before him. "Jean, I beg you. Do not send me away. Everyone will assume I am in disgrace." Moisture poured from her eyes. Several large teardrops landed on the oak floor directly in front of him. "Take me with you!"

Jean glared at her. "Stop that crying."

Still on her knees, she put her hands over her eyes and sobbed.

She disgusts me. She reminds me of a hound, crawling on its belly.

He grabbed a bag made of tent material from a table near the door. He pulled a clean shirt and a pair of trousers from hooks that lined the north wall of the room, and he threw them in the canvas bag. "I am leaving now, Yvette." He tossed a sack of gold coins on the bed and grabbed the door handle. "You will not see me again until I return."

Jean smiled mockingly. *If ever.*

He went out the door, slamming it behind him.

Eleven

Rachel watched Pierre during supper at Suzette's kitchen table. Something flickered in his dark eyes that disturbed her. Yet each time he caught her looking at him he smiled. She had no way of knowing what he had been thinking but sensed that something must be wrong.

"The meal tasted wonderful, Suzette. Thank you, but I am tired and want to turn in early." Pierre glanced at Rachel. "I hope you will both excuse me from the table."

Suzette nodded in agreement. "Of course."

"I am not surprised that you are tired," Rachel said. "After chopping and stacking wood for the islanders after that meeting with Rene and the other men, anyone would be."

As he started toward their bedroom, he motioned with his head toward their door. Rachel took that to mean that he wanted to have a discussion. She had seen Pierre and Rene talking soon after the fisherman returned from the mainland and hoped Pierre would tell her whatever he knew.

❧

Captain Jean Vallae went out the front door of the inn and motioned to the stable boy, standing nearby. "Saddle my horse and bring him around. I plan to leave here at once."

"Right away, sir."

Jean loaded his belongings in leather bags, hitched them to the back of his saddle and mounted. He knew animals and men and how to get the most from both. He seldom ran a horse, but he wanted to be as far from Yvette as he could get and as soon as possible. He settled into the saddle in haste and whipped his gelding into a hard gallop, as if he thought it would somehow dissolve his loveless marriage.

A light rain had turned the dusty road into a thin layer of mud, and holes along the way held about an inch of muddy water. The animal tromped through cold water, spattering high on its legs and onto Jean's black boots in the leather stirrups.

A few minutes later, he slowed the exhausted animal to a gentle trot, allowing the horse to rest, and glanced back. He could no longer see the lights coming from the inn.

When he reached the pier, Jean would reveal his travel plans to Brother Julian and the two young men the monk had hired. He wasn't impressed with any of the three, but he supposed they would have to do.

Jean recalled with disgust how the fat little monk's eyes almost closed when he laughed and how his thick lips turned up at the edges. Brother Julian had promised to have the rest of the information he sought tonight without delay, and Jean wanted to hear what he had found out.

He reached the appointed location and found the monk and the other two hirelings standing on the shore next to the pier. The men were prompt. A good sign. Anyone who worked for him arrived on time or wished they had.

"What have you discovered?" Jean asked as he dismounted. "Have you learned the name of the fisher who transported the outlaws from the church?"

"That I have, captain," the monk said. "His name is Rene LaToure, and he is a Huguenot."

"A Huguenot. That does not surprise me. All Huguenots are filthy rats."

"Indeed they are," the monk replied. "This Rene and his fellow Huguenots live on Beraud, a small island a half a day from here by boat, but we will not need a big ship to find them. A small sailing craft will be sufficient."

"How did you learn this information?" the captain asked.

"I found a letter from the young nun you are looking for, and the letter was addressed to Father La Faye and the nuns at the Sanctuary. The young nun's real name is Rachel, and she is married now to Pierre Dupre. Pierre is the Huguenot you have been seeking, as well as the young monk who spoke up for Rachel that day at the church."

The captain ground his jaw teeth together. "Have you discovered the identity of the young Jewish girl in the portrait?"

The monk shook his head. "I have not. But I will continue to search, of course."

"What about Magdalena Poyer. Who is she?"

"Unfortunately, I have not found the answer to that question either. But Magdalena must be connected to Rachel in some way, perhaps a relative."

"I will be eager to read the letter you found at the Sanctuary. You have done well, Brother Julian." Jean gazed out toward the sea. "Well, indeed. As you know, I have resigned my commission. Have you found us a boat?"

"Of course," the monk said. "I have rented a small but well equipped fishing craft from a fisher I know, and his boat should meet our needs well, I think."

"Good. We shall sail at dawn."

Jean's mouth curved upward in a mocking smile. His revenge would soon be a reality.

As soon as Rachel finished helping clean up after the evening meal, she turned to Suzette. "Like Pierre, I am tired. I think I will say goodnight now."

Suzette's smile held a hint of teasing and good humor. If Rachel read her facial expressions correctly, the older woman thought she wanted to spend time with Pierre, and she couldn't tell the real reason. Though Suzette and the others she had met on the island seemed trustworthy, she'd promised Pierre that she wouldn't mention what happened at the Sanctuary or that she had pretended to be a nun. Only Pierre knew what really happened.

Rachel opened the bedroom door and shut it behind her. Pierre sat on the edge of the bed.

"I saw you talking to Rene," she said. "Did he tell you what he learned on the mainland?"

"Yes." He got to his feet without looking at her.

"Well, what did he say?"

He motioned toward the bench and chair in the corner. She moved ahead of him and settled onto the bench. He sat down beside her but still didn't say anything. He pulled off first one shoe and then the other, letting them drop near his feet.

His delay in telling her what happened irritated her. If he didn't think she could handle the truth, he should say so openly. She was not a child. To keep her in the dark this way without any kind of an explanation demeaned her as a person and made her feel cut-off from him; isolated.

"I am not moving from this bench until you tell me what I want to know."

He grinned briefly. When he did, dimples on both sides of his mouth punctuated his smile, giving him a friendly, boyish look that Rachel found attractive.

"Very well then," he said, "I will tell you. But we must speak softly. Rene might not want everyone on the island to know what he told me."

The bench squeaked as Rachel inched closer to him.

"Captain Jean Vallae and his men returned to the Sanctuary after we left, and the captain threatened Father La Faye and terrified the nuns. Perhaps if Father La Faye hadn't reminded the captain of the close relationship between his uncle and the King himself, the priest and all the others at the compound might have been put in prison. They could still be in danger. I should never have taken you to the Sanctuary. I should have found another place for us to hide. Now everyone there and here is in danger."

"You cannot blame yourself, Pierre."

"And why not?"

He got up and moved to the window. His back to Rachel, he looked out as the sun dipped beyond the horizon.

"What else did the priest tell Rene?" she asked.

Pierre folded his hands behind his back. "I have no good news to report, Rachel. Not tonight."

She swallowed. "Then tell the bad."

Pierre turned away from the window and paced back and forth in front of the bed. "Captain Vallae is an atheist and hates both Jews and French Huguenots, but he has a personal vendetta against you, Rachel."

Rachel tensed. "Do you know why?"

"Maybe." He paused and shook his head. "Maybe not. As you know, at first the captain seemed attracted to you. He might still be, but the letter you wrote to the nuns is missing from their quarters. Father La Faye believes that it is now in the hands of Jean Vallae. If that is true, he knows more about us than we would like him to know."

"If only I could remember what I put in that letter," she said.

Pierre's voice had dwindled to hardly more than a whisper. Still pacing, he cleared his throat. "It seems the captain found a miniature portrait in a trunk at your house before he burned it to the ground. He tried to get the priest to identify the young girl in the portrait, to say it was you, but Father La Faye refused."

Rachel stiffened. "A portrait, did you say?"

"Yes. The captain had it with him when he returned to the Sanctuary, and he showed it to the priest. Father La Faye tried to deny knowing the identity of the young girl in the miniature, but in his heart he knew that it was you, Rachel."

She knew exactly what portrait he meant. Only one portrait had ever been painted of her. The work had been done by her late uncle, Simon Levin—a Jewish merchant and part time painter who lived in Switzerland. If somehow the captain had managed to discover that her uncle's name was Levin, he also knew about her Jewish roots.

Did Pierre know, too, or had the priest kept her secret?

"The priest told Rene," Pierre continued, "that the captain read a letter aloud in front of the nuns. The letter came from a trunk found in a house full of criminals from Benoit, and the captain was convinced that the young girl in the portrait and a Swiss merchant mentioned in the letter were related. He thinks the merchant cheated his family out of land in Switzerland when Captain Vallae was a boy and that you are that young girl in the portrait."

Rachel wondered if the captain also mentioned that the owners of the trunk were Jews.

"My uncle was a kind and honest man. He made his living as a merchant, but he was also an artist in his spare time. Yes, he painted the portrait of me. But he would never lie or cheat anyone. What else did the captain tell the priest about me and my family?"

"Captain Vallae claimed that your uncle convinced his grandfather that giving up some of his land to pay off a debt would keep him out of prison, and his grandfather quickly handed over a good portion of his property to your uncle. However, the rest of the Vallae family never believed that story. They think your uncle gave the grandfather bad advice for personal gain; that he would never have gone to prison in any case."

"If you had known my uncle, you would know that he would never commit such a vile act."

"The captain also told the priest that if your relative had not cheated his family out of their land, he would be even wealthier today. And he wants revenge."

"All this trouble we are in is my fault, Pierre. Not yours. None of this would have happened if I had never left the village after my parents were killed."

"If you had stayed, ma chere, you could be dead now. And have you forgotten that the captain is also chasing me? In his eyes, I am a criminal who conspired against the crown."

"But you and the others would be safe, if not for me…"

"Huguenots are never truly safe," Pierre insisted, "and as Huguenots, we are all bound together as servants of our Lord. Whatever happens to you touches all of us, and what happens to us touches you." He swept across the room in two long steps and embraced her. "I understand more than you think I do, Rachel, and you are not alone."

Though still a brotherly embrace, he held her a little closer this time than he had in the past, and she didn't try to pull away. Rachel had to admit that she liked the feel of Pierre's arms around her.

"Thank you, Pierre, for standing up for me."

"My pleasure." He smiled and released her. "I have no written copy of God's word but would you like for me to recite from memory what little of the scriptures I remember before we blow out the candle and go to sleep? I rest better after I have prayed and recited scripture verses, and I think it would help you, too."

"Yes. I would like that."

"Let me get the candle to light our way. It can get rather dark over here in this corner." Pierre moved to the table by the bed, picked up the lighted candle and returned to the bench.

In a deep and resonant voice Pierre recited verses from the first chapter of the Book of John. Rachel had heard the scripture verses at the Reformed Church in the village, yet the words never rang so true as when she heard Pierre speak them.

"Who is the Word who became flesh and dwelled among us?" she asked.

"Jesus."

"Do you really think Jesus is the Messiah mentioned in the Bible?"

"Yes, Rachel, I do."

"I once heard that some of the rabbis believe that there will be two Messiahs."

"I believe that as well, and both of them are Jesus."

"How can that be?"

"Jesus came the first time as an innocent baby, the Lamb of God. But when He comes again, He will come as the Lion of the Tribe of Judah with power and great glory. So, as you can see, the two Messiahs are actually one and the same."

She nodded as if she understood. In reality, his explanation only caused more questions because his words appeared to be in direct conflict to what she had always heard before she moved to Benoit.

"As I said, Jesus is the Lamb of God," Pierre said, "and He came down to earth once to pay for our sins. According to the scriptures, Jesus is coming a second time at the end of the age as the Lion of the Tribe of Judah. A gentle lamb and a lion are so different in nature, and yet in this case, they are both Jesus, our Lord."

He smiled down at her. "You look tired, Rachel." He touched her forehead with the palm of his hand. "Why not prepare for the night behind the screen now?" He turned his back on her. "See, I am already looking away."

❦

Pierre lay on the wooden bench only a few feet from the bed where Rachel slept, yet he might as well have been a hundred miles away.

He pulled the woolen cape over his shivering shoulders, trying not to think of the icy air all around him. Yes, the chill bothered him. But he'd always been told that a woman needed more blankets than a man in order to keep warm.

Pierre had been given a more detailed account of what went on during Rene's visit to the Sanctuary than what he had shared with Rachel. Rene had already sailed for the island to talk to the cousin of the soldier under the general's charge. Rene had every hope that the soldier visited his cousin recently on the island and that the soldier told his cousin all he knew about the captain's plans.

But for the present, he would not tell Rachel anything more. Even in the dim light of a single candle, he saw worry-lines form on her forehead. She might be served best if she got her bad news in small doses.

Pierre turned on his side. With his back pressed against the cold rock wall, he pulled the cape up around his shoulders. Bending his legs, he scrunched down under the cover.

Each day since their marriage, he found it more difficult to live with Rachel as brother and sister, but the nights seemed far worse. She loved the memory of Louis, and he could understand that. He had loved his brother, too, but Rachel was his wife.

His destiny in life seemed clear. Present the image of strength and kindness to Rachel at all times and never declare his love for her, never express his desires and needs openly, and smile often. Keeping his true thoughts and desires hidden was like tying a fast horse to a tree with a short rope. Sooner or later that rope would break, and the horse would run free or die in the act of trying.

The scriptures told that he should love his wife as God loved the church and gave Himself for it. But sometimes when the chill of a cold night threatened to freeze his very bones, he thought of Rachel—so warm—so near, yet out of his reach. He longed to make her his wife in all ways. Was he strong enough to accept his fate if she never shared his bed?

Before dawn the next morning, someone knocked at their bedroom door.

"Get up and dress quickly!" Suzette shouted. "Rene just left here with important news for all of us. We must leave the island at once. And he said to bring blankets and as much food as one armload will hold."

Still half asleep, Rachel rubbed her eyes. "What did she say?"

"Get up at once! We must prepare to leave the island."

"Leave the island?" Rachel sat up in bed. "What happened?"

"I will explain later. Now, get dressed in the clothes you wore when we left the Sanctuary, so we can leave. And bring the dress Suzette gave you."

Finally awake and alert, Rachel tensed. Something must have happened while she slept, something important; perhaps dangerous.

Captain Vallae must have found us.

Twelve

"We must make haste." Pierre rushed out the bedroom door. "Suzette and her son, Anton, have already left the cabin."

Stunned by all that had transpired, Rachel followed him into the main room of the cottage. Inside the doorway, she stopped, pressing the palm of her right hand to her forehead. "For some reason, I cannot think right now. What would you have me do?"

"Gather the water and supplies Suzette and Anton left for us and carry them down to the pier. The time is short. Some of the boats might already have left the island."

Rachel nodded and hurried to the fireplace. A bundle had been placed on the floor beside it. She would get that and any other supplies she could carry.

By the time they reached the beach, small boats bobbed in the sea near the shore exactly like the day Louis and her parents died. Down at the pier, the rest of the islanders had already lined up to board the boats that still remained.

"We will be leaving in Rene's boat," Pierre said.

"What other important information are you failing to tell me?"

"I will explain everything. Later."

Rachel's insides grew tight, her nerves taut, as she watched Pierre and Rene row with all their strength. She hoped all the boats would make it to safety in time and glanced back to see if they were being followed. Instead of Captain Vallae's boat, she saw only the little trail of waves made by Rene's boat and the oars.

With the patch over one eye and the missing tooth in front, Rene's appearance had frightened her on the day they met. Knowing him now, she wondered why she ever worried. She had to trust that Rene's plan would work—for all of them.

A fresh wind whipped up as the little boat cut through the sea. Calm waters became choppy, not unlike the wave after wave of unanswered questions churning through her. Rachel would have offered to help row, but seeing only two oars, she decided to wait.

She thought of the hungry look in Captain Vallae's dark eyes on the day he first saw her at the church. He'd wanted her then. A chill shot down her spine. He probably still did.

"The captain is after us, is he not?" Rachel finally asked loud enough to be heard above the roar of the waves. "I have to know."

Pierre nodded, but neither of the men spoke.

They didn't have to. The answer shouted from the darkest corner of her brain.

Sweat poured from their bodies as Pierre and Rene continued to row in earnest. But would they be able to locate a safe place to hide until the danger passed?

After almost an hour, Rene stopped rowing. "It is time for us to rest."

Pierre sighed and loosened his grip on the oar. Rachel got the urn of water from the center of the boat and offered it to the men. They drank greedily as though their thirst could not be satisfied.

She crouched in the middle of the boat, trying not to let her concerns show.

"Why are you wringing your hands, Rachel?" Pierre asked.

Rachel glanced down. She was wringing her hands and hadn't even noticed.

"I can see that you are nervous," he said. "Perhaps you are also worried." Pierre wiped his sweaty brow with the back of his hand. "But there is no need to be. Rene visited another island last night while we slept, seeking information, and he knows what he is doing."

Rachel turned from Pierre to Rene. "What did you learn at that island?"

"A young soldier who works as an aid to a general in La Rochelle visited his cousin on the other island," Rene said. "And he informed me that Captain Vallae resigned his commission and has no plans to wait for a replacement to arrive. Some will call this an act of treason."

Rachel stared at Rene. "He could already be on our trail. No wonder you told us to leave the island in a hurry."

"The soldier heard that the captain hired three men and that he hates Huguenots," Rene went on. "The soldier said that the general he works for knows the captain well and that Captain Vallae is the kind of man that never gives up. He will not rest until he has done exactly what he wants to do."

❧

Rene guided them to a small island and dropped anchor. "We must keep the boat hidden. But I think we are safe enough here."

Pierre helped Rachel from the boat. After sitting for so long, it felt good to stretch her legs. She looked back toward the sea, but nobody appeared to be following them.

"I think we should remain here for a while," Rene announced. "If the captain and his men are looking for us, they will soon tire of searching this area, and they will go elsewhere. Then we can leave.

"Until then, we must hide the boat with bushes and dry leaves and seek cover ourselves." Rene pulled out one of the oars and let it drop on the wet shore. "If we turn the boat over, we can sleep under it in bad weather. And we must dig a tunnel in the soil and cover it with canvas and leaves in case we need to hide under the boat as well. That will give us some protection if the captain and his men search the island."

Rachel thought of what the captain might do if he caught up with them. If given a choice, she would gladly sleep under the boat even in good weather.

That night, she lay under the boat while the men slept in the grass nearby. Exhausted from helping Pierre carry out Rene's orders, she wanted to sleep but couldn't. Rachel heard a rustling noise and stiffened. "Who is there?" she whispered.

"Pierre and Rene," Pierre said softly.

Rachel released a deep breath as the two men crawled under the boat and joined her there.

"We must whisper, Rachel," Pierre said so softly she could barely hear. "A small boat is sailing not far from the bank. It could be Captain Vallae. If so, it is unlikely they will search the island at night. But we must consider that possibility."

They could be killed as they slept; or worse.

Rachel felt a tug of irritation. She hated being treated like a child. The two men had to be as worried as she. Why wouldn't they admit it?

She pressed her back against the side of the boat to make room for the men. With Pierre in the middle and Rachel and Rene to his right and to his left, she could scarcely move. Still, three adults crammed under a small boat seemed far better than no shelter at all.

Pierre inched still closer to her. She could barely breathe. Even Louis had never been that close.

All at once, her nose itched. She longed to scratch it, but in such close quarters, it would be almost impossible to move her arm.

Nobody spoke after that. The men fell asleep. She knew because she could hear them snoring.

She strained to hear any noises louder than the ones the men were making. Under these conditions, sleep would be difficult if not impossible. The whoosh of the wind on the sand sounded like footsteps coming ever closer. Rachel signed and found herself contemplating all sorts of unpleasant outcomes.

Would they be captured and returned to a prison in La Rachelle, or killed as they slept? The boat seemed well camouflaged. Still, she worried that they would have no advance warning should their enemies come upon them during the night.

According to Pierre, the Bible said to think on whatever was lovely and of good report. He'd also added that he often sang hymns when worry taunted him, but it would be impossible to sing a hymn aloud with two men sleeping nearby.

Pierre jerked beside her. Rachel jumped.

"What is wrong?" she whispered.

Pierre snored and turned his back to her.

At last, she fell asleep.

❦

From his sailboat a short distance from the beach, Jean Vallae gazed toward the small darkened island. They had checked the other beaches for tracks before sundown and found none. Nor did they find any small fishing boats. They had arrived at this island after dark and too late to do any checking. They would have to wait until morning.

Something told Jean to linger—that Rachel and Pierre were on that small island. He glanced toward his three hirelings. Too dark to see them, he imagined them watching him; waiting to hear his decision. The monk seemed clever enough but the other two, Samuel and Zeb, were young and impatient to continue on.

"I have heard that there is a larger island a little further on," Samuel said. "Perhaps the ones you are looking for are hiding there."

"Samuel wishes to go to that island because we have heard that there are many young and beautiful girls living there," Zeb added.

After spending time with Yvette, the captain imagined what such an island might be like. Music, dancing girls; perhaps they should go there and spend the night. He would enjoy a diversion.

On the other hand, he couldn't squelch the feeling that they should stay exactly where they were.

❦

"I see a strip of daylight coming from under the edge of the boat," Rene whispered. "I am going to crawl out now to look around—see what I can see. I will come back as soon as possible. But if I fail to return, prepare to defend yourselves."

Prepare to defend yourselves. Rachel watched Rene crawl out from under the boat.

They had been in danger before, but this time, she was alarmed; perhaps because she'd just awakened from a bad dream.

In the dream, Captain Vallae grabbed her and carried her off. She'd wanted Pierre, called to him. But he had not come to her aid.

A few minutes later, Rachel heard a sound, like somebody walking.

"Listen, Pierre!" she whispered. "I hear something."

She couldn't see the expression on Pierre's face. It was too dark under the boat. But he took her hand and held it. Surely, he must be as concerned as she was.

"It is me," Rene said. "The boat is gone."

"Splendid," Pierre replied. "It is time to thank and praise the Lord."

Rene crawled under the boat and stretched out, pushing Rachel against the side of the boat again.

"I saw no vessels anchored off shore or on the beach," Rene said after a moment. "The boat or boats must have sailed on last night instead of waiting until morning. So if all goes well, we should be able to get our fishing gear and be on our way in a few days."

Two days later, Pierre helped Rene drag the boat down to the water's edge.

"May I be of help?" Rachel asked when they had almost reached the beach.

"Yes," Rene said with a trace of aggravation. "Get in the boat before we shove off."

Pierre sent Rene a hard look and helped Rachel into the boat. He knew the strain the fisherman must be under. Pierre felt it too. Still, that didn't give Rene the right to take his frustrations out on Rachel.

They set out again, posing as three fishermen, and at first, they caught few fish. However, when they pulled in their nets on the third day, they counted twenty-two in all. As a result, they were able to sell fish to the beach dwellers they met each time they camped for the night.

❧

Captain Vallae and his men had arrived at one of the islands after a man, two women and a boy had left. Knowing that Huguenots had been there and hadn't been captured infuriated him. He and his men had combed the beaches but to no avail. However, he'd been given a clue by one of the fishermen he met in one of the villages that seemed promising.

"In the past," the villager had said, "Huguenots congregated at a small seaport village not far from here. You might look there."

"And what is the name of this village?"

"The people call it Casa. It is the Spanish word for house."

"Interesting."

Jean Vallae and his men arrived on the island of Casa that same day, and Jean went straight to the largest church he could find. Though he'd already resigned his commission in the army, he wore his dress uniform. The uniform of an army captain with a sword buckled to his belt opened doors for him.

He never visited churches for religious reasons, but he found the clergy helpful in learning important information over a glass of port. As soon as he entered the office of the head priest, he complimented him on his fine town and inspiring church. After a minute or two, he got right to the purpose of his visit.

"I am looking for a young man and a young woman who fled from the law back in the village of Beniot and later fled a church near La Rochelle."

Jean pulled out the portrait of Rachel and handed it to the priest. The priest gazed at the painting with what Jean considered mild interest.

"The man is a Huguenot," Jean said. "We think the young woman is a Jewess."

The priest's lifted his right eyebrow and gave the portrait back to Jean as if he thought it might be poison or in danger of catching fire. "I am a humble parish priest and know nothing of Huguenots or Jews. You can tell your superiors as much." He motioned toward the door as if he wanted Jean to leave.

"I will report your words to my superiors as you suggested," Jean said. "And should I find that you are mistaken, I will tell them that as well." He bowed politely and left the room.

On the porch outside, he smiled as he went down the stone steps. He would give the priest a day or two to digest his words and then he would visit the priest again. Perhaps his memory would have improved. In the meantime, he hoped to discover what the fishers on the dock knew. As the monk said, a bottle of wine should loosen their tongues rather quickly.

After three days of living in an uninspiring inn, eating food that tasted like shoe leather and talking to numerous town folk, Jean had learned nothing new. Though the fishers insisted that Huguenots had lived in Casa in the past, they knew of no recent arrivals. The priest seemed as unwilling to answer Jean's questions on his second visit to the church as he had on his first.

If he didn't learn something new soon, Jean would have but one choice—leave the town of Casa and join his men on a nearby island. However, he planned to continue searching for these criminals in other villages along the coast and beyond; no matter how long it took to find them.

❦

Rachel gazed out at the same setting she had been looking at for six day; water, beaches, and villages here and there. But she'd had enough of boats and seawater.

All at once she saw a town in the distance that looked almost as large as Benoit. "Will we be stopping there?" she asked.

"Yes. It is the town of Casa." Rene looked off toward the village. "The boat has a small leak and needs to be repaired. We also need supplies. Besides, the village of Casa has been our destination all along."

"Is this village safe?" Pierre asked Rene.

"That is my hope. I have friends in the village. My grandmother lived there until she died, and she left her home to my brother, my sister, and I. We lived for a time in the village with our grandmother when we were children and we attended the French Church there every Sunday morning. It helped keep us safe to make friends with the villagers and the local priests, and some of those friendships have lasted through the years.

"We will dock and stay close to the boat until nightfall," Rene went on. "When it is dark, the Madame will put on the dress she brought with her, and we shall hike to the house I mentioned. If all has gone as planned my brother and his wife, my sister, Suzette, and my nephew, Anton, will be waiting for us."

⚜

Rachel helped Rene and Pierre secure the boat. Later, she helped them carry buckets of fresh water from a well near the center of town back to the dock where the boat had been anchored. They washed down the boat, and when they had finished, Rachel washed her hands and face in fresh water for the first time in days.

Exhausted, Rachel questioned whether or not she would be able make the two mile trek from the beach to Rene's country house at the edge of town; but she knew she must. She put on the dress Suzette had given her over her smelly shirt and trousers. After having been in and out of the boat for so long, the dress had a fishy odor, and she hated the sticky feeling seawater left on her skin. She could hardly wait to take a bath in water that didn't taste like salt.

Rene had moved ahead of Rachel and Pierre, but he stopped and waited for them. "On the road to my grandmother's farm," he said, "we must pass in front of a small inn. I would suggest we walk around it, but with the bay on one side of the road and the inn on the other." He shrugged.

"Why not loop around behind the inn?" Pierre suggested.

"Unfortunately, we cannot. The owner of the inn is a very rich man who owns all the land behind the inn, and he keeps dogs and men with guns guarding his property at all times. But we will be all right." Rene patted Rachel's shoulder. "It is true that the entry to the inn will be lighted, but have no fear. Look straight ahead as if you pass that way every day."

As they grew closer, Rachel had an uneasy feeling about being in the light where she could be seen by others. She sucked in her breath. What if the captain happened to be coming out of that inn as they walked by?

Four lighted lanterns hung from the eves, swinging back and forth in the breeze. As she reached the path directly in front of the inn's entry, the door opened. She froze as a man came out and stood on the front porch, watching them. With his dark hat pulled low over his forehead, it would be impossible to see his face. A shiver filtered through her.

It's him! She gasped. It must be. The man is the same size and build as Captain Vallae.

Thirteen

"Pretend not to see him," Rene whispered to Rachel and Pierre. "No need to draw attention to us. But it is just old Jasper from the village. He is strange but harmless."

Rachel hurried on down the road and out of the light from the lanterns hanging on the eves of the building. She stumbled over something in the path and fell against Pierre.

He grabbed her arm. "Are you all right?"

"Yes." She felt the gentle pressure of his hand on her skin as she glanced down. "I tripped over something in the road but it's too dark to see what it might have been."

"Did you hurt your foot?"

"It hurts a little but it will be all right."

"My late grandmother's farm is ahead," Rene said. "The house is around that bend in the road."

A single light burned in one room of the house, giving Rachel something on which to focus.

"Four steps and you are on the front porch," Rene said. "Grab hold of the railing and go on up."

Rachel gripped the wooden railing for support and trudged up the stone steps. Rene moved ahead and knocked at the door.

"Felix," Rene said. "It is I, Rene. Pierre and his wife are with me."

The door opened. Felix stood before them with his arms out-stretched. In the dim light, Rachel also saw Yvonne, Suzette and the boy, Anton, lined up behind him.

Felix motioned for them to come inside. The two women came around him and moved forward. First Suzette hugged Rachel, and then Yvonne. On her first day on the island, Rachel had felt iso-lated—a stranger to Rene and his family. The warmth she felt now seemed to radiate within the walls of the small cabin, filling her heart with a sense of acceptance, joy and love.

From just inside the doorway, she examined the tiny cabin's interior with its rock walls and wooden floors. She saw one room and a loft. A half opened door revealed another room across the back of the house. It would be a tight squeeze with six adults and a child living in such close quarters. However, after all Rachel had been through, any walls at all seemed like a castle.

"You and the others look tired," Suzette said to Rene. "Water is warming in the kitchen house. I suggest that each of you take a bath and change your clothes. Then let us meet around the eating table for food and fellowship."

Rachel bathed and dressed in the kitchen house, but the men carried their buckets of hot water to a shed behind the cabin. At last, they gathered around the table.

Felix peered at his nephew. "Anton, I see you are reading."

The boy blushed and closed the book. "Yes, sir, I am."

"We are glad of your interest in literature but the table is no place for it."

"It shall not happen again, sir."

As the older of the two brothers, Rene led the blessing of the food. Then they passed around a large platter, and Rachel took a slice of dark bread and a piece of boiled fish.

Rene leaned forward, took a bite of fish and chewed. "Felix, it is time for you to tell us what has happened since last we met and the latest news from the village."

"We have all fared well." Felix wiped his mouth on a white cloth. "And we have been attending a Catholic church in town as well as having our own services here in the cabin. We were unable to learn whether or not the ship carrying Pierre's mother, Henri, and the others reached its destination. However, we are hopeful and if no news is a good sign, they have arrived in England."

"What about the people we met on the island?" Pierre asked. "Are they safe?"

Rachel put down her fork, waiting to hear his answer.

Felix shook his head. "We have heard nothing."

Pierre drummed his fingers on the table. "What can you tell us of Captain Vallae and his men?"

"According to our friends from the village, the captain and his men visited here several days before we arrived, asking questions. But they sailed away before we docked."

"Can you still trust those childhood friends of yours?" Pierre asked.

"Perhaps," Felix said, "perhaps not."

Felix pushed back his plate, got up from his chair and backed up to an open window, blocking part of the evening breeze. "Besides attending church in town," he went on, "Yvonne and Suzette have been taking food to the sick of the village. Therefore, the people here have no reason to think we are not loyal to the crown in all ways."

Rene traced the top of his cup with his forefinger. "I only hope that you are right and that the villagers will accept us."

Suzette smiled. "Can we not talk of something more pleasant? This is a celebration. Our friends arrived tonight." She gazed at Rachel from her side of the table. "I see the dress Yvonne gave you fits well enough, Madame Rachel."

"Yes, and I am happy to report that it smells nice, too."

Everybody laughed.

"The clothes you wore when you arrived are soaking in a tub of water this moment," Suzette said. "Tomorrow we shall scrub them until they are clean again. And on the day after tomorrow, the women will go into the village to buy the things we need."

"Are you including me?" Rachel asked.

Bang!

Rachel flinched.

"What was that?" Suzette demanded. "It sounded like a gunshot."

Felix smiled as he moved away from the window and sat down again. "It was not a gunshot you heard." He peered at his nephew. "It appears that Anton dropped his book on the floor. Would you mind picking it up?"

"Yes, sir. I—I mean, no sir."

Rachel joined in the general laughter.

"My stomach indicates that it is time to eat the honey cake the women baked," Felix said.

Rene picked up his fork. "Mine is sending the same message."

A feeling of excitement surged through Rachel on the morning she dressed to go to the village. After being deprived of such simple pleasures for so long, she wanted to shout for joy.

Later, as she walked down the main street with Suzette and Yvonne, she reminded herself that she had promised not to speak while in town. With her strong German accent, it would be unwise to talk openly.

"A weaver of fine cloth lives down the street. I wish to buy soft fabrics from which to make clothes for my baby." Yvonne put her hand on her round belly. "I would like to stop there next."

"I should like to help make your baby some clothes," Suzette said.

"So would I," Rachel added. "I might have left on a ship bound for England by the time the baby arrives. Nevertheless, I would like to help."

The weaver's little shop looked dark and dreary but light from a line of windows across the back wall, and the thought of touching silk material, drew Rachel forward.

Her eyes stung. The strong scent coming from the fabric must have caused it. She sneezed and sneezed, again and again.

An old man with a long white beard glanced up when she sneezed. He sat under the middle window weaving cloth, and something about him reminded Rachel of her grandfather who died in Alsace. His loom appeared to be made of the finest woods and his slender hands and long fingers looked like those of a Jewish harpist she'd known as a child. Spools of red, yellow, and blue thread lay on the floor at his feet. Shelves lined the walls holding still more.

Rachel's mother had owned a loom, and she had always enjoyed helping Mama spin and weave cloth. Her fingers itched to try her hand at weaving once again, but she knew better than to make her desires known. Instead, she stepped into the shadow of an alcove and let Yvonne and Suzette do all the talking rather than speaking and perhaps being identified.

Yvonne found several pieces of cloth that pleased her. Once her choice of fabric had been made, Yvonne paid for the items.

Rachel sneezed.

The old man squinted at Rachel.

"And who might she be?" he asked Yvonne. "I daresay she has not been in my shop before."

Rachel swallowed, trying not to move.

"She is one of our cousins," Yvonne explained. "She and her husband are here visiting us for a while."

"Humph," he said as if the sight of her displeased him. "Seems to me you have a lot of relatives all at once; and she looks too young to be a married woman."

Suzette's nervous laugh rang out. "Young girls grow up very fast this day and time, Monsieur."

"Too fast for my taste," he said.

Yvonne and Suzette nodded in agreement. They talked with the old man a while longer as he bundled the packages. Rachel drifted toward the door.

"I felt uncomfortable in there," Rachel whispered as they left the shop.

"So did I," Suzette agreed. "It might be best if we avoid buying cloth for a while."

Yvonne had said that other Huguenots lived in the village, but Rachel hadn't met any of them. As they walked along, she wondered if some of the very ordinary looking buildings on both sides of the street held tunnels and hidden rooms like those in Benoit.

"The old woman we will be visiting goes by the name of Cecile," Yvonne said, "Madame Cecile DePuy. She lives down that way." She motioned toward a narrow road that branched off from the main street. "But first we must go to the butcher's shop and buy food for her."

Yvonne opened the door to the shop and hurried inside. Rachel and Suzette went in after her.

They left the butcher shop and ambled down the street to the old woman's home.

"Madame DePuy is old and blind," Yvonne said. "So unless her daughter is with her, she will remember little of our visit other than that we brought her food to the glory of God."

Half hidden by a large Elm tree, Madame Cecile DePuy's little brown fieldstone cottage stood on a rise not far from the bay. Rachel followed Yvonne and Suzette to the door.

"The Madame will be resting," Yvonne said. "So if she fails to come to the door by the second knock, we are to walk right in."

Yvonne carried the cloth and Suzette the leg of lamb they had purchased earlier that day. Rachel carried the basket with the baked goods in it that they had brought for Madame Cecilia. She hung back and let Yvonne lead the way inside.

The sweet-sounding twitter of a bird in a wooden cage welcomed her as soon as they stepped inside. With the curtains all drawn, the front room seemed a bit depressing despite the bird's cheery song. A woman who looked every bit as old as the weaver sat in a chair toward the back.

"Who goes there?" Madame Cecile asked in a weak voice.

"Your friend, Madame Yvonne LaToure. I came to bring food for you. I have also brought my sister-in-law, Madame Suzette Debose, and our young cousin, Martha."

"Bring the girl closer," the old woman said. "I want to feel Martha's face."

Rachel gazed at Yvonne, wondering what she should do.

"Go on," Yvonne urged. "Kneel down in front of her and let her feel your face. She cannot see as I told you, but she will think she knows you if you allow her to touch your face. And while you do that, we will prepare a meal for Madame."

Rachel nodded instead of making a verbal reply. The request seemed strange, but she didn't argue. She knelt.

The woman traced the outline of Rachel's nose and mouth with her forefinger. "You are very young and beautiful, my dear. You remind me of my youngest daughter, long dead." The woman sniffed, and a tear rolled down her puckered and wrinkled cheek.

Rachel took a white cloth from the waistband of her dress. As she wiped away the woman's tears, memories of her own mother came to her mind, and she realized how much she missed Mama and Papa. All at once she felt a strong desire to reach out to Madame Cecile. Console her in some way. She'd lost a mother and the woman a daughter. Rachel felt a connection to the old woman; a closeness that she found impossible to describe in words.

"Like you, my mother could not see well," Rachel said to Madame Cecile. "She often had me read to her, and you are kind like she was. It shows in your smile. I am sure your youngest daughter must have loved you very much, indeed."

"Thank you for saying that. Did you lose your mother?"

"Yes."

"We must leave the food and go," Yvonne inserted.

Guilt flooded her as Rachel glanced back at Yvonne and Suzette. She'd broken her promise not to speak and wasn't surprised to find them glaring at her.

"I am sorry," Rachel mouthed. "Please forgive me."

The two women frowned. Then they nodded but very slowly. At the last possible instant, they both smiled. But Rachel sensed that their hearts weren't in it.

Now, I have upset my friends.

Rachel got to her feet. Leaning over, she kissed the old woman on the cheek. "Farewell," she whispered.

"You are going now?" Madame Cecilia asked.

"We must," Yvonne replied. "It is late. But we will return and bring you more food on another day."

"Will you be bringing the beautiful young woman with you?"

"I cannot say," Yvonne replied. "Our cousin will only be visiting here for a short time."

"How sad. I enjoyed meeting her. And I look forward to see-ing her again and touching her pretty face. She is so like—like—" She covered her mouth with the palm of her hand to muffle a sob.

Rachel reached out and patted the woman on the shoulder.

"When will your oldest daughter be visiting you again?" Yvonne asked.

"I cannot say. Michelle promised to come yesterday, but she never came."

"Who prepares your meals when she fails to come?" Suzette asked.

"I—I manage to do it," the woman said.

Yvonne and Suzette exchanged doubtful glances.

Suzette had said that Cecile's daughter, Michelle, had never married. Yet she refused to live with her ailing mother.

"We will be back as soon as we can," Yvonne said. "Perhaps tomorrow."

"Bring this young woman with you when you come. And thank you for your kindness."

Suzette opened the door of Cecile's little house and stepped out. Rachel and Yvonne followed her. All three stood on the porch watching the rain. Rachel hadn't known it had started raining until that moment.

She glanced at Suzette and then Yvonne, prepared to be scolded for speaking out of turn as she did, but neither of them said a word.

A middle-aged woman in a black dress climbed the front steps and practically ran them over in her haste to get in out of the rain.

Rachel forced a smile. This must be Madame Cecile's way-ward daughter, Michelle.

"Good day, Mademoiselle Michelle," Yvonne said in passing. "Your mother seems a little better today."

"That is good." The woman frowned. "Now, if you will be so kind as to get out of my way, I would like to go into my mother's house."

Just before Mademoiselle Michelle went inside, she gazed at Rachel. Rachel forced a smile, but the woman kept staring.

Michelle must have been pretty once. What could have made her so sour?

The rain stopped, and they went out again. But it began to sprinkle before they were halfway down the street.

"Run," Yvonne shouted. "Run for the covered porch in front of the butcher's shop. Showers like this become downpours in seconds here."

Rachel felt wet and cold by the time she and the other two women reached the store. They huddled on the porch under the wooden roof. All at once the rain stopped.

"We should go home before it starts raining again," Yvonne said. "We can buy the rest of the things at another time."

"I regret speaking out the way I did in front of Madame Cecile." Rachel gazed at her two friends, hoping for an indication of what they might be thinking. "Please, forgive me."

"Think no more of it," Suzette said. "We all make mistakes. But try not to make this one again."

Rachel nodded. "I never will. You can be sure of that."

A young man strolled by as they stood there on the porch. Rachel's heart pounded. His proud gait reminded her of the captain. He stopped and glanced back. She knew it was him. How would she ever forget his face; so handsome and yet so filled with evil?

Rachel gestured toward the entry door of the butcher shop. "Hurry," she whispered to her two friends. "I know that man. He is Captain Vallae, and he cannot find me here. We must go inside at once."

"But we visited the butcher's shop earlier today," Yvonne reminded her. "The butcher would have noticed us when we came in. He will wonder why we returned so soon."

"Say that we forgot something," Rachel suggested. "But hurry in, please."

Yvonne and Suzette shrugged and followed her inside.

Rachel directed them to a corner away from the butcher and the old woman buying chicken. "I cannot be sure, but I think the young man on the street outside is Captain Jean Vallae. The man I told you about. Did he see us?"

Yvonne shook her head. "I think not. He stopped and turned around, but I doubt he saw us, standing in the shadows as we were. Still, let me look out the window to make sure." Yvonne peered out a tiny window by the door. "I see no one. He must have gone on his way."

"Good." Rachel released a big sigh. "You two go on back to the cabin. I must stay here a while longer—until I feel it is safe for me to leave."

"But how will you know when to leave? You cannot stay here forever. We will wait here with you, at least until the butcher becomes suspicious."

"I have money left," Suzette said. "I could buy pork. We can shop a while here, and then leave."

Rachel frowned. "But what if he is still out there and sees us?"

"Wear my black shawl. It will hide your hair and most of your face," Suzette suggested. "Then walk between us." She giggled. "And walk like a boy the way my brother taught you."

Rachel shook her head. "That I will not do."

"But your natural walk is very winsome and feminine," Suzette pointed out. "The captain is sure to remember it."

"Will he not also remember a woman in a dark shawl who walks like a boy?" Rachel asked.

Yvonne laughed. "Yes, but not in a favorable way."

"I will take my chances and just walk," Rachel said.

"And in the future," Yvonne added, "it might be best if you stayed at the cabin when the two of us go into town to buy the things we need."

Suzette nodded. "I agree."

"As do I," Rachel said.

Fourteen

As soon as they reached the cabin, Rachel went in search of Pierre. She found him on the back porch, gazing off—perhaps at the woods beyond the chicken house.

"Pierre," she exclaimed, "I think I saw the captain in town today. He and his men must be camping in the village. If so, he is here looking for us."

"Rachel." He sighed deeply. "I feel sure it was not the captain you saw. Felix said that the fishers on the beach saw Captain Vallae and his men leave the village of Casa before we arrived. Perhaps you saw old Jasper again, the man we saw on the porch of the inn on the day we got here."

"I know what I saw, Pierre," she insisted, "and it was not Jasper."

Pierre does not believe me. But I know what I saw.

It rained that night, but by the next morning, the skies had cleared. Suzette and Yvonne went to the village again. In their absence, Rachel had volunteered to feed the chickens and gather the eggs.

The air felt cool and crisp as she went out the back door. Trees surrounded the cabin partly shading the hen house. Yvonne had been feeding a stray dog she called Brownie. All at once, Brownie ran up to the shed where the chickens were kept and barked. The hens went wild, fluttering about and squawking.

The sound of their cackling and clucking increased the closer she got. Rachel reached down, picked up a rock and threw it near the dog. Brownie ran off. Yet she could still hear him barking in the distance.

She opened the rickety pine door. The cackling noises peaked. Rachel took a step back amidst a flurry of angry beaks and flapping wings. No birds had actually harmed her or touched her, but she disliked having them try.

Once as a child when she went out to gather eggs, she had found it hard to open the door to the hen house. She pulled and yanked it every way she could, but it wouldn't budge. When the door finally opened, it made a lot of racket. Before she could step inside, an angry hen ruffled her feathers and ran at her.

Since then, she had avoided gathering eggs whenever possible. But Rene and his kinfolks had shown her and Pierre such kindness and friendship that she refused to mention her misgivings when they asked for a volunteer to feed the chickens and gather eggs.

Rachel held the handle of the brown wicker basket with both hands and stood in the doorway of the hen house, waiting—hoping that the birds would settle down enough for her to continue. Out of the corner of her eye, a shadow caught her attention. Rachel whirled around. Pierre smiled back at her.

"I never meant to scare you." Pierre's deep voice held a measure of gentleness. "I noticed when you came out here and decided to follow you to see if I might be of help." He reached out as if to take the basket from her. "Why not let me gather the eggs? Would that be all right with you?"

"What is the matter?" She put her hand on one hip. "Do you think I am not capable of gathering eggs? Like you didn't believe me when I told you about seeing the captain?"

"I regret saying that," he said. "But you do jump to conclusions."

"Now you are accusing me of things."

"Please," he urged. "Let me gather the eggs for you. It is my way of saying how sorry I am."

"I can do it."

"I know you can," he said. "I have no doubt that you can do

whatever you wish to do. But I would very much like to gather the eggs for you, if that is all right."

He gripped the handle of the basket but didn't attempt to pull it from her. When their fingers touched, a strange but pleasant tingle shot through her. She realized that until now they hadn't been truly alone since they left the island. The small size of the cabin in the woods had meant that all the women slept in the room at the back of the house and the men in the loft. She suddenly knew that she missed the intimate chats that she and Pierre had shared in Suzette's bedroom while on the island.

Slowly, she removed her hands from the basket and took another step back. As she waited, Pierre went into the hen house.

When he had gathered the eggs and fed the chickens, Pierre turned toward her. "Since everyone else in the household has gone elsewhere, I thought it might be nice if you and I took a walk in the woods near the cabin to have a look around. See what we can see. We could take along a picnic lunch, if you like."

Pierre's invitation appealed to her. She wanted to accept but still, her feelings for him were too new, too complicated. And despite his apology, she couldn't forget what he said when she told him about seeing the captain.

She considered him to be a good friend. However, it was too soon after the deaths to think of him as anything more than that. Besides, she had chores she'd promised Suzette and Yvonne she would do that morning.

"A walk in the woods sounds lovely. A picnic does as well, but I really must refuse. I told Yvonne that I would begin sewing a garment for her baby this morning so it will be ready when the child is born. I am eager to get started. Perhaps on some other day."

She thought he looked disappointed but only for a moment. Then his warm smile returned.

"Of course," Pierre said, "I understand. Then we will put off our picnic for another day." He turned and strode away.

Rachel longed to call out to him; to tell him that she had changed her mind and that she would go on the picnic after all. If he'd stopped and looked back at her, she would have. But he kept walking and never turned around.

❦

On the following morning Rachel strolled back to the cabin, feeling good about the fact that she had successfully fed the chickens and gathered the eggs without having to rely on Pierre to come to her aid. Still, she missed seeing him and had hoped he would visit her at the hen house.

Rachel heard men's voices coming from the woods behind the pen where the chickens were kept. She stopped and looked back. Through a break in the bushes, she saw Pierre, Rene, Felix, and Anton gathered around some sort of wooden cart.

"What a treasure we have found," she heard Pierre say.

Rachel moved toward them slowly. The men had captured her interest, and she had to know more about that cart. She took another step, stumbled on an exposed root of a tree and fell.

"Ouch!"

"What was that sound I heard?" Rene whispered. "We must have been followed."

The men rushed toward her through the bushes.

The basket lay on its side. Broken eggs had formed a yellow mess that had spilled onto the hem of her dress. She sat up and reached for a wooden stick at her side. Carefully, she brushed the runny yellow mixture away with the stick. Then she wiped her hands on a cloth attached to her belt.

"What are you doing here?" Rene demanded.

"I wanted to see the cart is all. Then I fell." She held her ankle. "But I am all right."

"Let me see that ankle." Pierre reached down and scooped her up in his arms. "I must carry my wife back to the cabin," he said to the other men.

Wife. She smiled regardless of her pain. He called me his wife.

Despite all she had said and thought to the contrary, she liked being called Pierre's wife. Maybe she liked being his wife—a little anyway. But when had it happened? When did the transformation begin?

Until that instant, she hadn't realized that her arm had found its way around his neck. It had seemed so natural, she'd hardly noticed. All at once she realized that of course it seemed natural. How else would she hold on?

The soft material of his shirt brushed her fingertips. She'd blushed the first time she put her arm around his brother's neck. But she wasn't blushing. Regardless of the turmoil going on around her she felt closer to Pierre than to anyone alive, and that wasn't right. She should be concentrating on her losses instead of thinking about Pierre.

Rachel started to pull her arm away and felt her body fall backwards a bit. She grabbed his shirt.

"Hold on, Rachel. I would not want you to fall and hurt your other ankle."

He'd sounded just like his brother when he said those words. For an instant, she thought Louis had said them.

Memories of Louis appeared to be fading, and she had a difficult time remembering his face now or the way his eyes wrinkled around the edges when he smiled. She'd attempted to bring those recollections to the surface again and again. But the harder she tried, the more they seemed to disappear. And in their place...

She hated to admit that Pierre appeared to be taking his brother's place in her thoughts and in her dreams. It seemed wrong, somehow, disloyal. She must try harder.

Yes, that is just what I must do.

Pierre took her inside and placed her on the bench in front of the fireplace. The room felt cold even though a residue of hot embers still remained in the hearth from the previous night. Rachel focused her full attention on Pierre.

"I need to wrap a warm cloth around your foot and ankle," he said.

"I interrupted your work. Leave me here and go back to join the men. I will be all right."

"No, Rachel. I will do as I said I would. But it will take a while to get the cloth warm enough. You rest there on the bench until I get back."

She turned in order to watch him hurry to the door and leave through it. When she heard the door close behind him, she rubbed her ankle again.

The pain had decreased. She thought she could walk if she tried. But the gentleness and kindness Pierre showed when he came to her rescue had touched her heart. She longed to experience that emotion again.

Yes. I have feelings for Pierre, strong ones. But this cannot be love.

Love described what she had felt for Louis—still felt for him. She only cared for Pierre because he reminded her of his brother. However, there could be no substitute for real love in this world or in the world to come.

Louis and her parents resided in Heaven with God now. At least, she hoped they did. Pierre had said that a person could know for sure whether or not they would go to Heaven when they died, but that explanation hadn't resolved the issue for Rachel.

She glanced down at her foot. It still hurt and her shoe felt tight, especially around her ankle. Maybe it was swollen.

The door opened. Pierre had returned with a white cloth.

He knelt before her and removed her shoe and one black stocking. Rachel felt her face warm. Nobody but her father had ever performed such a personal act, and Papa hadn't changed her shoes and stockings since she was a small child.

Her foot felt cold without a covering.

"Is your foot cold?" he asked.

"Yes, a little."

"I can fix that."

He rubbed his hands together for a moment. Then he placed them on her foot as if to warm it.

Rachel peered straight ahead so maybe he wouldn't know how his touch affected her. His hands moved to her ankle, and a sense of delight and wonderment swept over her.

Surely by now she must be blushing, and he probably made a note of it. Pierre glanced at her and smiled, and she knew her conclusions were correct.

"Feeling any better?" he asked.

"Yes, thank you."

"The pain will be much relieved once I have put this cloth in place."

The cloth felt warmer than she expected when it first touched her skin. Hot almost. She jerked her leg back from him.

"Calm yourself, woman, and let me do this for you."

He glanced at her and grinned. Then he wrapped the cloth around and around her ankle with hands that looked rough from many hours of chopping wood in the forest. The cloth soothed her ankle. In fact, she felt soothed all over.

Pierre had said that she jumped to conclusions. Perhaps she did, still, she thought she caught him looking at her in a very personal way. Slowly, he wrapped the cloth around her ankle one more time and tied it, gazing at her lips the whole time.

Does he plan to kiss me?

Impossible. He promised he wouldn't.

But did she want him to kiss her?

Rachel swallowed because she really didn't have an answer. It was much too soon after Louis's death to allow Pierre to kiss her. To kiss Pierre now would dishonor his brother's memory—tarnish the love that she and Louis had shared. She couldn't define her feelings for Pierre, but she knew she was grateful to him and that would never change.

She had never been kissed by any man but Louis, but even Louis had never looked at her with such obvious interest. She needed to think of something to say that would change the current situation.

Rachel thought a moment and cleared her throat. "Tell me about that cart you found in the woods before I fell and hurt myself," she finally said.

"Cart?" Pierre frowned and looked away. "Oh yes. Well, the cart is old. It must have belonged to Rene's grandmother. Rene and Felix plan to buy two horses to pull it, and they will be buying a milk-cow as well. Felix and Yvonne will need horses if they hope to farm the land that surrounds the cabin, and the cow will give milk to Yvonne's child as it grows"

She shouldn't have changed the subject so abruptly. Pierre had looked hurt. Perhaps he was angry as well. She would need to think of something that might smooth things a bit.

"I am sorry I refused to go on a picnic with you when I had the chance," she said. "I truly am, and I would love to go one day soon. What about today?"

He shook his head. "How would you walk on that ankle? Besides, I have things I must do today, and those chores cannot wait."

Rene held a worship service on Saturday night in the main room of the cabin. Everybody in the household attended. Rachel sang hymns of praise and prayed along with the others. But on Sunday, Rene insisted that everyone go to a church in the village.

"If we attend services at the French Church," Rene had said, "the villagers are less likely to become suspicious of us."

After what happened with the blind woman, Rachel felt sure that Rene and his family would insist that she stay behind.

"The villagers know about Madame Rachel now," Rene continued. "If she does not go to church with us, some might assume that we have something to hide."

Rene and Felix had bought two horses from a man they knew in town. They hitched the animals to the cart early on Sunday morning. When they finished, Rachel sat down in the back of the cart with Suzette and Yvonne. Her ankle no longer bothered her, but at Pierre's suggestion, she had stayed off of it as much as possible.

At last, they started moving. The little cart seemed even smaller with three women and one child crammed inside. Rene sat up front, driving. Pierre and Felix walked along beside it. Then Anton got out and walked with the men, giving Rachel enough room to stretch her legs. Pierre strolled beside the cart on Rachel's side.

The cart hit a hard bump in the road. Rachel put her hand on the wooden side nearest to her and held on. Pierre put his hand over hers, and she experienced the same exciting awareness she'd felt when he wrapped her injured ankle.

As they were leaving the church service, Yvonne complained of back pains.

"What can I do to help?" Rachel asked Yvonne.

"Not a thing," Felix answered for her. "Suzette said that Yvonne will be fine as soon as I get her home." As his older sister and the mother of Anton, Suzette should know.

Rachel hesitated to make sure she wasn't needed and hurried to the cart.

Pierre smiled when she walked up. "Let me help you up into the carriage."

Without waiting for a reply, he grabbed her around the waist and lifted her into the cart. Rachel settled into the back. Pierre stood on the road and as close to where she sat as he could get.

"I am concerned for Yvonne," Rachel said to Pierre. "Perhaps the baby is coming early."

"Felix said her baby could arrive at any time, but I am sure she will be all right. My mother complained of back pains before Henri was born."

Rene sat on the wooden bench up front and held tight to the reins, waiting for Yvonne and the others to join him. With Felix on one side of Yvonne and Suzette on the other, they trudged on toward the cart.

"Madame Yvonne, wait a moment!" a woman shouted.

Rachel saw Michelle, Cecile's daughter, race down the steps of the church building and hurry toward Yvonne, Felix, and Suzette. Rachel glanced at Pierre. "That is Michelle, the woman I was telling you about."

Pierre nodded, still standing beside the cart.

Rachel looked down at her hands folded on the skirt of her blue dress. Then Pierre looked down, too.

"You are rubbing your thumb against your forefinger, Rachel. Does your thumb hurt or is something bothering you?"

Before she could answer, she heard Michelle say, "Nobody introduced me to the young woman." She looked straight at Rachel. "Will someone please introduce us?"

Yvonne stared at Michelle for a moment. "This is Martha, our young cousin." She nodded toward Rachel. "Martha has been visiting us to—to help me with the baby when it comes."

"My mother seemed so taken with Martha. I had to learn more about her."

As Michelle moved toward the cart, Rachel noticed that all the sourness she saw previously had been replaced with what looked like a created smile.

"Where are you from, Martha?" Michelle asked.

"Paris," Rene replied for her. "Martha comes from Paris."

"Paris," Michelle said, "my favorite of cities. Have you ever been to—"

"Please excuse us, Madame," Felix inserted firmly. "But we must go now. With the baby coming and all, Yvonne is tired and needs to go home to rest."

"I noticed you left church early."

"Now you know why." He hesitated while the others climbed into the cart. "We would enjoy chatting with you longer, but we really must go. I hope you understand. And good-day."

Rene cracked the whip a few inches above the heads of the horses. The animals moved forward with a jerk. When Rachel glanced back, the woman still stood on the side of the road in front of the church, watching them. She glanced at Pierre and found him looking back at the woman as well.

Rachel gazed down at the bottom of the cart. Michelle couldn't be good news for any of them. If only she could do something to end the woman's suspicions.

❦

The next morning, Rachel sat in the main room on a bench near the fireplace with Yvonne and Suzette. Her two friends sewed squares of cloth together, making a quilt. Rachel sewed white lace on a tiny white dress for Yvonne's baby.

"Yesterday in church, Madame Cecile's daughter seemed interested in learning more about us; especially me." Rachel pushed the needle through the soft cloth and slowly pulled the thread through. "Does Michelle know where we live?"

"She might not know at the moment," Suzette replied, "but it would not be difficult for her to find out. Her confessor knows where we live. If asked, I am sure he would be willing to tell her."

Pierre came in from chopping wood.

"Good morning, ladies," he said.

"Good morning," Suzette and Yvonne said together.

Rachel nodded but didn't say anything. However, when she looked at Pierre, she saw a twinkle in his eyes.

Perspiration caused Pierre's blue shirt to stick to his muscled body. She could see the shape of his upper arm through the thin material and thought how she had felt when he put his hands on her waist and helped her down from the cart.

"I would like to invite my wife to a picnic lunch in the woods this morning. Will you agree, my love?"

Rachel blushed. Pierre didn't often speak such tender words in front of others. It embarrassed her that he had and yet, in a strange way she liked it.

"The last time I invited you," he went on, "you said that you would go on a picnic with me on another day, and so it is; another day."

"I promised Yvonne I would finish the hem of this dress," she said.

"I think you should go with your husband," Yvonne insisted. "Considering all the work you do around here, you deserve a day of rest."

"I agree." Suzette put down her sewing and got to her feet. "And it is such a nice day for a picnic. I shall go out to the kitchen house and gather food for you to take with you."

Pierre looked back at Rachel. "Does this mean you will agree to go?"

Shyness swept over her, and she felt her cheeks warm. Still, the thought of being alone in the woods with Pierre sounded exciting.

"Yes, I should enjoy a picnic very much," Rachel said after a short pause.

Smiling, Pierre offered her his arm. "We should go as soon as the food is ready."

She took his arm and returned his smile with one of her own. A fondness for Pierre dominated her thoughts now. At the same time, she didn't want to appear overly eager for his affection. Her mother had always told her that a proper woman never spoke those kinds of thoughts aloud. And she did want Pierre to think well of her.

Pierre carried the basket, and they stepped out the front door of the cabin and into a cool yet sunny day. Leaves on some of the trees had dressed in all the fall colors in shades of gold and rust, and they seemed to shiver on their branches in a gentle breeze.

A few damp leaves from recent rains fell on Rachel's blue cap and on the shoulders of her pale blue dress. She tossed her head and shook her shoulders in order to dislodge them, but that didn't work. She finally brushed them away with the palm of her right hand.

Pierre grinned down at her. "You missed one." He'd been swinging the wicker picnic basket as they moved along. But he stopped and pulled a gold leaf from her auburn hair below her bonnet and handed it to her.

Rachel laughed. "What a lovely gift. I shall cherish it always."

His deep chuckle blended with her laugh. "Someday, I plan to buy you a gold wedding ring for your finger."

A gold wedding ring. Two months ago she had been engaged to Louis, yet thoughts of him had melted into old but precious memories.

In a clearing just ahead, a shady spot next to a rushing creek appealed to Rachel, and she smiled when she first saw it.

"Would you like to have our picnic under that big Elm tree?" he asked.

"Yes, I was hoping you would suggest that. Do you have the ability to read my mind?"

"No, but as your husband, it is my job to know what my wife wants."

Wife, she thought with a shy smile. He said it again.

She had never known anyone who anticipated her wishes as he did; not even Louis. Pierre's thoughtfulness always made her feel special and never more than when he called her his wife. Yet at times, he appeared to be holding in his emotions as if to hide his true thoughts and feelings.

They sat down and spread out their meal; a small urn of milk, dark bread, cheese, and baked fish. Rachel carefully poured the white liquid into metal cups that Suzette had packed in the basket. She handed one cup to Pierre and put the other on the grass in front of her.

Pierre took a slice of bread and wrapped it around one of the fishes with a bit of cheese.

"The fish looks good like that," she said, admiring his unique way of eating a rather bland meal.

"Would you like a taste?" Before she could reply, he moved much closer to her and poked the bread and fish in front of her mouth. "Try it."

She expected him to hand her the bread, but he kept holding it as if he planned to feed her.

"Open your mouth, little bird," he said jokingly, "and take a bite."

Rachel laughed at his lighthearted request. She liked being near him but felt self conscious by all this special attention. They had spent time alone together at the island but not often since then. She had always feared the unknown and wondered how this picnic would end—and what it might be leading to.

"Come on now." He moved closer. "Open up."

Rachel felt slightly ridiculous. Still, she opened her mouth and took a bit. So close to him now, she felt his cool breath on her forehead as she chewed. The bread and cheese tasted delicious, either from its superior flavor or because Pierre fed it to her. She wanted another bite.

"How did you like it?" he asked, his lips inches from hers.

She swallowed. "I liked it very much."

"Would you like for me to fix your bread as I did mine?"

"That would be delightful."

With Pierre looking at her lips, she no longer thought they were talking only of food. He stroked the side of her face, and the rough texture of his fingers sent a chill down her spine. He cupped her chin, and his face moved still closer to hers. She knew he meant to kiss her, and she shut her eyes, anticipating the instant.

Suddenly she heard Anton's voice, calling to Pierre from a distance.

"Oh, no," Pierre said under his breath and got up. "Not now."

"Monsieur," the child shouted when he reached the clearing. "My uncles need you in the cabin at once. They said it was important."

Pierre took Rachel's hand in his and helped her to her feet. "Sorry, Rachel, but I must go."

Rachel nodded. "You mean we must go."

Fifteen

Rene stood in front of the fireplace, his expression grave. Felix and the two women sat on a bench nearby. Yvonne looked nervous, curling a lock of her hair around her forefinger.

Rachel chose the bench opposite theirs, and Pierre sat down beside her.

"For a long time now," Rene began, "I have been thinking about what we should do if this day ever came. Now it has. We can be thankful that I finished repairing my boat earlier today."

"What has happened?" Felix asked.

"Someone has been asking questions about us."

Captain Vallae. Rachel stiffened. I knew it.

"Jasper, Madame Cecile's daughter, Michelle, or somebody reported seeing a young woman in town who fit the description of the woman Captain Vallae was looking for," Rene said. "Now at least some of us must leave this village as soon as possible."

"Who leaves and who stays?" Pierre asked.

"It would be unwise if not impossible for Felix and Yvonne to leave since she is with child. Besides, they have lived here in the village off and on since they married and are highly regarded by the local priest and by many in his congregation. However, I think you and Rachel should leave tonight. I will be leaving, too, but not with you. It is time for us to go our separate ways. It will be much safer that way, I think."

"What about Anton and me?" Suzette asked. "Are we to leave as well?"

"No," Rene insisted. "I want both of you to stay. Since you spent part of your childhood here with our late grandmother, Suzette, you are known to some in the village as Felix and I are known and now Yvonne. The villagers might suspect something if we all left at once."

Pierre leaned forward. "How are we to leave if not with you?"

"As all of you know, I have been going down to the docks, checking on my boat and working on it since we arrived. A cargo ship is docked in the harbor right now. The captain of the ship is hiring sailors, and I think Rachel and Pierre should sign on. Rachel will need to dress as a boy once again and pretend to be Pierre's little brother as before. She will be expected to work like any of the other sailors on board. However, since they will think she is a child, she might not have to work as hard as the men.

"I will take you and Rachel out to the ship in my boat. We leave tonight. On our way to the ship, it might be necessary to wade in the bay some distance from shore to prevent those at the inn from seeing us as Jasper did when we arrived." Rene glanced at Rachel. "Can you do all of these things, Madame Rachel?"

"Yes." Rachel swallowed. "I will do exactly as you requested."

"This will not be easy for any of us," Pierre continued. "We should pray."

Rene nodded. "Yes."

After the prayer ended, Pierre got up and pulled Rachel to her feet. "Come. We have much to talk about before we leave."

At dusk, Pierre stood at the water's edge, studying the outline of a ship with Rachel at his side. The Atonement, anchored off shore, would be sailing to England, and they had already signed on as sailors. He gazed down at his wife in name only. Things had improved between them, but now, they must pretend to be brothers on a ship filled with men.

In trousers and one of Anton's brown shirts, Rachel looked like a young boy. Still, she might well be in danger.

Sailors stood talking among themselves a few feet away. All of them probably waited to be taken to the ship.

If he could think of a way to save Rachel other than boarding that ship he would do so, but all their other options appeared to have vanished.

He gazed at Rachel. In front of strangers, he would call her by the name they agreed on. "The bay looks choppy tonight, is that not so, Jacque?"

"Yes," Rachel replied.

"Look at the man and the lad standing over there," Pierre heard one of the sailors say. "Did ye notice them when they first walked up?"

"The lad looks a mite young to be a sailor's mate," a huge, bulky man replied. "Do you think we should teach the boy a bit of a lesson once we get out on the high seas?"

Pierre stiffened, but the other men laughed.

He glanced at Rachel again and touched her shoulder. Her body trembled under his hand.

"They are merely talking," Pierre explained.

"I know that," she whispered.

"Come."

He strolled on down the beach in the direction of the pier and motioned for her to follow him. She ran to catch up, just as a young boy might do.

He smiled. Good for you, Rachel.

The salty air had a fishy odor that he knew Rachel didn't like. And what the sailors said must have cut deep.

"I worry that the sailors on board will discover that I am a woman while on the ship." she whispered, "and the possible results of that terrible outcome. I also dislike dressing as a boy, Pierre. I know that I must; you explained all that. Still, I have no wish to board a ship filled with rowdy sailors."

"I cannot blame you," he said, "especially after what Rene told me about the other Huguenots."

"What did he tell you?"

He hesitated. "I hadn't planned to say—not now anyway."

"Say," she demanded. "What happened to the other Huguenots?"

Now he would have to share that information with Rachel and all because he had spoken out of turn.

"Shortly before we left the cabin, Rene told me of their fate privately." Pierre paused in hopes of delaying what had to be said. "It appears that one or two of our friends were captured after they left the island."

"Who? What are their names?"

Pierre shook his head as a wave of despair swept over him. "Rene did not know."

"Did not know?" She put her hands on her hips. "Rene?"

"He said he did not."

"He knew," Rachel insisted. "It would be impossible for him not to know. He just refused to tell you."

Pierre had thought the same thing, but until now, he'd tried not to dwell on it. Rene had probably attempted to shield him from another disaster. Pierre should have demanded that he be told everything, but they were in a hurry to leave. Now it was too late.

"Why did he withhold that information from us, Pierre?"

"I do not know."

A mountain of memories and emotions smothered him; the soldiers, the deaths, the house burning. All these events seemed to appear before him as if they were occurring now.

Something lodged in his throat. He swallowed, hoping it would disappear along with his negative thoughts. Rachel must be having the same kind of recollections.

Pierre recalled how the captain had looked standing in front of Rachel's house, so straight, tall, and threatening. He also re-membered the look on Captain Vallae's face as he studied Rachel's shapely body in her black habit at the Sanctuary. Pierre's jaws tightened.

He would not let Captain Vallae or anyone look at Rachel in that way again.

"Pierre," she said, interrupting his musings. "I think you know the names of those who were arrested and are just not telling me."

"Then you would be wrong. I spoke the truth. I know noth-ing." Pierre cleared his throat. "But my hope is that the others made it to their various locations without being seen."

Nobody spoke for a moment. Pierre wondered what Rachel might be thinking.

"Oh, Pierre," she said with deep emotion. "You knew them better than I did. This must be so hard for you." She started to put her hand on his arm to comfort him.

Pierre longed for her touch but not here, in front of the other sailors. He stepped away and out of her reach.

Rachel's hand fell to her side.

"I want to put my arms around your shoulders, Rachel, and console you. But others might be watching."

"I think you hold in your feelings more than you should," she said, "as if you have no thoughts, no hurts. You are a kind man and gentle, Pierre, and you comfort me often. Why then, do you not allow me to comfort you?"

Her words cut to his heart and soul, forcing him to look at his motives. He didn't like what he saw. He'd kept his emotions locked away lest Rachel discover how much he cared for her; how much he loved her. In doing so, he might have seemed less real to her, less human.

Still, she could never love him as she had loved his brother. She'd made that clear enough. His only defense against total humiliation had been to keep his feelings well hidden, too well, perhaps. But what alternatives did he have?

"Come, Jacque," he said. "It is time to walk to the end of the pier. Rene will be along shortly."

Wet soil swished under his feet, and he had to walk through cold sea water almost to the tops of his worn black shoes in order to reach the wooden piling. Darkness had covered the last glow of evening, but lanterns lined the pier at intervals on both sides.

"Jacque, due to your strong German accent, Rene recommended that you speak as little as possible while we are on the ship."

"I know," Rachel whispered. "He told me the same thing."

"As you know," he continued, "this ship came from England. It is good that you know the English language. If you must speak, speak English while aboard the ship."

"I will."

He smiled.

Though dark clouds still blackened the moon, the lanterns made it possible for him to see Rene secure his boat close to the pier. Pierre motioned for Rachel to move forward.

"It is time for us to board Rene's boat. Are you ready?"

"I am."

They waited at the end of the pier. As they stood there, Pierre hoped to encourage Rachel in some way. She had seemed so lost and worried. If he were honest, he worried for their safety more than he wanted to say.

The sailors they noticed earlier had gathered at the opposite end of the pier.

Pierre leaned down and whispered in her ear. "All will go well with us while on the ship. I know it."

"How can you be sure?" she whispered.

"You know the answer to that."

"You mean God?"

"Yes," he said, "the Lord is with us."

"You have a deep faith, Pierre, and I am glad of that. I cannot see your face now, but sometimes, your expression does not match your calming words. It is almost as though you are hiding under another man's skin."

"What if I am?" He felt the muscles in his face tighten. "And if I seem worried at times, you would be right. But that can never lessen my faith in a merciful God. I believe that the Lord hears my prayers and will supply all our needs."

He wanted to say more. But two of the sailors now walked down the pier and straight toward them.

"It might be unwise to continue our conversation," he whispered. "It could cause the sailors to become suspicious." Pierre helped Rachel down into the boat. "Be careful where you step, little brother. We would not want you to stumble on a rope or something and fall."

Rachel tried to relax as the men rowed out to the ship but to no avail. The wind howled. The sea churned and roared, and the boat moved from side to side like a sailor who had consumed too much wine. She heard the loud clang of the ship's bell, reminding the sailors to come aboard. The swish of the oars as they sliced the choppy water had been absorbed by all the other sounds.

Yet none of this played on Rachel's mind as much as going aboard that ship.

"A rope ladder will have been thrown over the side of the ship," Rene explained as they grew closer to the ship. "Latch on to the ladder with both hands and climb on up, Madame Rachel. Sailors will be waiting to pull you on deck. And remember, from this moment forward you are Jacque, Pierre's younger brother. Are you afraid?" Rene whispered.

"No," she replied. But it was a lie.

Men would be on board that ship. Men of all ages who wanted a woman any way they could have her. Some would be gentlemen, others would not. If they managed to discover that she was a woman, she could be. . .

"Never let the darkness of the deck or the fierce-looking faces of the men frighten you," Rene went on softly. "No doubt, most of them are good fellows, and you will learn the names of the ones who are not soon enough."

But if Pierre wasn't nearby, how would Rachel fight against them?

The odor of fish still hung in the air as Rachel climbed the ladder. The ropes felt rough, stinging the palms of hands that had toughened since she left Beniot. Near the top of the ladder, a cool wind blew in from the north. She felt a sudden chill all the way to her bones.

"A boy is coming aboard," Pierre yelled out in English. "Jacque is young, but he will make a fine sailor."

The moon came out from behind the clouds. A burly man with a black beard pulled Rachel on deck. He picked up a lantern, raised it and stared at her. "Are you Jacque?"

Rachel nodded.

"Do ye speak the King's English?"

"Yes, sir."

"What kind of accent is that?"

She shrugged.

"No matter. You, laddy, are bloody smaller than most. Ye might well be the smallest lad on this ship. Can ye keep up with the work, boy?"

She nodded again.

"Then get below." He motioned with his head toward an opening.

Rachel studied the opening, concluding that it must be what Rene had called a hatch. The hatch led down a flight of stairs.

"It is bloomin' dark down there," he said. "So, watch your step, lad. Below, you'll be seein' a man by the name of Burney, and he will show you where ye are to sleep."

Rachel moved near the opening but didn't go down the stairs.

"Jacque is waiting for me." Pierre stepped onto the deck of the ship without assistance. "You see, he is my younger brother."

"Make sure he does his share of the work," the burly sailor warned. "If not, ye will do his and yours as well."

Pierre led the way down the dark stairway. The steps creaked as they descended them. A skinny man in smelly clothes stood at the bottom, holding a lantern.

"I am Burney," he said with an accent Rachel could not identify. "Follow me."

Lanterns swung from hooks at various points below deck, making points of light in an otherwise dark place. Rachel cast her eyes downward as Rene had instructed, trying to ignore the smell of fish and body odors that drifted up from the hold. Burney led them through a sea of men below deck, and the distasteful odors increased. Rachel saw a flash of bare shoulders and realized that some of the sailors had removed their shirts. Embarrassed, she cast her eyes downward again.

She would not change her clothes in front of these men. Not even in front of Pierre. And without a change of clothes or a way of washing the ones she now wore, this could mean she must wear the same faded brown shirt and brown trousers until they reached England. She could be thankful that Rene had said it would be a short trip through the Channel.

Narrow hammocks, one beside the other, had been strung from the bulkheads and hung loosely, swaying back and forth in time with the waves that roared outside the ship.

A young Negro boy seated on a low hammock caught her attention as they walked by. His makeshift bed had been placed at the forward part of the ship in a spot that Rene had called the ship's bow, far away from any of the lanterns and away from the other sailors. The boy held his arm against a post at an awkward angle. Rachel feared he might be chained.

In the light coming from the lantern Burney held, she caught a glimpse of what appeared to be a lonesome look in the boy's dark eyes. Her heart softened toward him. The boy could hardly be more than fifteen years old, and she knew what it felt like to be alone in a hostile world. When she looked up, she saw Pierre watching the boy, too.

Burney had moved on toward the middle of the ship, carrying his lantern.

"We must catch up with him," Pierre whispered.

"Yes." Rachel ducked under a rope attached to one of the hammocks. "I am coming."

"You will sleep here," Burney said at last.

"Very well." Pierre nodded. "I shall take this one," he said to Rachel, "and you take the one next to mine. You will be safer there."

Burney frowned as if he expected an explanation.

"My little brother is new to ships and sailing, and sometimes he walks while sleeping. If his hammock is close to mine, it is less likely that he will decide to take a stroll on his own during the night."

Burney nodded as if the explanation satisfied him. "You best both try to get some sleep now. You are going to need it. And if someone wakes you during the night, get up at once and come on deck."

"The wind grew stronger before we boarded the ship," Pierre said. "Are we likely to run into a storm tonight?"

Burney shrugged. "Who can say what the sea will do next?" He lifted the lantern, and his eyes narrowed as he stared at Rachel.

She tensed, wondering if her disguise had been discovered.

Burney watched her a moment longer and left.

Most of the lanterns in their part of the ship had been extinguished for the night. The last glow from Burney's light disappeared, and darkness engulfed them. Pierre helped Rachel up onto her hammock. He dropped his shoes by his bed with a thump.

"Are you all right, little brother?" Pierre asked.

"Yes," she whispered.

"And if you need my help in the night, tap on the wall."

"Your little brother ain't talkin' much," a sailor said in the darkness. "Is he able to speak?"

Pierre didn't reply. Rachel wondered if he ever planned to and what Pierre was thinking.

She couldn't tell where the voice came from in such a dark structure. However, she assumed it came from a sailor in one of the hammocks nearby.

"Of course Jacque can speak," Pierre said finally, "but it is unlikely that he will. He is very shy, you see."

"Some will make sport of him for being shy," the sailor pointed out. "You will need to keep watch on the boy at all times."

"Thank you, Monsieur, for telling me. And I will keep watch, you can be sure of that."

"Sounds like you be a Frenchy," the man said. "But you speak my language, and that is good."

Nobody spoke again for a moment.

"Who is the young Negro boy who sleeps alone in the bow of the ship?" Pierre asked.

"His name be Ebony, and he is a slave. At night, they keep him chained to his bed, they do. He is only free to move around when he is working."

"Slavery should be outlawed," Pierre said, "in England and everywhere else."

"True. But the skipper of this ship makes the laws here."

"I see."

Rachel longed to find out more about Ebony, the slave-boy. But she'd promised not to say much, and she intended to keep that promise.

"I would not want to be a slave," Pierre said.

"Who would, I say," the man said. "But there be not much either of us can do about it, is there? And who might you be, if I might be so bold?"

"My name is Pierre La Salle, and this is my little brother, Jacque. And you?"

"I be the one they call Smitty."

"What an unusual name," Pierre replied.

"It could be as you say, unusual," Smitty said, "I lived in an orphanage in London for as long as I can remember until I signed on this bloody ship ten years ago. Many orphans had no names where I grew up. At the orphanage, the headmaster also served as our preacher, and he sometimes called me lazy or foolish. I like Smitty better than any of them names."

"I assume the orphanage was Christian," Pierre said. "Are you a man of God?"

"I think so. I went to church, I did, whilst I lived at the orphanage. We were beaten if we refused to go. So I went regular."

"I worship God because I want to and not because I must," Pierre said softly. "The Lord gives me peace even when my life is full of storms."

The man released a deep sigh. "I will be awantin' that kind of peace someday."

"Why wait?" Pierre asked.

"You sailors stop all that talking over there and go to sleep," someone shouted. "I am tired of hearing ya."

The men stopped talking. Rachel curled up in a ball under the covers, thinking. She thought about Ebony and Smitty and their tragic lives and about her own situation. What if one of the other sailors guessed that she was a woman and attempted to abduct her? Was Pierre strong enough to protect her from two or three burly men?

Something bumped her hammock in the darkness. Rachel stiffened. Her heart pounded so loud she thought she could hear it. The to and fro sway of the ship caused the hammock to swing back and forth often, but this movement seemed different. Before she could scream, a hand covered her mouth.

Sixteen

"All is well," he whispered to Rachel, "It is me, Pierre. And I regret it if I startled you."

"Of course you startled me," she whispered back. "It is blacker than a cave in here."

"I approached you suddenly," he said. "And I was afraid you might scream."

"Surprising me made that very likely. Unless you like hearing me scream, you must stop catching me unaware. When you did it at the Sanctuary, I almost jumped out of my skin. My heart is pounding so fast now I think I can feel it."

"I am sorry."

"Good. What do you want?"

"To tell you something I forgot to tell you earlier."

"What?"

"Rene said that the captain and his officers break the fast in the galley, but the sailors, like us, eat on deck. If we hope to fill our bellies in the morning, we must collect our bowls and go out on deck early. Otherwise, we will have nothing to eat. You must get up as soon as the bell tolls in the morning."

"Very well. But if I fail to hear the bell, wake me. And another thing, remember when I asked you to tap me on the shoulder when you have something important to say."

He chuckled. "Yes."

"Well, you forgot. As I said, putting a hand over my mouth is unacceptable."

❧

Jean Vallae sat with his three hirelings at a table at an inn further on down the coast. Brother Julian had taken a chair directly across from him.

"What news have you for me tonight?" Jean asked.

"Good news I am happy to say." The monk puffed out his chest and a smile appeared on his face. "A fisher from the town of Casa said that the man that sounded like the one you are looking for and a young boy signed on a ship as sailors."

"A young boy did you say?" Jean asked.

"Yes."

The monk's smile deepened, and his yellowed, rotten teeth sent out a disgusting odor that seemed to fill the air in the inn's entire eating area. Jean had leaned forward, but he shrank from the smell and sat as far back as his chair would allow.

"The ship is bound for England, and it is my belief," the monk went on, "that the boy is actually the nun you are looking for, dressed in men's attire."

"And she was in Casa while we were there?" Jean asked.

"No. The man and the young woman arrived after we left."

Jean's jaw tightened, remembering the woman he saw in front of a store in Casa. He'd returned to the village alone for one last search before moving on to the next town. At first, he thought he'd found the young woman he sought near the butcher shop and waited to see her come out, but she never did. When he finally went inside and looked around, she had gone. However, the butcher recalled seeing a young woman who fit her description.

If the young nun and the girl he saw at the butcher shop were the same person, he could have captured her then. It would have been so easy. He would not make that mistake again.

"What is the name of this ship the man and the woman signed onto?" Jean asked.

"The Atonement."

"The Atonement. I have heard of it. You have done well, monk," Jean replied. "I will hire a fast sailing ship bound for

England at once. If the winds are with us, we shall arrive before they do. And what a surprise they will have waiting for them when they step on shore."

He laughed, and the others joined in.

Jean lifted his mug of ale. "To the capture of the enemies of the King of France."

The other three men lifted their mugs. But the portly monk looked down instead of taking a swallow of ale, and another layer of flesh appeared under his double chin. After a moment, Brother Julian excused himself and left the inn.

Jean's jaw firmed. He trusted no one, not even a former monk.

When the other men had gone, Jean continued to sit at the table. If they planned to leave for England in the morning as he'd said, he would need to find a ship to carry them there. He'd made it sound like the task would be easy. It would not.

Though he didn't know him well, Jean would call on Monsieur Beaumont that very night. How fortunate that he knew someone in the village who claimed to be a ship owner. The gentleman gave the impression of power and influence. If he didn't own an available sailing ship, he might know someone who did; someone who would be willing to sail to England on short notice, for a handsome fee.

Relations between France and England were seldom good. As a result, it might be wise to pretend to be no friend of the crown while in that country. He would leave his captain's uniform behind. The uniform served him well in France. However, things would be different in England.

Jean had felt good about visiting the home of Monsieur Beaumont regardless of the late hour. He had a business transaction to discuss that would make the man money.

However, as he stood on the front porch of the Beaumont mansion, the nasty taste of regret filled his mouth like a glass of spoiled milk. Regret that his marriage and his military career had failed, and regret that the woman of his dreams was a Jew and that he might never have her.

The interior of the house looked dark except for a light in one of the downstairs rooms. The Monsieur's wife and children had probably turned in for the night hours ago, and he didn't know the man well enough to pay him a social call in daylight, much less after dark. Jean wouldn't be surprised if Monsieur Beaumont slammed the door in his face before he'd had time to explain his visit.

He glanced behind him. The moon left a trail of light on the gravel path leading to the entry doors as if he was being invited to politely retreat while he still could. But if he left before giving his offer, he might lose the chance to capture Rachel, the woman he'd called Magdalena Poyer, and her new husband.

He thought of her beauty even in the clothes of a nun as he turned back around. He hit the heavy metal knocker against the oak door. When he heard no movement inside the house, he straightened his shoulders and hit it again, only much harder. He would stand there all night banging on the door if he found it necessary in order to reach his goal.

⚬⚮⚬

Rachel found Rene's warning to be correct the next morning when she and Pierre arrived on deck. The sailors had gathered around a big tub full of stew. Ebony held a large spoon that he dipped into the tub again and again, filling the bowls.

Sweat shone through the boy's ragged green shirt and brown trousers. Rachel assumed that he had been up and about doing his various tasks for some time. As Ebony filled her bowl, she noticed red marks around his wrists where the chains had been, and cuts and bruises on both his arms.

She guessed that he had been beaten.

Pierre poked her arm with his elbow. When she glanced his way, he sent her a shushing gesture as if to warn her not to say or do anything that might cause others to notice her.

The ship groaned and churned, moving from side to side. The cloth sails snapped in a brisk breeze.

Rachel took her bowl and walked on unsteady feet to the rail and glanced at the ocean. Wave after wave of blue-green water crashed against the hull of the ship, but her thoughts centered on Ebony, wondering what she could do to help him. Pierre joined her at the rail, and she wanted to share her thinking with him; to protest the slave's plight verbally. With so many sailors on deck, that could be risky.

A group of men had gathered at the rail directly across from where they stood. One of them, a stranger, walked up to them.

"I be Smitty," the stranger said. "And you must be Pierre. I seen you and your brother as soon as you came on deck, I did. I be wanting to know more about that peace you told me about last night so I can have it for meself."

Pierre smiled. "It might not be safe to have a discussion here, but surely we can discover a place to talk later."

"That ain't likely," Smitty said. "The captain puts the strap to our backs if we be talkin' while there is work to be done." Smitty leaned forward. "Can you read?" he whispered to Pierre.

"Yes."

"Good." He handed Pierre a small scrap of paper. "Meantime, I be wanting to help you and your brother since you are new here."

Pierre's friendly smile warmed her heart. "Thank you," he said. "That is very kind of you. We would appreciate any help you can provide."

"Be on deck before daylight of a morning and again at dusk, if you want a full belly," Smitty warned. "Come late, and you be going without."

Rachel wondered if Ebony had been fed at all.

Pierre looked around the deck. Perhaps to see if any of the other sailors were listening to their conversation. Rachel looked, too, and nobody else appeared to be paying them any mind.

When she finished eating her meager breakfast, Rachel moved away from Pierre and Smitty so they could talk privately—man to man. A short distance away, she pressed her body against the railing and gazed out at the sea.

"What did you wish to discuss?" Pierre asked the other sailor.

"I want to be talking about that peace you told me about," Smitty said. "I want it for meself, I do."

Pierre nodded, thrilled at the thought of witnessing to another. "As a Christian, I believe that Jesus is the Prince of Peace. Do you know how to pray?"

"I learned to say me prayers as a child, I did, back at the orphanage."

"Then you know that prayer is talking to God."

"Yes," Smitty said. "But I know nothing about God or the Bible."

Pierre thought of the joy that Smitty would soon be feeling if he decided to follow the Lord. "I believe that the Lord wants you to learn about Him."

"Are you going to teach me about God?"

"That is my desire. But first, you said that you have no real name. Is that right?"

"Yes."

"Might I have the privilege of giving you a first and last name?" Pierre asked.

"You want to give me a name?"

"Yes. And I am sure your parents would have given you a proper name if they had been able to raise you?"

"Can you do that?" Excitement bubbled in Smitty's voice. "Can you give me a name like everybody else?"

"Indeed, I can." Pierre hesitated a moment in order to pray.

When he'd finished praying, he said, "I once knew an Englishman named Smith, and Smitty sounds like that name. I have never owned a Bible. However, I was told that the book of Matthew is the first book of the New Testament. Though I will always call you Smitty, I would like to name you Matthew Smith. Is that name all right with you?"

"I be liking that name very much. And I would like to tell Ebony everything you said. Would that be all right?"

"Of course, and if we speak ever so quietly, maybe we could meet tonight at Ebony's hammock. We could pray, and I could recite verses from the Bible. Would you like that?"

"Indeed I would. And bring along that little brother of yours. I am lookin' fondly to see him again."

"You mean Jacque?"

"Yes, bring him."

Pierre hesitated before replying. "I am not sure. I shall have to think about it."

The skipper walked out on deck with several of his officers.

"We must line up in front of the skipper and his men now," Smitty said. "Otherwise, we will be beaten."

"I will get my little brother and meet you there."

Smitty nodded as Pierre walked further down the deck and grabbed Rachel's arm. "Hurry, little brother. It is important that we do what our friend Smitty is doing at once."

As they lined up near the center of the deck, he thought about whether or not he should take Rachel with him to the meeting that night at Ebony's hammock. At first he'd thought she would be safer if he left her behind. They could be caught and beaten for being out of their hammocks. Yet despite possible danger, Rachel would be safer at his side than she might be in her hammock alone.

❧

One of the ship's officers assigned jobs for the day. Rachel would help in the galley. Since she knew a great deal about cooking and cleaning a kitchen, she thought that job sounded good. Later, she realized that she might not see Pierre again until supper.

In the galley, Rachel scrubbed tubs of dirty pans in soapy water until her fingers wrinkled like those of an old woman. Yet more pans and tubs were stacked for her to wash.

She emptied a pan of dirty dishwater over the side of the deck and walked back to the galley, hoping to see Pierre along the way. Several sailors worked on deck, but she couldn't find Pierre among them.

Rachel looked up and saw him. He'd climbed up in the ship's rigging and appeared to be working with the sails. The task looked dangerous. The cloth sails snapped and popped above her head. The rigging squeaked and moaned hauntingly.

We should never have signed onto this ship. Pierre and I must find a means of escape—for us—and for Ebony and Smitty.

Before the last lantern had been snuffed out that night, Pierre heard the squeak of Rachel's hammock. She leaned over and touched his arm.

"What did Smitty say in his message?" she whispered.

"He wants God in his life, and we must pray that he find Him." Pierre paused before speaking again. "As you know, this is a short journey we are taking to England. We have no time to waste if we hope to help Smitty and Ebony. Therefore, we shall be meeting in Ebony's hammock for prayer later tonight."

"Ebony, did you say?"

"Yes." He grinned because he knew she was smiling as well. "I thought that plan would please you."

"It does."

"The bell rings at midnight, tolling the hour," he went on. "And few sailors will be about then. So we shall get up from our hammocks and go to Ebony's hammock without making a sound. Can you do that, Jacque?"

"Of course. I am not a baby, Pierre."

He made no reply.

Pierre awoke when the bell rang at midnight. He had been dreaming of Rachel. Perhaps he always would.

He reached over and took her hand. "Wake up," he whispered. "It is time."

She said nothing.

He squeezed her tiny hand gently. "Hurry! We must go."

She squeezed his hand in return, a signal they had devised when speaking might not be wise. He rolled out of his hammock and found her again.

Pressing his free hand against the belly of the ship, he felt his way in the darkness. Rachel clung to the tail of Pierre's shirt as they moved though a maze of sleeping men to Ebony's hammock. He heard the sound of men snoring and breathing heavily. Little else.

"Pierre," he heard Smitty whisper. "I am over here."

Pierre moved toward the sound of his friend's voice.

"I have brought Jacque," Rachel heard Pierre say.

"Welcome," the sailor said in the darkness.

"Thank you, Smitty," Pierre whispered.

"I was Smitty. Now I am Matthew Smith, but you can still call me Smitty. This is Ebony, me friend. He be knowing few words in our language. But he understands much, he does. And he wants a name, too. Will you be giving him a name like you gave me?"

"Yes." Pierre hesitated. "I have been thinking on that very topic. I will name him Ebony Smith. That way, the two of you will be brothers forever."

Smitty chuckled softly, but Rachel heard another laugh as well—a deep belly laugh that must have come from Ebony.

"Will somebody tell that black boy over there to shut his mouth," somebody shouted.

"We must be quiet," Pierre warned in a whisper.

With two men already seated, the hammock must have hung almost to the wooden planks that lined the bottom of the hold. When Rachel and Pierre joined them there, the hammock dipped lower, and she felt her body touch the hard flooring underneath.

"It be too crowded. Ebony and I will sit on the floor," Smitty said.

When the two men got up, the hammock lifted, and in the darkness, Pierre put his arm around Rachel.

They managed to pray and worship together in whispers and without interruption. Though Rachel barely knew Matthew and Ebony, she felt as if they had been her friends forever, and she loved the worship, the teaching, and the fellowship with the three men. She also liked sitting close to Pierre on Ebony's hammock and feeling his hand on hers. She dreamed of Pierre at night now and hoped that he sometimes dreamed of her.

After breaking the fast one morning, Rachel went into the galley to wash the dishes. Later, she threw dishwater over the side of the ship. As she walked back to the galley with an empty tub, several sailors started laughing. The largest one blocked her way.

"Hey, lad," he said. "Did anyone ever tell ya that you walk like a girl?"

Rachel froze as male laughter echoed all around her.

She couldn't be sure, but the biggest of the three sailors sounded like the man she had heard talking about her on the beach the night they arrived at the ship. Rachel longed to tell him what she thought of him. Instead, she remembered her father's warnings and attempted to walk around him. Avoid a confrontation.

The big man stepped in her path a second time. Smitty had called him Bolder.

Bald on top, Bolder had a large nose under squinty brown eyes and a wide chin sprinkled with a stubby blond beard. Muscles bulged from his huge arms, and his shoulders looked so broad she doubted he would be able to enter the galley unless he went in sideways.

Gathering all her strength, she lifted her head and peered at him. "Would you mind getting out of my way?"

"Of course, boy," Bolder said tauntingly. "Or should I say girl?" The big man laughed.

Then the other sailors did.

Seventeen

"Get out of my way," Rachel demanded. "I have work to do."

"Work?" Bolder laughed mockingly. "Am I stopping you from your work, boy?"

"You are standing in front of the door."

One of the skipper's officers came on deck. He glared at Bolder. "You men get back to work or I will take a strap to you."

Bolder and the other sailors scattered. Rachel opened the door to the galley and went inside.

She considered telling Pierre what had happened but decided against it. He would get angry, and she didn't need a fight going on between Pierre and one of the other sailors. She would sit on her anger and wait. Besides, they would be leaving the ship soon enough; so she hoped.

❦

Ebony's hammock hung from a rope at the forward of the ship. Rachel realized that if it had been anywhere else, the privacy they desired might have been sacrificed. But since it was far from everyone else on board, nobody appeared to notice them that night when she, Pierre, Ebony, and Smitty met again for prayer and worship.

"It be a short voyage to England," Smitty said as soon as everybody sat down.

Rachel nodded. That bit of news gave her hope.

"We have already entered the English Channel," Pierre explained, "and could dock at a port in England at any time; perhaps as soon as tomorrow. This could be our last prayer meeting. Fortunately, we have already planned Ebony's escape."

She smiled. My wish came true.

Rachel had always liked being a female and hated dressing like a man and pretending to be one. If she left the ship tomorrow, it would not be too soon for her.

"Smitty gathered scrap metal before we came onboard and made a hammer that seems strong enough to smash Ebony's chains," Pierre went on. "However, Jacque and I signed on this ship for a year, as did Smitty. The ship's captain will not be pleased if we fail to honor that commitment. I too regret it, since my honor is at stake, but it cannot be helped. We will leave the ship at port in England."

"We could go ashore with them other men but not come back when they do?" Smitty suggested. "I be happy with that."

"We will be helping Ebony escape," Pierre pointed out. "As a result, we might have to jump overboard and swim to shore."

"Swim to shore?" Rachel whispered. "No, Pierre, that is impossible. You know I cannot swim. I could never jump overboard."

"Have no fear," Pierre insisted. "Smitty, Ebony, and I shall catch you in the water and tow you to shore, if it comes to that. But for now, think positive thoughts. You might not have to jump into the sea. It is possible that the shipper will already have had the ladder made ready for the sailors to leave the ship by the time of our escape. We might not have to dive into the water after all.

"And remember the plan we are discussing now," Pierre warned. "Trust in God." He touched Rachel's hand in the darkness. "And do not fight us, Jacque, while you are in the water."

Rachel bit her lower lip. "Have you considered the fact that I hate water; that if I jump in the channel, I will go under?"

"Yes," Pierre said, "but you will go under only briefly, and we will be there to keep you from going down a second time."

Only briefly? To Rachel, the plan was unacceptable.

"Let us end this service with a prayer that God will make our escape successful," Pierre said. "And may we soon be living on dry land and in a safe place."

Rachel closed her eyes, defeated.

I cannot—will not—go into the water.

She had no choice but to stay behind, take her chances, and go ashore when the other sailors did.

❧

Jean Vallae stood on the deck of the Mary Rose and gazed at the moon reflecting off the water. The brisk wind he'd hoped for cooled his face and slicked back his hair, and he held a rope connected to the rigging for support. His clothes hugged his body. His brown shirt had been pulled loose from his belt by the salty breeze, and his trousers flapped around at the back of his legs like the cloth sails above his head, snapping and stretching and snapping again.

By morning he would be closer to his goal of finding the outlaws than ever before, and now he knew for sure that the nun's name was Rachel. Rachel Zimmer Levin Dupre. The girl in the portrait and the nun were one and the same in his mind as well as in fact.

The monk had confirmed the names before they sailed. But only Brother Julian knew where the information came from.

Of course, he'd known Rachel's identity since he read the letters he found in the trunk, but he'd been trying to deny the truth, hoping she wasn't Jewish. The monk's report removed all doubts.

Monsieur Beaumont not only accepted his request for a fast ship on short notice, he had allowed Jean to purchase his private sailing ship.

"I have been wanting to buy a larger ship," Monsieur Beaumont had said. "Your request could not have come at a better time. However, if that were not so, I might have refused your generous offer to rent or buy my ship."

But he hadn't refused, and now Jean had taken on the adventure of his life. It should be easy enough to find a sailor and a young boy. Or rather, Rachel dressed as a boy.

"I learned in the village of Casa that her hair was cut short,"
the monk had reported. "And that she found favor with an elderly
widow by the name of Madame Cecile. The woman has a middle-
aged, unmarried daughter called Michelle."

"Did your information come from one or both of them?" he'd
asked.

"I cannot say." The monk had smiled and looked away. "I
never reveal my sources. But the daughter seemed to dislike
Rachel as much as you do, Captain. It is said in the village that
Michelle's younger sister died under peculiar circumstances and
that the mother had always favored the youngest girl. Perhaps
Rachel reminded Michelle of the dead sister she hated. According
to a butcher who lives in the village of Casa, Rachel is beautiful
even without her long auburn hair."

I will have her. Jean gripped the rope so tightly, the palms of
his hands burned. I will have Rachel before her hair grows another
inch. And then, I will watch her die."

✿

On the morning that The Atonement finally anchored, Pierre
awoke quickly—alert and excited about the possibility of going
ashore. But Rachel looked sleepy as they headed for the stairway a
few minutes later. Pierre searched for Ebony but couldn't find him
as he climbed the stairs with Rachel and Smitty.

"I hear we not be eating first thing this morning," Smitty said.
"The skipper be talking to us about something, and we stand at
attention until he be through."

"Why? What has changed?" Pierre asked. "We normal-
ly break the fast before we stand before the skipper to get our
assignments."

"Today be different," Smitty whispered. "A small boat done
rowed out to The Atonement late last night to deliver a letter to
the skipper."

Pierre stopped to hear more, pressing his body against the
wall beside the stairway so the other sailors could get by. Rachel
and Smitty followed his lead and paused as well.

"Why should we worry about a boat?" Pierre smiled in hopes of encouraging Rachel. "Little boats come and go here. Let us think on the fact that today we will touch dry land. But first, we must go on up and hear what the skipper has to say."

Pierre, Rachel, and Smitty joined a line of sailors on deck.

One of the skip's officers stepped forward. "The skipper will be along shortly with important news."

Though Pierre pretended otherwise, doubts lingered. To pull off a plan such as theirs, everything must work perfectly. Having a stranger on deck might make their escape difficult.

He'd tucked the hammer in one of the wide pockets of his trousers, and if necessary, he wouldn't hesitate to use it to save Rachel and Ebony. The skipper still hadn't arrived to make his announcement. Pierre stood at attention with the rest of the sailors, waiting. Though a patient man, he disliked pointless delays, and this inconvenience could destroy their plans.

Rachel watched as the skipper left his cabin. A small man to begin with, he reminded her of a skinny, little rooster hoping to outshine all the other birds in the chicken house. He strutted on deck in his red waistcoat, black wool trousers, and a black hat cocked at an angle. She wondered who he hoped to impress—certainly not her.

The skipper cleared his throat, and holding a letter in both hands, he began to read.

"Please delay discharging your men until I can come aboard to check for thieves. Two men stole money from me on my last trip to France, and I have reason to believe that these criminals might be hiding aboard your ship.

Regards,

Jean Vallae."

Jean Vallae?

Rachel stiffened. Captain Vallae had discovered them; or soon would.

"Go about your normal duties until Mister Vallae arrives," the English skipper said. "This morning, we will break the fast after he leaves the ship."

She glanced at Pierre, but he appeared to be looking at Smitty.

"What are we to do?" Rachel whispered when they had been dismissed.

"We shall leave the ship and swim to shore as soon as possible. This could not have happened at a better time. Ebony's chains were removed before we went on deck this morning. Are you up to the task ahead, Jacque, because we should leave this very hour?"

Rachel nodded, hoping she looked braver than she felt. It was time to be honest.

"I could not sleep last night for thinking about jumping into the sea," she said. "I cannot swim, Pierre. Therefore, I cannot do what you want me to do. You and the others go on. Leave me here on the ship. This trouble is my fault anyway."

"Nonsense." Pierre gave her a stern look. "I have no intentions of leaving you behind. Now, begin swabbing the deck as near where the rope ladder was located as possible, as we discussed. Smitty, Ebony, and I will join you there soon."

"But Pierre. . . ."

He turned to leave without waiting to hear what else she had to say.

Rachel carried a bucket of water and a mop to the place where she entered the ship when she first arrived and began her mopping there. Though she had no intentions of diving into the sea, she could help the others make their escape.

The rope ladder had been removed shortly after she came on board, but the sailors would soon be leaving in small boats that would take them ashore. The ladder could have been put in place before they came on deck. What a blessing if by chance it had already been installed there.

She hesitated and finally looked. The rope ladder had been tied to the side of the ship, as she'd hoped it would be. This would make it easier for the men to leave. It also meant that she wouldn't have to jump, but she would have to go into the water. Did the ladder make a difference?

Rachel turned around and began mopping. At the same time, she surveyed the deck to see who might be watching. Nobody appeared to notice her.

Briefly, she had gazed out at the sea. It looked deep, cold, and deadly to someone who didn't know how to swim.

I will not do this, no matter what Pierre says.

She tensed as memories of another body of water filled her mind.

Rachel had been a mere child in Alsace when water became her enemy. Until the age of nine, she'd enjoyed wading and splashing about in the creeks and streams near their home. On a particularly warm and sunny day, she grabbed her cloth doll, Rebecca, and strolled down to the lake to watch the ducks float about in the water. As a Jewish child, Rachel had considered Sunday morning a safe time for such an adventure since all the Christians were in church.

A soft breeze gently rearranged her long hair in an unbecoming style, and she pushed a curl away from her face. The ducks she came to see had gathered on the far side of the lake. Several white dots bobbed about in the water, but the ducks were too far away to see clearly.

She focused her attention on a fishing pier that went out some distance from the shore. She'd always wanted to walk to the end, but her papa had said the pier was rickety and dangerous and that she must stay far from it.

The wind whipped up, and her hair blew across her eyes again. Mama had wanted to braid her hair that morning, but Rachel had been in hurry.

She pushed back her hair and sat down on a log, placing her precious Rebecca as close to her as she could get. The doll's cloth arms fell limp beside her rag-stuffed body.

A dog barked. Rachel held her hair in place and glanced behind her. Her Christian neighbor might have gone to church, but the woman's pesky black dog hadn't. Pots had tried to bite her once. Since then, she'd avoided the animal, but this time, he'd caught her off guard.

"Hello, Pots." Rachel hoped the friendly sound of her voice would calm him. "How are you today?"

The dog growled, showing his teeth. Suddenly, he leaped forward, biting into her doll's cloth arm. Pots dragged Rebecca in the mud toward the water's edge.

"Come back here, Pots!" Rachel got up and chased after him.

The dog dashed away, splashing in the shallow water with the doll's arm in his mouth.

Rachel grabbed for the animal's tail. The dog darted out of her reach. He tossed Rebecca on a wooden plank that floated by. Moving forward, only the dog's head appeared above the blue-green waves.

The doll looked soggy but in good condition. A rusty nail in the board caught a tear in Rebecca's pink dress, holding her to the plank as if she'd been fastened there.

The water barely came up to Rachel's knees, but the hem of her blue dress felt as if it weighed a ton. Her brown leather shoes were probably ruined.

Reaching out with both hands, she took a step toward the wooden plank. It floated just out of her reached. She tried again and missed.

She took another step. The water was only a few inches deeper. Her Papa's words came back to her.

"The lake's bottom slopes off suddenly," he'd said. "Water that is two feet deep can become ten in an instant. You must never play in the lake."

And she hadn't, until now.

She knew her father's warning was justified. Several children in the village had drowned in the lake; one just last year.

Heavy poles held up the fishing pier. One of the pilings was only a few feet away. All at once her stranded doll floated by. The plank bumped the pole she'd been looking at, making Rebecca only a foot or so away.

I wish I knew how to swim.

She could leap for the pole, but if she did, she might push the plank away. Rachel took another step. Her foot slipped. She tried to step back but started sliding. Down. Down. Her feet came out from under her. She bobbed under the water and up. Gasping, she reached for the pole and missed. Rachel went under again.

Mama! Help! She bobbed up, coughing. Am I going to die?

A wave slammed her against the pole, bumping her head. Her head ached as she gripped the pole with both hands, but at least she wasn't drowning.

She needed to climb to the top of the pier. Loose planks or not, it had to be safer than losing her hold on the pole and falling back in the lake.

Her heart pounded as she gazed at the top of the pier. It looked much too high, and the bracing under the pier was also out of her reach. How would she ever manage to climb up?

I am going to die. And Papa will always think I disobeyed him.

"Rachel," she heard someone call.

"Papa, is that you?"

He called her name again as if he hadn't heard.

"Papa," she shouted. "Save me." She heard someone up on the pier coming toward her. "Over here, Papa! Quick!"

"Boy, get back to work!"

Rachel jumped. The gruff voice of the burly sailor she'd met when she first boarded the ship had hurled her back to the present.

He stood at the opening to the hatch and looked right at her. Apparently, he'd been watching her for some time. Her fingers shook so much she could hardly hold the mop.

The skipper of the ship had already gone back to his cabin, and his officers had followed him inside. Probably to hold some kind of meeting related to Captain Vallae's visit. She tried not to think what it would be like if she stayed behind and had to face the Frenchman again.

Pierre strode slowly toward her with Ebony a few steps behind. Smitty hadn't moved. Couldn't they see that the big sailor still peered at her?

Pierre promised to go down first followed by Rachel, Ebony, and finally Smitty. She still had no intentions of leaving. In fact, she was doomed either way. She hoped that she would be able to withstand whatever came after Pierre left the ship.

She overturned her mop bucket as she had been instructed to do. A loud bang sounded when the wooden bucket hit the deck. Mop-water streamed onto the wooden planks. Several sailors looked up to see what had happened.

"Be careful with that bucket, boy," the burly sailor shouted.

Rachel nodded. "Yes, sir."

Pierre stepped forward and righted the bucket before all the water poured out. The big sailor studied them for a moment and went down into the belly of the ship.

Pierre stood with his back to the ladder. "Smitty is not going with us," he whispered.

"Why not?"

"Since he is in no danger of being arrested, he has decided not to leave with us after all. He will collect his pay and leave the ship when the other sailors do."

"What about Ebony?" she replied softly.

"He is coming with us."

"That is good. But I am not."

His forehead wrinkled. "Not what?"

"Going with you."

"Then you must change your plans," Pierre said.

"I cannot swim as you well know, Pierre, so I have decided to stay here on the ship."

"To do so could endanger all of us; and might result in our arrest. Now, are you going with us or not?"

Rachel gazed at the burly-looking men on deck. After all the trouble she'd caused, she couldn't willingly do something that might cause others to be harmed.

"All right," she said. "I will go. Better to drown than face what would happen here if they discover who I really am."

Pierre smiled. "That is better. And you will not drown, Rachel. That I promise."

Smitty tripped over a coil of rope. He fell and cried out in pain.

Rachel frowned.

"He will be all right," Pierre whispered. "He is creating a distraction to help in our escape."

When no one seemed to be looking, Pierre turned and went down the ladder. Rachel checked again. Everybody else still peered at Smitty, laying on the deck and holding one leg. She motioned for Ebony to move closer and went down the ladder. Before she'd reached the bottom, the Negro slave started down, too.

Pierre looped a rope over her head. "Tuck the rope under your arms. I will tie the other end around my waist. Grab my shoulders and hold on. And try not to make a sound."

Rachel ducked under the rope, put it under her arms and gripped his shoulders as best she could. Then Ebony let go of the ladder and swam beside Pierre. The chilly water looked dark and deep. Rachel gripped Pierre's shoulders a little tighter.

"Hang on," Pierre said. "We must reach shore before they notice that we are missing."

As they neared the beach, the waves got stronger. Her head went under. She took in a mouthful of salty water. She gasped. Then she coughed. Flinging out her arms, she grabbed Pierre around the neck and held on with all her might.

"You are choking me!" Pierre forcibly removed her hands. "Hold on to my shoulders and try to relax. You must not grab me around the neck again. Do you understand?"

"Yes, Pierre."

"If you grab me like that again, we could both drown."

"I—I understand."

Rachel intended to do as he said. Yet her heart still pounded, and every muscle in her body tensed.

When they finally reached the beach and hadn't been discovered, Rachel sent up a prayer of thanks to God as she had seen Pierre do. It seemed strange to finally pray—but good at the same time. Wet and cold, she continued to pray for their safety as they climbed up the bank.

Pierre motioned toward a clump of underbrush ahead. "We will stop and rest behind those bushes."

The two men looked exhausted. Rachel stretched out on the ground beside Pierre and gazed at him.

Pierre is a good man—like Papa—handsome, too. And he makes me feel safe.

Rachel regretted the way she'd behaved in the water. At the same time, she felt a sense of pride at actually doing something she never thought she could do.

She had a clear view of the ship. Four men in a small boat rowed toward it, and they didn't look like any of the sailors she knew.

"Look," she exclaimed. "The leader of those men looks like… It is Captain Jean Vallae."

Pierre squinted toward the ship. "This time, I think you are right. Hurry, we must leave this place at once."

Rachel raced through the trees behind Pierre as twigs and branches brushed her face and arms. Her breath came in gasps—from fear as much as from exhaustion. Still, she kept running.

At last, Pierre said, "I think it is safe for us to stop now, but only for a moment."

Panting, she slowed her pace.

Pierre offered Ebony his hand. Rachel thought she saw sadness in the eyes of both men as they shook hands.

"We must say farewell, friend, "Pierre said. "It would not be wise for us to travel together now. The men from the ship and others will be chasing after us, and a Negro and two white sailors would be too easy to spot."

After a moment, Rachel shook Ebony's hand. "Good-bye, Ebony. I will never forget you."

His nod served as his good-bye.

A lump formed in her throat as the former slave turned and walked away, a free man.

"Will we see Ebony, Smitty, and Rene and his family again?" she asked.

"Perhaps not in this life." Pierre gazed at Ebony's back. "But we shall see them in the world to come. Now, we must journey on or the captain and his men will catch up with us."

On the following morning Rachel gazed at a sign that had been nailed to a wooden post. An arrow pointed to the word Cert in black letters.

Cert. She had heard the name of that town previously but couldn't remember where. After a moment the answer came to her.

"Magdalena Poyer," she said aloud.

Pierre turned and looked at her. "You mentioned that name in front of the captain on the day he came to the church looking for us, but I cannot recall you mentioning her since then. Who is she?"

Rachel gazed up at dark clouds hovering overhead, hoping to come up with a way of explaining Magdalena to Pierre without revealing more than she wanted to say.

"At first, I could not remember where I heard that particular name or why it kept ringing in my ears. But just now, I remembered that she lives here in England. Madame Poyer was the aunt of my childhood friend, Marie Piron, and Marie often talked about her aunt who lived in England in the small village of Cert."

"Would you like to call on Madame Poyer?"

Rachel wanted to say yes. Magdalena was her best friend's aunt, and the woman might have heard from Marie. She might be willing to share some of Marie's letters with her or give Rachel her current address. At the same time, she knew they should continue on as planned.

Marie was a Jew. It seemed logical that Magdalene would be Jewish, too, and Rachel still hadn't told Pierre about her Jewish roots. If Marie's aunt told Pierre the truth before Rachel did, the results could be a disaster, destroying her friendship with Pierre.

"Well," he went on, "do you wish to pay the woman a visit or not?"

"No," she said. "I have never even met her. She might think it odd if we simply arrived at her door."

"I agree."

Rachel felt relieved. Under these circumstances, visiting Magdalena would not have been wise even if she had gotten the opportunity to learn Marie's mailing address.

The air felt cool and crisp as they moved on toward the English village. Rachel felt drained—physically and emotionally. The events of the day had been traumatic. Running and then trekking through the English countryside for miles hadn't lessened the load. Danger still followed them, but she could be thankful that they hadn't seen the Captain or his men since they left the beach.

"Run, Rachel!" Pierre warned. "I hear hoof beats, coming up behind us."

Eighteen

A farmer drove a few cows and a sickly calf down the middle of the road.

Rachel glanced at Pierre and smiled.

"I know what you are thinking, Madame Dupre." His grin became a laugh. "And you make mistakes, too."

"But Pierre, you said you heard hoof beats. Merely because they turned out to be made by a farmer and a few animals is no reason not to trust your judgment." She cupped her ear as if listening to something. "And I am sure it is hoof beats I hear now."

"We have almost reached the village of Cert, wife. If you would prefer that the town folk not see me take you across my knee and spank you, you must hold your tongue."

She feigned holding something small with her thumb and forefinger. "See, I am holding my tongue, Pierre, exactly as you requested."

He laughed. "I am warning you, no more jokes or you will be sorry."

"I will investigate the village instead. It looks very nice from here."

"Good decision."

Homes lined the road on both sides, but for Rachel, one house stood out from the rest. The cottage had a thatched roof like many of the other dwellings she had seen since arriving in

England, but its dark green shutters reminded her of her former home in Alsace.

Rachel studied the Alsatian house closely as they walked by. Perhaps Magdalena lived there. Now she might never know.

The German influence shone in the carvings on the eves and on the shutters of the charming cottage. Hearts had been artfully etched into the wood before the shutters were framed and painted, and seeing them only served to remind her of the loved ones she had lost.

A church stood on a rise at the edge of the town, and she saw a sign in the garden out front. Good News Church—Free Clothes

"Pierre, they are giving away clothes, and I have no dresses. Might we stop so I can buy one?"

"But the dresses are free."

"The priest from the Sanctuary gave us money. We could give this church a donation in exchange for proper clothes. The captain is looking for two sailors. We are sure to be spotted if we keep wearing what we have on."

He grinned. "Why not buy several dresses?"

Rachel smiled. "Several?"

"Of course."

Rachel found two dresses that fit her small form, one in rust and the other in brown. The rust dress had a white collar edged in lace and looked like the kind of gown dignified ladies wore to church on Sunday. A matching cap came with the dress. The brown dress had been made of a stiff material and had a patch in a lighter shade of brown on the right sleeve.

Not far out of town, Rachel stood behind some bushes to change into the brown dress.

"Duck," Pierre shouted. "Riders are headed this way."

Rachel gasped, slumping down behind the bushes.

Pierre had said that she jumped to conclusions. He could be right because she sensed that the riders were Captain Vallae and his men. She and Pierre had no weapons to fight against them—except Pierre's God.

Pierre crawled toward her on all fours and crouched down beside her.

"Were the riders who I think they were?" she asked.

"I cannot say, but it is possible. I heard them speaking French."

"I knew it!"

"I doubt they saw us, Rachel. If they had, we would have been captured." He glanced back toward the village. "Strange, they turned their horses around and raced back to Cert."

"Why would they do that?"

He shrugged. "Who would know but them? But as fast as they were running their horses, they were looking for someone. I think we should hide here behind these bushes until it is dark. Later, we can look for a barn where we can stay the night."

⊰❦⊱

Jean Vallae and his men tied their horses outside the cottage owned by Magdalena Poyer. The information they had gotten from the farmer they met on the road could not have reached them at a better point in their journey, and it had sent them right back to the village of Cert, to the edge of town and Magdalena's cottage.

He knew from the letters he found in the trunk at Benoit that Magdalena was Jewish and somewhat older than Rachel and her friend, Marie. Still, he hoped to find her comely if not beautiful.

He glanced back in time to see his three hirelings examining Magdalena's vegetable garden. "Stay out of sight," Jean warned. "I shall pay the woman a visit."

Magdalena's cottage had green shutters. He walked up to the door and knocked.

"Who is there?" a woman said in a shaky voice.

"I have news of your friends from Alsace, the Levins."

"I know no such people."

"Ah, but they know you. Their daughter is a friend of your niece, Marie. I have a letter to prove it."

He heard the latch squeak. The door opened. A middle aged woman with lines in her leathery face and salt and pepper hair stood before him.

So, this is Magdalena Poyer. She is not what I expected by any means.

"May I come in?" he asked.

"I see no reason for it." She put her hands on her hips. "State your business from there."

"I do see a reason for it." He pushed his way inside.

⚜

Dark clouds threatened overhead as Rachel and Pierre made their way down the road. Lightning cracked the night sky. Thunder boomed in the distance.

"Hurry Rachel," Pierre said. "We must find shelter before the rain starts."

Rainwater had already gathered in puddles along the way, and mud caked the ground.

"The rain must be ahead of us," Pierre added. "But we must hurry on. More rain could be following us as well."

Rachel trudged in mud up to her ankles for what seemed like miles, attempting to keep up with Pierre. In the glow of a lightning flash, she saw a barn some distance from the nearest farmhouse.

"We will stay there," he said. "I will leave the barn door open for you."

Rachel felt relieved. They would stop for the night. Her feet hurt from walking, and her body ached from crouching in the field all day. She heard a loud scraping sound and assumed that Pierre had opened the barn door. She managed to find it in the darkness, and touching the wooden walls as she had done in the tunnel in Beniot, she felt her way to the ladder.

Boards creaked as she climbed up. She took another step, and her shoes, slick with mud, slipped on one of the rungs. She gripped the ladder to steady herself.

"Easy there," Pierre whispered in the dark. "Are you all right?"

Rachel released a deep breath. "Yes." She climbed to the top.

"You could have fallen, you know."

"Yes, but I did not."

"I made a bed of hay for us." He took her hand and helped her to sit down on the floor of the loft. "You looked tired earlier."

"I still am," she said. "It has been a long day."

"That is true. But somehow you seem more relaxed than I have seen you since we left the ship. Have you stopped looking back to see if the captain is chasing us or am I imagining things?"

"I made the decision to stop worrying. Unfortunately, I cannot say how long my new resolve will last." She yawned. "I have never been so tired and sleepy."

"Hungry?"

"Yes." She stretched and yawned again. "But have you ever been too tired to eat?"

"Many times."

"Then you know exactly how I feel at this moment."

Rachel heard the rustle of hay as she nestled under it and smelled its fresh scent.

"Good-night, Pierre."

He took her hand and kissed it. Joy and a feeling of well being swept over her.

"Good night, sweet wife."

Sweet husband. She smiled and closed her eyes.

His tender and encouraging words gave her strength and comfort as she waited for sleep to come. Once, she had encouraged her parents and made them laugh. She hadn't felt like laughing or encouraging anyone since that day in Benoit, but perhaps now, she would try.

Suddenly, she recalled the danger they were in. She wanted to erase all negative thoughts from her mind, but they refused to go away.

❧

Jean Vallae gathered his men around a tree not far from Magdalena's house. "We will spend the night at an inn here in Cert." He glanced toward a lighted building directly across the road. "Tomorrow we will continue our search."

"Very well," the monk said. "The two young hirelings and I shall be ready. Is that not right, Samuel?"

"How much longer will we be staying here in England?" Samuel asked.

"As long as it takes to find the criminals I hired you to help me find," Jean replied.

"My brother Zeb and I miss our friends and family back in France."

"Are you saying that you wish to leave me now and return home?"

Silence filled the air.

"Yes." Samuel said. "We would like to return as soon as we can find a ship."

"Have you the money you will need to pay for your trip home?" Jean asked.

"Well, no." There was another long pause. "We thought you were going to pay for our fare back to France," Samuel said. "You said you would."

"You will return home on my ship when we have completed the mission we set out to do." Jean reached down and picked up a small stone. "That was the bargain." He fingered the rock between his thumb and forefinger. "But should any of you leave before that. . . ."

Jean assumed his announcement took the two young men by surprise, and he imagined how they might look with their jaws hanging loose. Surprising them and keeping them on their toes and under his authority was exactly what Jean had in mind.

"So," Jean said, "when will the two of you be leaving?"

Both of the young men grew silent again.

Jean smiled, and he threw the small stone. The rock sailed through the air and hit a nearby tree. He hadn't said he wouldn't pay their fare home now, but the implication had been loud enough for them to know his meaning.

The monk and the two young men went above stairs for the night. Jean stayed in the inn's eating room and ordered another mug of ale. He'd been impressed with the young auburn-haired barmaid with the emerald eyes. She reminded him of Rachel. And her sassy, provocative way of walking drew her to him in ways his wife, Yvette, never had.

Her green dress made her eyes look greener, and she kept glancing back at him as if she sensed his interest.

Jean pulled two gold coins from a saddlebag he'd thrown on the table and held them up so she would see them. As she continued to gaze at him, he placed the coins over his eyelids and sent her a silly grin.

She laughed and started toward him.

"Sit down." Jean motioned toward the empty chair.

She stood by the chair. "I would like to sit down," she said, sounding very British, "but I am working now, sir."

"How much must I pay for you to sit at the table with me and talk a while?"

"I could ask me employer to see what he says."

"Go then and do it. I am eager to speak with you."

"I will go, sir, of course."

Jean watched her go up to the counter and talk to the innkeeper. He couldn't hear what they said in such hushed tones, but he saw them look at him and talk some more. After a moment, the girl returned to the table.

"He said I could talk to you for one of them gold coins."

Jean handed her a coin. "Go and return quickly."

She giggled girlishly. "I shall be but a minute."

Jean grinned and watched her walk away.

The girl returned a moment later and sat down beside him. "What do you wish to talk about?" she asked.

"You. What is your name?"

"Polly. Polly Ingles."

"Have you lived always in Cert, Polly?"

"No. I was born in Ireland in the town of Cork. But I have spent most of my life here."

"Cork. I have heard of it."

"And you," she said, "where were you born?"

"France. My family moved to England when I was a child. I am a citizen of this country now, and proud that it is so, I might add." He smiled. "You remind me of someone."

"Do I, now?" She cocked her head at an angle, and a flash of embarrassment added a touch of innocence to her smile. "Someone said those same words to me just today."

"What do you mean?"

"A man came in here to eat his meal this noon. And when I brought him his food, he said that I reminded him of a young boy he saw looking at free clothes in front of a church here in Cert. He asked me if I had a brother, but I told him I did not."

"Do you know the name of the man you talked to?"

"No. He was not from around here. But I do know the name of the church. It is called the Good News Church, and it sits on a rise as you leave town going north. I got me a dress for free there, too, today; a pretty yellow one."

Pierre enjoyed talking to Polly regardless of her lack of polish and refinement. But he needed to find that church and see what he could learn.

He got up and stood by his chair. "Do you know the name of the priest at that church?"

She laughed. "You will not see no priest at that church. A preacher is what you are likely to find there."

"Would I find him at the church or at this house?"

"I would not be knowing something like that." She followed his gaze to the entry door and looked back at him. "You are in a hurry to leave here?"

"Yes, I need to be on my way."

She stuck out her lower lip like a rebellious child. "Are you tiring of me already, or could it be that you need to confess?"

He smiled. "Neither. I want to talk to that preacher, but I will be back. It is my hope that I will see you later."

"I will be here waiting. You can be sure of that."

A smile turned up the edges of Jean's mouth. He exited the house behind the church where the preacher and his family lived and looked around. Moonlight would guide him back to the inn, and he would stay the night.

He'd learned quite a bit from Pastor Carter, the minister at the Good News Church in Cert. Two young sailors stopped at the church that day, and they bought dresses—one in brown and one in rust. They also bought a suit of clothes for the older of the two young men. The minister thought the dresses were for their mother or sister. Jean knew they were for Rachel.

According to Pastor Carter, the two young men took the north route out of town and could be a long way down the road by now, but they would have stopped for the night. Tomorrow, he intended to search again. Jean and his men should be able to overtake them soon enough on horseback. For now, he would return to the inn and finish his conversation with Polly.

Nineteen

The next morning Rachel awoke to find Pierre shaking her shoulder, an action she had grown to expect.

"We must get up and go at once," he said. "Otherwise, we could be discovered by the farmer or overtaken by the Captain and his men."

"Are you hearing hoof beats again, Pierre?"

He grinned. "I am serious, Rachel. Get up at once, and no arguments, please. We have no time to waste."

Rachel gazed out the window beside the barn door. "But it is raining outside, Pierre, a regular downpour. Let us stay here where it is warm and dry until the rain stops? The captain will think we have gone on and not look for us so close to the town of Cert."

"What about the farmer?"

Rachel smiled. "The barn door made a lot of noise when we opened it last night. We should have enough time to hide under the hay before the farmer sees us."

"And if he climbs up here to the loft and finds us under the hay? What then?"

"We shall apologize earnestly and leave the barn as soon as we can." She sat up and stretched. "So, can we stay?"

"All right, Rachel. We will stay until the rain stops."

"And if the rain continues until the morrow?" she asked.

He grinned. "Then of course we will stay here a day longer.

But no matter how wet it is out by tomorrow morning, we must start out again."

Rachel pretended to hold something as she had as they entered to town of Cert. "See, I am not arguing. I am holding my tongue."

He laughed. "You have changed, Rachel. You truly have. Once you worried about everything. Now you seem happy and full of fun. When did you decide to become a clown?"

Rachel looked away and smiled. *The moment I realized that I am falling in love with you.*

It rained all day and all night, and nobody came in the barn to disturb their needed rest. On the second morning, the rain stopped, but mud spread across the land as far as they could see.

Nevertheless, they set out, hiking on the road again. Pierre noticed how Rachel struggled to plow though deep mud and puddles of water, and he resolved that they would spend the night indoors.

That night, he helped Rachel up the slippery steps of the Crooked Creek Inn, and they stood just inside the door. The innkeeper sipped something from a metal mug, and he didn't glance in their direction when they came in. His red eyes and slow movements told that he had been drinking for some time.

"Go and find us a table, Rachel," Pierre whispered. "I will speak to this man."

Pierre watched Rachel walk to the back of the main room and sit down at a table.

The innkeeper gazed at Pierre for the first time. "I have not seen you here before." He slammed down his mug, spilling gold liquid on the polished wooden counter. "My name is Finley. Mister George Finley," he said, slurring his words. "And I am the owner of this here inn. Now, what—what might I be doing for you?"

"My wife has already found a table, and we would like something to eat."

"Food we got aplenty. You came to the right place."

Finley's voice sounded so coated in strong drink, he appeared to be having a hard time getting his words out. He spread out his hands on the counter as if to prop himself up or risk falling forward.

"Miles," Finley called out. "We have guests. Bring out stew and ale for two and—and take it to the table in the back."

"We would like tea instead of ale, sir."

"Make it two bowls of stew and two cups of tea."

Pierre's stomach growled from hunger, yet he felt he should talk to the innkeeper a little longer to see what news he might learn from the man before joining Rachel at their table. The innkeeper had probably been drinking for hours, and Pierre hoped that in such a condition, he might be willing to not only answer Pierre's questions but elaborate.

"You have a nice establishment here. Such a delightful inn as this must attract fashionable ladies and gentlemen from inside as well as outside the borders of England."

"For sure." The innkeeper straightened his shoulders and poked out his chest. He grabbed his mug, gulped down several swallows and wiped his wet mouth with back of his hand.

"Have you had any interesting guests who are not from around here recently?" Pierre asked.

"Not recently. The roads are bad with all the rain and mud."

"Do you expect more guests tonight," Pierre asked.

"Not tonight." He studied Pierre with bloodshot eyes for a moment. "You sound like a Frenchy, you do."

"My wife and I are travelers. We have visited many places, including France."

The innkeeper slanted his head to one side. "That might explain it." He glanced behind him. "Hurry up with that stew, Miles." He turned to Pierre again. "We have nice rooms here. Change the bedding once a month. Will you and the wife be staying the night?"

"Yes."

"Your room will be the one on the right at the top of the stairs."

"Thank you, sir. I will join my wife now."

Pierre ambled to the back of the eating area and sat down across from Rachel.

She glanced out the window. However, darkness made it impossible to see much except when someone stood under one of the lanterns that hung from the eves.

"Do you think it is safe to stay here?" she asked.

"Yes. If the innkeeper had seen Vallae and his men, he would have bragged about it. And I doubt he will remember us in the morning from the amount of ale he is drinking."

"Thank you for keeping your promise and finding us a nice place to spend the night."

"I know this inn cannot compare with the barn we slept in the last two nights, but I am glad you like it here."

She laughed.

A man brought out two steaming bowls of stew and set them on the table before them. He returned with a platter of dark bread and cups of tea. Rachel picked up her spoon and began eating.

"You are hungry, are you?" Pierre asked.

"Starving."

"So am I."

A stable boy raced inside holding a lantern. "Master Finley, riders are headed this way, and their horses look very fine indeed from what I can see. I think they are coming here."

Pierre stiffened. Rachel could be in danger. On the chance that the riders were Jean Vallae and his men, he needed to prepare himself mentally for whatever might come.

"Fine horses, did you say?" Finley asked.

"Yes, sir."

"Go back and tend to the needs of the travelers. Tell them that I shall be right out to escort them inside meself."

The stable boy went out again.

"Miles," the innkeeper ordered. "Have me maids prepare the private dining room for the riders and the best rooms we have." Finley grabbed the candlestick on the counter and went out, slamming the door behind him.

Rachel gazed out a window for the second time. Pierre followed her glance. Though he couldn't see much on such a rainy night, the lanterns produced a little light, and he heard men's voices. Frenchmen's voices, he realized.

"It is the captain, Pierre! This time, I am sure of it."

"We must leave the dining room at once," Pierre said casually as if nothing could possibly be wrong. "But try to act as if all is well. Now, help me gather our bowls of food and follow me. We will be having supper in our room above stairs."

As Rachel and Pierre started toward the stairway, Miles sent them a puzzled look—as if seeing them with bowls of food displeased him.

Pierre paused before going up. "My wife is not feeling well tonight. We shall be dining in our room."

"Very well, sir. Anything else I can do for ya?"

"That will be all—for now."

He started to ask him to tell the innkeeper that they would be leaving before daylight the next morning but decided against it; the less known about their plans, the better.

As soon as they reached their room, Pierre closed the door and locked it. He crossed his forefinger over his mouth in a shushing gesture.

"Eat your meal quickly, my love. The new arrivals downstairs might well be the captain and his men. As soon as we finish eating, we will be leaving."

As they ate their meal, Pierre glanced at the window by the bed.

"What are you looking at?" Rachel asked.

"Our escape route." He got up and yanked the top cover off the bed. "I plan to make a rope ladder by tying all the bedding together."

"I will help you." She pulled a white blanket from the bed. "But why would we need a ladder? Surely you. . ."

"Yes, we will leave by a window." He began tying the bed clothes end to end. "I will leave the money we owe the innkeeper on the bed, and tonight, we will travel as far from this inn as possible. We must pray that it does not start raining before we find shelter tonight." He tied one end of the rope bedding to the bedpost and threw the other end out the window. "Watch what I do." He grabbed hold of the rope bedding, one hand over the other.

"You must hold the rope exactly as I am doing when you climb out the window and drop to the ground below."

"The ground below? Are you suggesting that I climb down that rope you made?"

"Precisely. Now, you try it, Rachel."

Why did all Pierre's suggestions seem so difficult? First he forced her into the channel when she couldn't swim and now this.

"Go on," he insisted.

Rachel took hold of the bedding and did exactly as he had demonstrated. Actually going down the makeshift rope would be quite another matter.

"I will go down first," he said. "That way, I will be there to help you to the ground."

Pierre threw money on the bed and climbed down the rope. "Now you come."

Rachel swallowed. The task had looked anything but simple when he did it. Nevertheless, she intended to do as Pierre suggested. With no other options, she had no choice.

She lifted her skirt and put one leg over the edge of the window-sill as she had seen Pierre do. She paused and grabbed the rope with both hands.

Yes, she managed to climb down the ladder when they left the ship, but she'd had ropes to hold onto and places to put her feet. This time, she would have neither. And what if she fell? She could break a leg, or her neck!

"Are you coming?" he whispered from the ground below.

She made no reply.

"There is a small ledge below the window," he instructed. "Turn around and reach down with your leg until you find it."

Reach down with my leg? How does he expect me to do that?

Putting all her weight on her right foot, she strained to find the ledge with her left. She found it, or at least something, but would it hold her weight going down?

"Good. You found the ledge," he said. "Now, never look down or let go of the rope. Simply bring your other leg down to the ledge."

Rachel had to bend her right leg at an awkward angle in order to get it high enough to slide over the sill. If anyone saw her, they would think she was insane. After two attempts, she did it and stood on the ledge on shaky legs. The ground looked a long way down.

"Now," he said, "bend your knees and reach down with your left foot until you find a stone jutting out from the side of the building below the ledge. When you do, press the toe of your shoe against it."

"I cannot do this, Pierre. I will fall for sure."

"Never tell yourself that you will not make it," he warned. "Tell yourself that with God's help, you will."

Why would God listen to her? She had ignored Him for years.

The cloth rope cut into the palms of her hands. Nevertheless, she found a stone. But unlike the ledge, it didn't feel wide enough to stand on.

She wanted to share her conclusions with Pierre when he said, "Now, push out from the wall with your right foot and gradually come down. Hand over hand over hand."

Rachel shut her eyes. It took all the courage she had not to scream in protest. To remove her left hand from the rope and put it below her right meant that for a moment, she would be supporting her entire body with one hand and the toe of one foot.

Why had she let Pierre talk her into such nonsense?

She gripped the rope as hard as she could as she searched for a lower stone to rest the toe of her shoe on. When she finally found one, she kicked out with her left leg and began the whole process again.

What other choice did she have? At last her toes touched the muddy ground below. Pierre grabbed her around the waist. "Well done," he whispered.

"Just be sure not to request that I do such a thing again," she said.

He laughed softly. "We will see."

They were standing on a dark and narrow street with two-story buildings on both sides. Pierre motioned toward a line of windows on the first floor of the inn.

"We must be especially quiet when we pass by those windows, Rachel." Pierre took her hand. "I think it might be that private dining room the innkeeper mentioned."

She nodded. "I understand."

As they walked by, Rachel couldn't help glancing inside. Numerous candles lighted the private dining room, and she saw five men. Four were eating at a table. She and Pierre weren't in the light, and she hoped they wouldn't be visible to those inside.

She knew she had never seen the two young men, but the portly one near the door reminded her of someone. The other man with dark hair had his back to her.

The dark-haired man suddenly turned to speak to Miles, the waiter. Rachel froze. Jean Vallae sat at the table closest to the window. No mistake about it this time.

"He does not see us," Pierre whispered. "Keep walking." He gently tugged at her hand. "Act as if nothing is wrong."

Rachel wanted to run, but Pierre's words confirmed her best hopes. He must not have seen them.

Further on down the street, Pierre said, "Come, Rachel. We need to get away from here as fast as possible. Run."

On the road leading out of the village, they slowed to a fast walk. Rachel couldn't stop thinking about what she saw, standing at the window and looking into the private dining room.

They found what looked like an abandoned barn and would stay the night. Pierre gave thanks to God that they had arrived safely and that the rain had not come again until they were nestled inside.

Rachel had been helping Pierre spread out the hay to make a bed when she stopped and pressed the palm of her hand to her forehead. "Now it comes to me. The portly man we saw at that table with Jean Vallae had to be the monk who tried to listen to my confession while we were at the Sanctuary. How could I have failed to recognize him?"

"Yes, Rachel, I noticed the monk as well, but try not to think about it. We need to sleep now, while we can."

The next morning, they managed to hitch a ride on the back of a hay cart pulled by two tired-looking brown horses, but the farmer only took them a mile or two. Then they hiked down the road toward Scotland again.

"I wish we had a horse and cart to ride in," she said, "like the one Rene and Felix had in Casa."

Pierre grinned. "Why wish for a horse and cart? Why not a fancy carriage and four fine horses like the ones coming around the bend?"

Rachel glanced at the road ahead as a carriage rounded the curve in the road and approached them at a fast trot.

"Rachel," Pierre warned. "Get out of the way. Give the horses and the carriage room."

He tromped through the mud and moved back from the road. Rachel turned, intending to follow him. She slipped and fell to her knees. Reaching out to brace herself, her hands sank into the wet soil almost to her elbows.

"Rachel," she heard Pierre say.

She tried to get up but fell back to a sitting position. Mud caked the back of her dress as well as the bottom of her skirt. The fast moving carriage splattered even more mud—this time on her face and hair.

Pierre rushed to her side and offered her his hand. She ignored it and got up on her own.

The carriage stopped a short distance farther on.

Three men in gray uniforms stood stiffly on a ledge across the back of the carriage, holding on to some sort of metal bar. Another man sat up top beside the driver. The man inside the carriage behind the drawn curtains worried Rachel. From what she had heard from Rene, Captain Vallae could well afford to rent or buy horses and a carriage like this and a mansion to go with it.

"He is turning the horses around," Pierre said.

The carriage, painted black, pulled to a stop as close to where she stood as it could get. Stunned, Rachel found herself at the door of the most expensive-looking means of transportation she had ever seen.

An impressive crest had been carved into the carriage door. As she stood there, afraid to breathe, someone pulled the curtain back. She saw a blur of black cloth. A face appeared. She shut her eyes.

Captain Vallae. It must be.

Her heart pulled into a knot, waiting for whatever would come.

Twenty

"Forgive me, ma'am," a man said from the other side of the black door. "My horses and carriage splashed mud and soiled your dress. Please allow me to make amends."

Rachel opened her eyes. *He is not Vallae.* She exhaled.

A dignified-looking stranger sat at a window, gazing at her.

Pierre stood directly behind her. He put his hands on her shoulders. Knowing he was there gave her courage, and for the first time in her life, she realized that she wasn't alone.

"I am Lord Wilburn, Earl of Willowbrook," the gentleman said, "and I own a country estate two days ride from here. As it happens, I am on my way there now."

The man wore a dark waistcoat over a shirt as white as his snowy hair, and what looked like a diamond centered his royal blue cravat. But the warmth she saw in his pale blue eyes put Rachel at ease.

Except for Smitty and the other sailors she'd met on the ship, Rachel had never known an Englishman. Learning new languages had always been easy for her, and she felt fortunate that she spoke and understood a little English.

The earl focused on Pierre. "And who might you be, sir?"

"Pierre De Salle. And this is my wife, Martha."

"A Frenchman, are you?"

"Yes."

The earl smiled. "My late wife, Mimi, was French. Interesting country. But with poor relations between France and England the topic of conversation here in England, France might not be a good place to be from right now. Might I drive you and your lovely wife to your destination? It is the least I can do."

"We are on our way to Scotland, sir." Rachel inserted.

"Do tell. My estate is in the north of England on the road to Scotland."

Still standing on the road outside his carriage, Rachel spread out her muddy hands, palms up, and looked down at her filthy brown dress.

"I am dirty, sir, and dressed in soiled clothes," Rachel said. "I could never ride in a carriage as fine as yours. But thank you most kindly for the offer."

"Do you have clean clothes with you, ma'am?" Lord Wilburn asked.

"Yes, in the bundle my husband is holding."

"Splendid. I would consider it an honor to wait while you change into them, or if you prefer, come dressed as you are and I shall drape my cloak over the seat. You could sit on it during the journey."

"You are too kind, sir, but that will not be necessary." Pierre held out the package with Rachel's rust dress and matching cap inside. "I saw a lake a short distance back." He turned and pointed off to their left. "You cannot see it from here, but the lake is beyond that rise. If you will wait a bit while my wife changes into another dress, we will gladly travel in your carriage until you stop for the night."

"Indeed, I will wait for as long as you need."

"We will see you again soon, sir." He turned to Rachel. "Come, wife."

They trudged through the mud in the direction of the lake. Rachel glanced down at her soggy shoes. She'd heard that it rained often in England. Now, she believed it.

"Why did you introduce yourself as Pierre De Salle's and call me Martha?" she asked.

"I should never have said that. It was a lie, and Christians should tell the truth at all times. But the earl is not someone we know well. Therefore, we must not share all our secrets with him during our travels, Rachel."

"Forgive me, Pierre. I made another mistake. I knew I should never have told the earl that we were on our way to Scotland. In the future, I will try to think before speaking instead of being so spontaneous."

"All is forgiven. The earl seems sensible enough. I doubt he is the sort that will go about telling others our destination. In fact, we are fortunate to have met him."

"I feel the same," Rachel said.

They stood at the top of the rise. Trees surrounded the kidney-shaped lake just ahead.

"That is quite a view we have from here." Pierre handed her the package and sat down on a log. "I will wait here until you are dressed and ready to join the earl at his carriage."

"Thank you, Pierre."

She tromped through even more mud in order to reach the lake. If she hadn't needed a bath before, she needed one now.

After checking to make sure nobody was watching, Rachel removed her dirty cap. Her dress came off next and her wet shoes. She waded out from the shore.

The shoulder deep water felt cool on her skin and refreshing. Though the fear she once had of drowning had lessened since they left the ship, a small remnant still remained and refused to go away.

Mud caked one side of her face. Cupping her hands, she splashed water on her face and neck and rubbed off the moist dirt with her fingertips.

Rachel soaked in the lake for as long as she dared. The bath seemed to revive her body as well as her spirit, but she needed to hurry. A nobleman such as the earl should not be kept waiting.

When she returned to the shore, she dried off with the clean bodice of her dirty brown dress and wiped the mud from her shoes as best she could. She put on the rust dress and matching cap, bundled the soiled dress and went to join Pierre.

He reached for her bundle. "Let me carry that for you,"

She handed the dirty dress to him.

Rachel felt out of place in such esteemed company and hesitated before approaching the carriage. The driver motioned them on toward the coach.

"Throw your bundle up here," the driver said. "We will keep it for you."

Pierre threw the dress to the driver, and he caught it.

"Oh, there you are," the earl said.

She and Pierre stood outside the door of his carriage.

"Please come in and sit down," the earl said.

The door clicked open. Rachel couldn't believe what she saw. The walls of the carriage as well as the padded couches were covered with dark blue velvet. Did people actually travel in such a high and lofty manner?

"Welcome," the earl said.

Pierre bobbed a quick bow as if he thought the earl was a king or something. "Thank you, sir,"

"And thank you for being so understanding when I spoiled your wife's dress." The elderly man studied Rachel for a moment. "She is small like my late wife, and it is my greatest wish that you will allow me to give your wife some of my wife's clothes to pay for the dress my carelessness destroyed."

"Thank you, sir. We gladly accept your offer," Pierre said. "And it is clear to me that you are a good man."

Rachel thought he seemed embarrassed by Pierre's compliment.

"You both speak English well and with only slight accents. You must have had very skillful teachers."

"My grandmother was once a governess to the child of a family in England," Pierre said, "and I learned the English language from her. She also taught me to read and write. My wife has a special gift for learning languages, and I am happy to say that she speaks several."

"One can never get too much learning, but wisdom comes from the Lord." The earl glanced down at the black book he held on his lap.

Rachel had noticed Pierre looking at it. She wondered if the book he held was the Bible, but she dared not speak again so soon in order to find out.

The earl leaned forward, gazing straight at Pierre. As if he had guessed her thoughts, he said, "You are looking at my Bible, are you not?"

Pierre nodded. "I hope to own a Bible of my own some day."

"Please, take mine as my gift to you. I have another," the earl said.

Pierre shook his head. "You are more than kind, but I could never take your Bible, sir. Such an expensive gift is well beyond my station in life."

"Stations in life can change, young man, for the better or for worse. When you are older, you will know this is true. Now, please take this Bible with my blessings. It would pleasure me if you did." He reached over and handed Pierre his Bible.

Pierre smiled and took the Bible from him. "Thank you, sir. I shall treasure this gift always. May your life be filled with blessings, and may your title be passed from generation to generation."

The earl returned his smile. "My title came from my English father, but you might be surprised to know that I was reared by a Jewish mother and once searched for my Messiah. At last, I found him. Money, possessions, and stations in life have no meaning for me now."

Rachel couldn't believe her ears. The earl had been raised in a Jewish home, just as she had. What an incredible man.

Stranger still, he willingly admitted his Jewish heritage. She and her family had always kept their roots hidden from the world. Questions she longed to have him answer filled her mind. If only she felt comfortable enough with him to ask questions openly.

"It is not often that I speak so freely with strangers," the earl said, "but I felt at peace as soon as I saw the two of you standing by my carriage. I only wish I had noticed you sooner."

"Could it be," Pierre asked, "that finding us on the road and soiling my wife's dress are part of God's plan?"

"You might be right."

Pierre gently traced the outline of the Bible with his right hand. "I am afraid I have not been completely honest with you, sir. My name is Pierre Dupre, and this is Rachel, my wife. Forgive me for not revealing our true names as soon as we met."

The earl smiled. "You are forgiven."

"I would be interested to hear how a Jew such as you became a Christian," Pierre said.

"Interesting that you should ask. A Jewish friend of mine became a Christian, and he slowly convinced me that Jesus is the Jewish Messiah. Since that time, he has taught me so much more. I might add that Jesus is pronounced Yeshua in the Hebrew language. And as I said, I now believe that Jesus is the Jewish Messiah."

"It is not surprising that a Jew would become a Christian," Pierre said. "All the disciples of Jesus were Jews, and Jesus was raised in a Jewish home."

Rachel nodded as if she agreed with all that had been said, but until she met Pierre and his family, she had never thought much about Jews becoming Christians. Now, she wondered. Should she become a Christian with her whole heart, as Pierre so wanted for her to do or hold out a bit longer and see how she really felt after she had time to stop and think on it?

"I would like for you and your wife to meet my Jewish friend, the one who introduced me to my Messiah," Lord Wilburn went on. "His name is Sir David Goldberg, and by now, he would have returned from a visit with friends and relatives who live in the village of Cert."

Cert? Rachel slanted her head to one side. Cert is where Magdalena lives, and a small village at that.

Could it be that Magdalena and Lord Wilburn knew each other?

"I am sure he has much to tell about his trip," the earl added.

If he knew Magdalena well enough to have read some of Marie's letters, Sir Goldberg might be able to connect them; and just when she and Pierre were growing closer—to each other and to the earl.

"My friend lives near the inn where we will be staying for the night. Perhaps we could stop by for a short visit."

"I am sure I also speak for my wife in saying that I would be delighted to meet your friend. But we are simple folk. He might not be eager to meet us. Perhaps it would be best if we left the carriage before you visited your friend."

"Nonsense. Sir Goldberg will be pleased to meet both of you. I insist that you allow me to introduce you."

Rachel bit her lower lip to keep from saying what she really thought. Meeting a man who might know Magdalena would be one of the last things she would ever hope to do.

After traveling for the rest of the day, they arrived at a large, pleasant-looking house near the village of Brawn. Pierre had seemed tense for the last hour or two as if something bothered him, and Rachel had no idea why he kept looking out the window now and again. She hadn't seen another carriage all day.

Two smiling grooms in green jackets ran out to meet them as soon as the carriage pulled to a stop in front of the entry door of Sir Goldberg's estate. Its thatched roof and rock walls seemed to radiate the same warmth and a sense of welcome that his grooms had in such abundance. The earl's driver and two footmen in gray jackets secured the horses as they climbed the steps to the heavy wooden door.

A metal doorknocker with a design on it similar to the one found on the door of the earl's carriage captured Rachel's attention. However, the door opened before she could examine the object fully.

An elderly servant in black clothing stood in the entrance. "Welcome back, Earl Wilburn. Sir Goldberg will see you in the drawing room." He peered at Rachel and Pierre.

Rachel felt the impact of the servant's condescending stare as she stepped onto the polished floor of the entry. The odor of beeswax filled the air.

"If you like, I will escort the man and the young woman to the servants' quarters, sir," the servant added.

"The man and young woman are not servants. They are my friends and shall go into the drawing room with me."

The servant frowned. "Very good, sir."

"My wife and I will be happy to wait with your friend's servants," Pierre put in.

"No. I want you to meet Sir Goldberg. And he will enjoy meeting you as well, I am sure."

A well-dressed middle-aged gentleman with curly red hair stood in the doorway. Rachel assumed he was Sir Goldberg. A short and slight man, Sir Goldberg wore the finest brown hunting jacket she had ever seen, and his high-topped brown leather boots looked as if they had been rubbed to a perfect shine.

Sir Goldberg leaned over and took the hand Rachel offered. She noticed a bald spot at the crown of his head. "I am glad to know you, Madame Dupre. Please come and sit down."

He directed them to a circle of comfortable chairs. She listened as the earl told all that had transpired since meeting Rachel and Pierre.

At last, the earl asked, "What news have you from the colonies? I heard that more trouble is brewing between the colonists and the Indians."

"I heard the same," Sir Goldberg said. "But it is nothing new. And how is Will?"

"My son is well, thank you," the earl said. "At the moment, he is on a journey on the continent to celebrate his recent graduation from the University. He has been gone six months now, but I expect him to travel for at least a year."

"Give him my regards, the next time you hear from him."

"I shall." The earl turned to Pierre. "Now, let us discuss my favorite subject, the Bible."

"Indeed." Sir Goldberg rubbed his hands together as if he couldn't wait to talk about scripture verses with others.

The men began a deep and serious conversation on Biblical themes. Rachel had little interest or knowledge on such topics and studied the drawing room with its heavy red drapes and red and green Persian rug.

A large gold Menorah centered a shoulder-high shelf. Memories of her mother carefully dusting a smaller Menorah filled her mind.

Her throat tightened, and she found it difficult to swallow. Captain Vallae took their lives as if Mama, Papa, and Louis were no more important than flies or some other pesky insect.

Captain Vallae must be punished. And clearly, I am the one who should do it.

All at once she heard the earl say the word Jew. Surprised, Rachel turned in her chair, focusing her full attention on the men's conversation.

Sir Goldberg hunched forward, placing the palms of his hands on his knees. "When I followed the Jewish faith, the rabbis taught that Jesus could not be the Messiah because he healed on the Sabbath."

"I was taught the same thing," the earl said. "'Remember the Sabbath and keep it holy.' But after I became a Christian, I discovered the true meaning of holiness. I now think healing others and helping them is part of what keeping the Sabbath holy really means."

"Exactly. How can one keep the Sabbath holy and not reach out to others in need?"

"Yes," the earl agreed, "and to the true believer, every day is the Sabbath." He gazed at Pierre and Rachel. "As believers, you must know what I mean."

"Indeed I do," Pierre said. "Some in the Reformed Church think attending a church service is all that is required to keep the Sabbath holy. And we should get together with other believers as often as possible, but it is also important to allow the Lord to have complete control of our lives.

"I always enjoyed sitting behind the reins of a small cart my family owned back in Beniot, France where I was born," Pierre went on. "But as Christians, we must let the Lord drive the carriage that is our lives. He must hold the reins, so to speak."

The two older men nodded as if they agreed with what Pierre had said, but Rachel had no idea what they were talking about.

"We know how much the Lord loves us because He gave His only begotten son, Jesus, to take the punishment we all deserved by dying on a cross at Calvary," Pierre explained. "But we must never fail to show our love for the Lord as well."

"How can we do that?" Rachel asked. "As you say, God owns everything; yet we are mere humans. How can we show God how much we love Him?"

"Jesus said, 'If you love me, keep my commandment.'" Pierre went on. "By obeying His commands, we are showing our love for the Lord."

She wanted to ask what commands he meant, but her father would have said that she'd said enough and should remain silent. Let the men talk.

Everyone grew silent for a moment.

At last the earl said, "Now, Sir Goldberg, tell us all the news from Cert. You must have much to relate since you recently returned from there."

Rachel tensed. Her time of reckoning had arrived, and Pierre still didn't know her secret.

Sir Goldberg gazed at the earl, and what she deemed sadness shone in his face. "A Madame Poyer was found dead outside her cottage. Murdered, they think."

Murdered. Rachel stared at Pierre. No.

The earl shut his eyes briefly and shook his head. "How dreadful. Tell us what happened?"

"Her house was burned to the ground. Those in authority think someone set fire to it."

Rachel shuddered. Like our home in Beniot when Captain Vallae burned it to the ground. She felt weak. Was it all happening again? Of course, Sir Goldberg could have been talking about another Madame Poyer.

The earl turned to Sir Goldberg. "Was Madame Poyer Jewish?"

"Yes," Sir Goldberg said, "I believe she was. However, she never admitted it except to close friends and family. I learned about it from my nephew who knew her well. You might have heard of her. She was a widow by the name of Magdalena Poyer and friendly to French Huguenots, they say."

No. Rachel tensed. This cannot be.

The earl glanced at Rachel. "Is something wrong, Madame? Are you ill?"

She nodded. To press her point, she faked a cough.

"My wife has been tired of late," Pierre put in. "Perhaps she has a case of the sneezes."

"Wretched luck, I say." Sir Goldberg pulled a red velvet cord that hung from the ceiling. "I shall ring my servant and have him take her up to their room at once."

The earl leaned forward. "We have no plans to spend the night, old friend. I had thought we would stay at an inn in the village."

"You shall all stay here with me," Sir Goldberg insisted.

The servant they saw earlier came into the room. "You rang, sir."

"Yes, Carson, take the young man and his wife to the bedroom at the top of the stairs and see that they are comfortable." He turned to Pierre. "When your wife is resting comfortably, please return to the drawing room. We have more to discuss on Biblical topics."

As Rachel followed Sir Goldberg's servant up the stairway, she thought of poor Magdalena—dead and her house burned to the ground. Even if the woman happened to be one of Sir Goldberg's closest friends, she doubted that he would connect her to Magdalena's niece, Marie. The possibility seemed more than slim. Still, she would need to be careful what she said until the visit with the earl's friend ended.

Rachel, followed by Pierre, entered a large bedroom that looked as if it belonged in a castle. The bed with its fine wine-colored velvet covering seemed enormous. She glanced around, hoping to find a cot among the elaborate furniture, and found one under a line of windows.

I shall sleep there tonight, she thought as Pierre helped her up onto the big bed.

"Will that be all, sir?" the servant asked.

"Yes." Pierre nodded. "And thank you for your help."

"That, of course, is my job," he said with a trace of sarcasm. Turning sharply, he left the room.

Pierre chuckled after the servant had shut the door. "I think he is telling us that we belong with the servants, below stairs, and not in a place as fine as this. Perhaps he is right, but as you can see, we are here. How are you feeling now?"

"I am not ill, Pierre. I merely pretended."

"I guessed as much. The news from Cert was shocking."

"Hearing what happened reminded me of—"

"I know what you mean." Pierre shook his head as if to emphasize his distress. "Several times today during our drive, I saw men following us."

"Captain Vallae, do you think?"

"I cannot be sure." He shrugged. "Perhaps I was mistaken."

"Pierre, tell me what you saw?"

"Several men holding their horses were standing in the underbrush near the road as we drove by. They seemed to be watching us. I saw them again further on. Twice more, in fact. They were probably merely curious. For all I know, a carriage as fine as the earl's could be quite unique in these parts.

"Both the earl and Sir Goldberg are gentlemen of the highest order," Pierre said, "and I would never want to put them in danger."

"Nor do I," Rachel said, "What should we do?"

"Tomorrow, we arrive at the earl's country estate which is not far from the Scottish border. He wishes to have his driver deliver us all the way to our destination in Scotland at his expense, but that is far more than we can accept, my love. He has done enough for us already. Do you not agree?"

"Of course. To accept more gifts from this dear man would be wrong, and I would never want to put him or anyone in danger. Have you a plan?"

"Yes. We shall write a letter thanking the earl for all his help and explaining that we must leave on our own. After we arrive at his estate, we will find the proper time to place the note where the earl is sure to find it. Then we will leave."

"Yes, Pierre, that is exactly what we must do."

Rachel noticed that Carson had not closed the door all the way when he left. She went to the door. Before shutting it, she glanced out. Carson stood in the hall outside by the stairway, gazing toward the door of their room. She shut the door quietly.

"I cannot be sure, Pierre, but I think the butler might have been listening at our door."

"Really?" Pierre's right eyebrow lifted. "How strange."

"But why would he do such a thing?" she asked. "What would he have to gain?

"That, my love, is one question I am unable to answer."

Twenty-one

The carriage started down the road in front of Sir Goldberg's estate the next morning. Rachel glanced out a window. Carson, the butler, glowered at her, and she still didn't know why he disliked them so much.

Could it be that he disapproved of the lower classes mixing with those of a high station in life? He'd frowned when the earl insisted they go in and meet Sir Goldberg. Apparently true Christian believers mixed with people from all walks of life no matter how low or how high.

They rolled through green glens sprinkled with trees and bushes she couldn't identify. Rachel thought about what Pierre had said on the previous day. Later when the earl exited the carriage, taking a short stroll in the woods, Rachel decided to question Pierre on the subject.

"Pierre, you said that the Lord should hold the reins and drive the carriage of our lives. But what does that mean?"

"It means that you should study God's Word, the Bible, keep His commandments, and follow the suggestions for living found in the Bible. Be a doer of the Word of God and not a hearer only. Jesus is also the only begotten son of God the Father. Yet He chose to serve us because He loves us. He even washed the feet of His disciples as a servant might do. The Lord expects us to show our love for Him by keeping His commandments and treating others as we would like to be treated. In a sense, we are to let the Lord hold the reins of our lives by following his suggestions and commandments."

"That sounds difficult," Rachel pointed out. "I am not sure I can do it."

"Allowing the Lord to drive the carriage that is my life is not always easy," Pierre replied. "When I first started going to the Reformed Church and listening to the sermons I heard there, I worried that I would never remember all God's teachings and commands. After I became a true believer, the Lord brought certain scriptures to my mind to answer my questions exactly when I needed them. But He could not have brought those scriptures to my mind if I had not first memorized scripture verses and knew them by heart."

"Sometimes I do things without thinking," she confessed.

"We all struggle with that. But when I go on and do something without praying about it first, I am in a sense making the Lord sit in the seat beside me while I hold the reins of my life. The Lord wants to be involved in our decision-making, but He is also a gentleman. When I take the reins He steps back and let's me take over, often with disastrous results.

"God loves every person in the world, Rachel, and He showed His love for us by sending His only begotten son, Jesus, to pay for our sins—to take the punishment we deserved. In return, we must show our love for the Lord by keeping His commandments by faith. Jesus said, 'If you love me, keep my commandments.'"

"Faith," Rachel said. "Christians talk a lot about faith in the Reformed Church, but what does it mean?"

"Unfortunately, few pastors and others bother to explain the meaning of true faith. To me, faith means believing that the Bible is absolutely true, every word of it, without any proof that it is true. When someone believes something without proof, we call that faith."

"I still do not understand," she said.

"While they were still living in Egypt, God told the Children of Israel to take a lamb without blemish, kill it, and eat every single bite of it. All that wasn't eaten was to be burned. They were also told to take the blood of that lamb and smear it above the doorway of their homes so the Angel of Death would pass over, and nobody inside would die."

Rachel shook her head. "In my opinion, eating parts of the meat they disliked and smearing blood over a doorway were strange things for God to tell them to do."

Pierre nodded. "It must have seemed strange to the Children of Israel as well, yet they did as God commanded because the Lord told them to do it, and for no other reason. They did it by faith. Today, we know that this lamb was a foreshadowing of what was to come—the Lord Jesus Christ—the Jewish Messiah. The Children of Israel might not have known that. They simply did what God told them to do by faith alone, in the knowledge that God knows best, and not because they understood the why of it."

"Are you saying that the lamb and the blood were symbols?" she asked.

"Exactly. Not only is Jesus the perfect Lamb of God slain from the foundation of the world and sacrificed to pay for our sins, Jesus is also the Word of God that was made flesh and dwelled among us. The Children of Israel were told to eat the entire lamb, even the liver and other parts of the meat they might not like. The Word of God can only be found in the Holy Bible, and like the lamb, we must eat all of the Bible—read every single word of it—even those parts of the Bible that might not seem interesting to us. By faith we know that though we might not understand why we should read every single word of the Bible, we know that we must. God said reading it all was for our good, and He cannot lie." Pierre smiled at Rachel and glanced down at the Bible on his lap. "Now, thanks to God's gift to me through the earl, I have a Bible of my own."

Rachel wanted to hear more, but Lord Wilburn opened the carriage door.

"We shall talk later," Pierre whispered as the earl climbed in and took his seat across from them.

They arrived at the earl's estate in mid-afternoon. Rachel knew Lord Wilburn to be a man of wealth and had expected a mansion.

She never dreamed it would be so enormous. Surrounded by well tended gardens, the three story stone structure looked big enough to hold twenty bedrooms or more. Yet the earl had hinted in the carriage that some in his social class looked down on him for being Jewish despite his lofty position in life.

As soon as the carriage stopped, his entire household came out and formed two lines in front of his mansion. The earl appeared to know each one and called them by name.

He whispered something to a maidservant with a plump body and a round full-cheeked face. The maid motioned for Rachel and Pierre to follow her.

"Sally is me name. Come." Sally led them up the stairs. "And I will be taking ya to your rooms, I will. Lord Wilburn wants me to take the Madame to his wife's room so she can choose clothes for herself." She turned her attention to Pierre. "But first, he wishes to give you clothes that belong to his son. Willy, his only son, is away on a long journey abroad and will not come again for many days."

They had reached the top of the stairs.

"What will Willy say when he returns and finds some of his belongings missing?" Pierre asked.

"The young gentleman is a Christian like his father, sir," Sally said, "and if you knew him, you would know that he will be pleased to learn that he filled a need in your life."

"He sounds like a very caring young man," Pierre said.

"He is, sir. He truly is. Now, follow me, and I will show you the rooms where these garments are stored."

Rachel watched as Pierre chose a white shirt, a pale blue neck cloth, a fine blue jacket and matching trousers.

"You go with Sally, Rachel," Pierre said. "I will change clothes here in Willy's room."

Rachel followed Sally a few doors down to the late Lady Wilburn's room.

"The room is just as me mistress left it." Sally pointed to a painting above the marble fireplace of a lady with long black hair. "This was me mistress."

"She was very beautiful."

"That she was; inside and out." Sally directed Rachel to a door by the big bed. "Follow me to the dressing room, Madame."

Hooks had been nailed to three of the walls, and expensive-looking dresses hung from them. The other wall contained three dressers with mirrors above each one and shelves as high as the ceiling. Boxes of all sizes had been neatly stacked on the shelves.

A yellow dress trimmed in white lace caught Rachel's eye.

Sally smiled. "You like the yellow one, do ya?"

"Yes, it is lovely."

After changing into the garments the earl had given them, Rachel and Pierre met Sally in the hallway outside and followed her to their suite of rooms.

"This is where you are to sleep." Sally opened a heavy oak door. "I will be leaving you now, but if you need anything pull the cord by the door." She pointed to a gold cord hanging from the ceiling. "And I will come back."

"We will wear these fine garments when we go down to dine with the earl tonight," Pierre said.

"I agree," Rachel concured. "But I think we should leave them behind when we leave in the morning."

"I disagree," Pierre replied. "We must bundle them up and take them with us. Otherwise, the earl might think we did not appreciate his kindness."

With Pierre beside her, Rachel went downstairs that night for supper with the earl, wearing the yellow dress. The huge rectangular table had been designed to seat twenty-two people. She felt like a queen as she sat down to Lord Wilburn's right. Pierre sat to his left.

"I have business in the village in the morning quite early," the earl explained. "And I must leave you for a few hours. While I am gone, please feel free to explore my gardens, visit my library or do whatever you wish."

"You are very kind," Pierre said.

Rachel felt guilty, hiding the fact that they planned to leave the earl's estate as soon as he left for the village the next morning. However, since Pierre didn't think they should tell him of their intentions, she would say nothing.

The earl had already left by the time Rachel and Pierre ate their first meal the next morning. Rachel went into the library and placed the letter on the earl's desk.

She and Pierre left the estate by a back door and hiked north. She'd packed the food left over from their morning meal to eat at lunchtime, and Pierre carried a canvas sack with the clothes the earl gave them folded inside.

❦

Jean Vallae and his men stood at a distance gazing at the earl's estate and holding the reins of their horses. He saw Rachel and Pierre leave by a back door.

"You said you would not arrest these people while they were in the company of the earl," the monk said, "but now they are out in the open. Is this not the time to catch them unaware?"

"I heard whispers in the town where the Jewish woman, Magdalena Poyer, lived," Jean Vallae replied. "Some there said that the woman had many Jewish friends in England. The man that the earl and his party visited yesterday was one of them. Perhaps there are others.

"We can capture these two at any time, Brother Julian. They are outnumbered and helpless. But if we follow them long enough, I am sure they will lead us to yet another nest of Jews and Huguenots. Why catch two ants when you can catch the entire hill and perhaps the queen as well?"

"Well said," the monk replied. "Your wisdom is beyond my comprehension, and you are always right."

Jean laughed softly. "Let us hope that I am right again. Now, get back on your horses and go forth. We must follow these two ants until we find the entire hill."

He hoped his feigned optimism would placate his hirelings for the rest of the morning.

He spotted another man following Rachel and her husband soon after they left the earl's mansion. The stranger trailing the couple appeared fearless in his pursuit of them—or him—Jean wasn't sure which.

❧

At noon, Rachel found a pond surrounded by trees that seemed like a perfect spot for a meal. "Shall we stop for our picnic now, husband?" she asked.

He grinned. "Are you sure you want to go on a picnic with me, wife?"

"But of course."

She knew he referred to the day she turned down his offer of a meal in the woods. However, there had not been a bit of bitterness in his tone and there would be none in hers either.

"I think sharing a picnic lunch with you would be delightful." Rachel knelt down under one of the trees and placed their parcel of food on the grass.

Pierre sat down beside her. "Then by all means, let us begin."

They ate a meal of bread, cheese, fish, and sweet cakes leftover from their breakfast at the earl's estate.

Pierre looked off toward the pond. "There is something I wish to discuss with you."

She swallowed a mouthful of bread. "Please, tell me what it is."

He paused. "As Christians, we are expected to be truthful at all times, and I know that you are Jewish, Rachel. I have known since before we left France. It is time for us to be honest with one another."

"Why did you not tell me this sooner?"

"I had hoped you would tell me."

"I wanted to tell you, but I was afraid—afraid you might turn your back on me once you knew."

"Never."

"Many have turned against my people once they discovered we were Jewish," she said. "Who told you I was a Jew, Father La Faye?"

"No, I saw the soldiers plunder the belongings they found in your house before they burned it to the ground. In a trunk, they found a special candle holder that could only belong to a Jew."

She gasped. "The Menorah."

"Is that what it is called?" he asked.

"Yes."

"I want you to know, Rachel, that I am honored to be the husband of one of God's Chosen people. Who can say but that my ancestors were Jews as well?"

"Oh, Pierre, you have lifted a weight from my heart. But if you knew I was a Jew, the captain must know, too."

"He might not have known when he came to the Sanctuary and saw you for the first time. But I feel sure that he must know by now."

"We might be in more danger than I first thought," Rachel said.

After they finished eating, they pushed on toward the north of England. However, as they walked along, Pierre kept looking back.

"Do you think someone is following us?" Rachel asked.

"No. I have not noticed anyone since we ate our noon meal."

"Did you see someone at noon?"

"Maybe."

Twenty-two

"What did you see as we broke the fast" Rachel asked.

"Shadows." Pierre's forehead wrinkled. "It was probably nothing to worry about."

Rachel paused, waiting for him to say more. He must have seen the captain or his men and wasn't telling her. Would he ever learn to trust her?

She thought about it. Rachel hadn't trusted Pierre either, and the Bible said a wife should obey her husband and the Lord. To obey without understanding took what the Bible called faith.

❧

Jean and his men watched Rachel and Pierre from the shadow of the trees, but he noticed movement in the distance; a flash of gray. Without a word to his men, he crept through the trees. A twig snapped behind him, and he knew his men were following him.

A man wearing some sort of gray uniform and a soldier's hat with a red plume had been following Rachel and her husband just as he had. Jean couldn't identify the uniform but he didn't think it looked like those worn by soldiers in the English military.

Jean and his men outnumbered the lone soldier. Despite the sword attached to his black belt, Jean and his men could overtake him easily. Yet if they kept their distance, perhaps the stranger would lead them to yet another ant hill—or several.

⁂

Rachel appreciated having spent two nights indoors, but another day of walking would not be easy. However, each step brought them closer to Scotland and the town of Luss where Pierre's mother and Henri waited. She tried to think on that as she trudged along.

Two days later around noon on the outskirts of a small English village, they found a lake in the middle of a wooded area. As they continued on down the road, Rachel saw a house in the distance.

"Look." She pointed toward it. "A thatch-roofed cottage."

"With a well nearby."

"Oh Pierre, it is lovely."

"The house is in need of repair, Rachel."

Pierre sniffed the air. "Something smells bad around here, and it could be a dead animal. But I think I will go over and have a look to make sure it is not the well. Then I will go and see if those inside the house will let us have water and if we can stay the night for a small fee."

"I will wait here," Rachel said.

He laughed. "I cannot blame you. The odor is exceedingly vile."

Rachel studied the house. All but one of the rickety gray shutters had been nailed shut. However, the one with the paint peeling off it hung loose, flapping back and forth in a soft breeze—banging against the rock wall again and again.

Pierre returned a few moments later. "The well is sour. We should be on our way."

"Can we not talk to those in the house first?" she asked. "Perhaps they have a good well that we cannot see behind the house."

"Very well," he said with a hint of exasperation in his tone. "We will call on those living in the house." Pierre moved ahead of her and knocked on the door. "Hello." He peered through the window by the door, the one with the broken shutter. "Is anybody home?"

When nobody replied or answered his knock, Rachel said, "The house looks deserted. Should we go inside?"

Pierre shrugged. "Perhaps we could." He touched an old board that had been nailed over the window next to the one with the broken shutter. "I doubt anyone has lived here for a long time, so I suppose it would be all right to go in and look around. Even if the house is vacant, we cannot spend time here without water. Later I will go out to see if I can find another well. I would like for you to stay in the house while I am gone."

"Why?"

"It is just a precaution." He lifted the latch and opened the door.

Rachel followed him inside.

The one-room cottage had two beds. The larger one had a small table by it. She also saw two chairs, a table for eating meals, and a cupboard near the fireplace.

"Can we stay here for a few days, Pierre? I am weary. I need rest before we continue our journey. I have not slept all night since we left Lord Wilburn's estate. If there is no well, we can always get water from that lake we saw near the village. The constant traveling has made me long for a home of our own, and I dream of sleeping in the same bed every night."

She became aware of Pierre, looking at her with a tender expression on his face.

He came and stood beside her. When he put his arm around her shoulder, she didn't move away.

"You really like it here, do you?"

"Oh, yes."

"In Scotland, we will have a house as good as or better than this one. In fact, I have already been thinking about a name for our future home. I shall call it Secret Place or Safe House because from now on, I want you always to be safe, Rachel."

She glazed up at him and felt something; a kind of warming that began at the top of her head and shot all the way to her toes. His face moved closer, and his eyes closed. His lips looked so soft she wanted to touch them with her own.

"I want to kiss you," he said, "and as your husband, I have the right. But I promised I would wait until you are ready. Are you, Rachel? Are you ready to truly be my wife in all ways?"

She wanted him to kiss her but felt unprepared for what might come afterward. Didn't he know that she had always feared the unknown?

Instead of gazing up at him, she focused her attention on several buckets stacked in one corner of the room. Her glance drifted to the broken window.

"It has started to rain," she said, hoping to change the direction her thoughts, and probably his, had been taking them. "It could be that we will not have to walk all the way back to that lake for water after all. We might be able to catch enough rainwater in the buckets to supply all our needs. There could be another lake around here we have yet to find."

"A man has many needs, Rachel, and not all of them have to do with bread and water."

Pierre gazed at her a moment longer. He felt as if he'd been stabbed by a sharp object. "And you are right, it does look like rain." He gathered up the buckets, one in each hand, and sent her a distant glance. He headed for the door. "I will set the buckets outside as you suggested, or should I say, ordered?"

Pierre," she said slowly. "I have hurt you, but I did not mean to. Please wait."

He went out and kicked the door shut behind him. His jaws hardened and so did his heart.

The rain had stopped but raindrops dripped off the roof. Soggy hay fell in small clumps on the wet ground.

Pierre arranged the buckets near the door and stood there a moment longer, surveying a dark sky. At last he looked through the nearest window.

Rachel sat at the foot of the bed. He thought she might be crying but couldn't be sure.

He walked around to the back of the house to search for another well but didn't see one. He strode all the way to the fence at the back of the cottage and peered into the woods beyond—

nothing. He doubted a well would have been dug that far from the house but had to make sure. His mother had always insisted that wells and tubs for collecting rainwater should be installed close to the dwelling so the lady of the house wouldn't have to walk so far. Would Rachel ever become the lady of his house?

Grimacing, he kicked an exposed rock. It sailed through the air and landed near an Elm tree much like the Elms in front of his family home in Benoit.

Pierre went around to the front of the house on the opposite side. He saw a shed he hadn't noticed before and started toward it.

He'd almost reached the shed when the rain came again. He raced inside and shut the door, intending to stay there until the heavy shower stopped.

Pierre tried not to look at Rachel as he made his way through the front door of the cottage. A trail of mud-clods tracked his path. He put the canvas sack he found on the table and removed the bow from his shoulder.

"I found this bow and some arrows in a shed outside. They were dirty, but I washed them off in the lake." He tossed the bow on a chair. "I put the arrows in the sack. I also found some potatoes in the garden next to the shed. Most of the potatoes were ruined, but these four look all right." He removed the vegetables from the sack and dropped them on the cot. "I thought we could use them."

Rachel swept across the room and scooped up the potatoes in a white apron.

"Where did the apron come from?" he asked.

"I found it here in the cottage." She dusted off the potatoes with her apron and lined them up on the table by the sack.

Even engaged in such a minor action as gathering potatoes, she'd glowed with a kind of winsome poise and grace seldom seen in a woman of any age. Pierre couldn't deny her beauty or his love for her. If only she loved him.

For too long Pierre had tried to impress Rachel by holding in his anger and exasperation with tender looks and encouraging words. He couldn't anymore. He should have known his true feelings would surface eventually. A man couldn't contain such strong emotions forever. He saw himself, maybe for the first time, and he didn't like what he found—that he was jealous of his late brother.

Now, he'd finally admitted it.

He still loved God and would always serve Him but in honesty and truth, not hiding behind a mask. He wanted to repent, but now might not be the best time. He needed to let the heat of his anger cool down first.

Rachel draped a blanket around her shoulders.

She must be cold.

Without another word, he moved across the room and made a fire in the fireplace. Rachel opened the cupboard and began banging things around in there.

"What are you doing?" he asked.

"Looking for something to cook the potatoes in."

"Cook them if you like. I am not hungry."

She stopped and studied him for a long moment. "Since the rain has stopped, why not take a walk in the woods behind the cottage? I know it is still wet out, but I would enjoy it if you would. And I should like to look around."

She cared nothing for him. Why did she suddenly appear so accommodating?

"All right," he said, "that sounds like a pleasant way to spend the afternoon."

As they hiked through the woods behind the cottage, Pierre put his hands in his pockets to keep from reaching out and taking her hand. The cooler air had added a touch of pink to her cheeks, and her green eyes sparkled.

Wet leaves had fallen to the ground. Some stuck to the hem of his trousers. And their shoes were caked with mud and leaves in shades of yellow and rusty brown.

Her emerald eyes had never seemed more appealing, and he found himself wondering if her lips tasted as good as they looked. He smiled, but before he reached out to take her in his arms, she turned her back to him.

"What is wrong, Rachel?"

"Nothing."

She still wouldn't look at him.

"Are you thinking about my brother at this moment? Perhaps wishing you were with him." His smile faded. "You were dreaming of Louis," His eyes narrowed. "comparing me to him."

"No, that is not true. " She whirled around to face him. "I was thinking about how much my parents would have loved a quiet place like this. And that reminded me of that day in Beniot when they died. That is what I was thinking."

He didn't believe her.

"I can never hope to measure up, can I?" he said.

Pierre crossed his arms over his chest, and the muscles in his face tightened as if all his gentleness had been squeezed out of him. He felt that he didn't have anything left to give.

He glared at her. "I thought our marriage had started to change for the good. I was wrong. I will not make such a hopeless assumption again." He turned and headed back to the house.

"Where are you going?" she asked.

"To get the bow and arrows I found. I plan to go hunting. And if I am fortunate, I will kill a deer or a bird. It could take all day. I might not return until the morrow."

"Stay with me, Pierre. Please. We need to talk."

He went inside the cottage and grabbed the bow and the sack with the arrows. "Good-bye, Rachel."

"Please stay."

Pierre stomped out the door and around to the back of the house. He heard Rachel coming up behind him, but he didn't turn or speak to her. Throwing his bow and the sack of arrows over the wooden fence, he climbed over and headed for the woods.

❦

Jean Vallae gritted his teeth. His hirelings were drifting further and further away from him. Now that he had finally found Rachel's trail, they didn't want to follow through. Samuel and Zeb constantly discussed how much they missed France. The monk had also lost interest in the search and had been talking about purchasing an inn in England.

"French chefs are always in demand," the monk had said, "and as the former cook at the Sanctuary, I think I will be successful."

Samuel and Zeb lay in the shade of a tree, too drunk to be of any help to him. He would need the monk to stay behind to keep the younger two from running away. Otherwise, he and Brother Julian would have to spend valuable time looking for them.

Jean mounted his horse. "I am going to see if Rachel and her husband are where we think they are. If I have not returned by nightfall, come after me."

The two young men looked as if they hadn't heard a word he said.

"I will try to keep the young ones in line while you are gone," the monk said. "And if you fail to return by nightfall, we will go and search for you."

"Then I am off."

Jean dug his stirrups into the animal's sides. The horse moved into a comfortable gallop. Being away from his hirelings lifted his spirits. Or could it be that the excitement he felt came from knowing he would see Rachel again, if only from a distance?

⚘

Rachel had never felt more alone. If only Pierre had turned around and come back to the cabin.

I have lost everything.

She knew she needed to repent of all her sins and tell God she would obey His commands. Pierre had said that when he prayed, the Lord answered.

I want what Pierre has. If God is real, I want Him in my life, now.

Rachel got down on her knees and repented of all her sins, pouring out her heart to the Lord. When she lifted her head, she knew her prayer for salvation had been answered. Rachel moved to the bed and sat down, praying there for a long time.

Later, she peered through a crack in the wooden slats that covered the windows at the side of the house, hoping to see Pierre walking up. All she saw was the well and the woods beyond it. The rock well looked as sturdy and full of purpose as it ever had. Like her life, the water inside it probably tasted as bitter and rotten as it smelled.

Rachel sat down on the bed again. In the dim light coming in from the partly covered windows, she gazed at the potatoes. She never did cook them, and a good wife would prepare a meal in case her husband was hungry when he came home. She grabbed a potato and put it on her lap. She had a small knife that she found in the pocket of the white apron. Rachel reached down to retrieve it from her pocket in order to peel the potatoes. She heard a knock at the door.

Pierre.

Rachel smiled. He must have had a change of heart and decided to return. She stood, and the potato fell on the floor and rolled around. She hurried to the door and stopped—her hand cupped around the door handle.

They hadn't been keeping the door locked. Why would Pierre knock? Why hadn't he simply opened the door and come right in? Strange—she hesitated a moment longer and opened the door.

Stunned, she froze as Captain Vallae stepped inside. His mocking smile sent shivers through her.

"What do you want here?" she demanded.

"You."

Twenty-three

"No," Rachel exclaimed.

"Oh, yes." Captain Vallae chuckled. "You are afraid, are you not?"

Her lips quivered. Nevertheless, she lifted her head. "I am not afraid."

"Yes, you are. And that is good. I like the way you look at me when you are afraid." He sent her a mocking smile. "My men and I been following close behind you and your husband, Pierre, for days," he said. "But who is the other rider, the man who has also been trailing you?"

"I have no idea what you are talking about."

"I think you know." He moved toward her. "But it matters not." His taunting grin reminded her of the boy who spat on her when she was a child. He took another step.

She stepped back. "I am married, Monsieur."

He laughed. "So am I."

The captain studied her in an unseemly way. Rachel crossed her arms over her chest as if that simple act would stop him from staring.

"Once," he said, "I thought you were a nun. Now I know what you really are—a dirty little Jew. And I plan to have you before I kill you."

"No." She took another step back. "You will not get away with this. Pierre will be returning soon, and he will rescue me."

"That is unlikely. My men are searching for him now, and they will find him before he gets here."

Rachel made a dash for the open door. The captain grabbed her arm, yanking her back.

"Let me go!"

He whirled her around to face him, gripping both her hands. Her pulse raced.

The knife.

With the knife, she had a chance; maybe only one, but still a chance.

He threw her against the wall. Rachel struggled to recover. She slid a hand into the pocket of her apron and gripped the knife.

The captain reached for her. Rachel lunged at him, plunging the knife into his shoulder with all her strength. Blood oozed from the wound, staining the sleeve of his blue shirt.

He swore, covering the wound with one hand.

Rachel quickly moved around him and ran outside. Racing toward the well and the woods beyond it, she heard the captain coming up behind her. She swerved, barely missing a rock that stuck out from the edge of the well at an odd angle. Its jagged edge caught the hem of her dress. She heard a rip.

The captain had almost reached her. She moved in front of the rock, covering it with her body.

He lunged for her.

She darted out of the way.

He tripped on the crooked rock and fell. His injured shoulder hit the rock railing that circled the well. He moaned, holding his shoulder. Jean reached out with his other hand as if searching for something to hold onto. He lost his balance and tumbled into the well.

Shocked, Rachel leaned forward and peered down into the shallow water. The captain lay at the bottom of the well and didn't appear to be moving. He could already be dead.

She sat frozen on the narrow rim of the rock well, gazing down into it. The captain moved one hand. After a moment, he tried to sit up and screamed.

She peered down at him. *So, he is alive.*

The captain looked up.

"Can you not see that I have broken my leg?" he shouted. "Are you going to sit there and leave me here to die?"

At barely one hundred pounds, Rachel didn't have the strength to pull the captain from the well even if she wanted to. And would saving his life be best for anyone?

The stench coming up from the bottom of the well nauseated her. She pinched her nose to lessen the odor. A thought came to her.

She could leave him down there to die and have her revenge at last.

In such a remote area, nobody would find him; except, perhaps, his men. If she walked away now, she doubted even Pierre would know Jean Vallae had ever been there.

Rachel knew that if she and Pierre rescued the captain and gave him aid, he would come after them as soon as his leg mended. If she left him in the well, his quest to destroy her would end and she would find peace.

All at once, Pierre's urgent warning pushed away all other thoughts, and she recalled that at the time he issued it, they were tromping down one of England's muddiest roads.

Pierre had been a few steps ahead of her. He stopped and turned in her direction. He'd smiled as he motioned for her to hurry and catch up with him, but his smile had slowly disappeared.

"Rachel, are you dwelling on revenge for what Captain Vallae has done to you?"

Stunned, she'd wondered how he had guessed her thoughts. How had he known that she'd been thinking about how much she hated Captain Vallae? Perhaps she'd had a hard expression on her face that he noticed.

Regardless, she remembered feeling slightly embarrassed that he had the ability to sense her thoughts. She'd considered denying his conclusions but then thought better of it.

"So what if I am thinking about revenge?" she'd finally said. "The captain is a beast."

Pierre had nodded. "That is true, and I understand why you

feel as you do. My brother and I were always close, and I have been fighting bitterness because of what the captain did to him." He hesitated. "Nevertheless, the Lord expects us to forgive our enemies."

"Forgive Captain Vallae?" She shook her head. "Never! You asked too much of me, Pierre."

"But you must forgive, Rachel. The Bible says so."

"And if I refuse?" she asked.

"The Lord said in the Bible that if we forgive others, God will forgive us," Pierre said. "But if we refuse to forgive others, the Lord will not forgive us of our sins." He shook his head. "Some will spend all eternity in hell because they were unwilling to repent and forgive others as the Bible says to do."

"How do you know all this?" she asked.

"The Bible says that Saint Stephen forgave those who were stoning him to death, and Jesus forgave those who were crucifying Him. While hanging on the cross Jesus said, 'Forgive them, Father, for they know not what they do. The scriptures indicate that we should do the same."

At the time, she'd brushed his words from her mind. How could God expect her to forgive a murderer?

Now, things were different. Rachel was different.

She'd changed since her hasty wedding to Pierre. She had learned God's ways. She thought of herself as a Christian in the true sense now, and hoped to remember everything Pierre had ever told her about the Lord.

She tried to picture the captain at the bottom of the well, but she couldn't erase thoughts of Louis and her parents, dying at the captain's hand. Clearly, she'd reached her moment of decision. What should she do? What would she do?

Curses echoed from the bottom of the well, angry words against Jews and Huguenots. Rachel could almost feel the hatred.

As a Christian, she now knew that she could not refuse the captain's cries for help no matter what he might have done in the past. Christians loved their enemies, forgave, showed mercy, and turned the other cheek.

Rustling sounds coming from behind her mingled with

Captain Vallae's curses and shouts. Rachel tensed. Someone approached. It could be the captain's men.

She sent up a quick prayer and turned around. If captured, she would face her accusers and look them in the eyes.

Pierre ran toward her. "Rachel, what is wrong? And what are those sounds I hear?"

She got up and ran into his arms. "Oh, Pierre, I prayed you would come. And now you have."

He held her close. "I should never have left you alone like I did."

"Help!"

Pierre flinched. "What was that?"

"Captain Vallae. He is down in the well."

"Then we must help him."

"How?"

Pierre moved to the well and looked down into it. "He looks hurt."

"He is. A broken leg, I think."

Pierre sat down on the rim of the well. "Let me think what is to be done." He turned to the side and gazed down into the well again.

"Help me!" the Captain shouted with a curse. "Your wife will not. Without your help, I shall surely die."

She told him all that happened after he went out to find food.

When she'd finished, he said, "Oh, my poor darling." He took her in his arms and held her.

"What about me?" Jean Vallae shouted from the bottom of the well. "I am in pain and it is all Rachel's fault that I am in this condition."

Rachel glanced downward. The captain sat at the well's bottom with his back against the rock wall and his legs spread out in front of him, and he appeared to be rubbing his right leg. She couldn't see his shoulder but pictured the small cut the knife had made.

She shuddered and looked away. "Have you seen a rope since we arrived at this farm?" she asked.

"No. I have not." He glanced at his surroundings and shook his head. "If we gathered bedclothes from inside the house and tied them together, I doubt we would be able to pull him out. There is nothing to anchor a rope to. The shed and the trunk of the nearest tree are much too far away."

A string of curses burst forth from the captain's angry mouth and heart. But neither Rachel nor Pierre spoke for a moment.

Rachel kept wondering how Louis and her parents must have felt as they lay dying. She hoped the captain wondered the same thing as he waited in pain at the bottom of the well.

"Save me," Captain Vallae pleaded. "Please." She heard what sounded like a sob. "Have mercy. I am begging you."

"Did you show mercy when you killed Louis Dupre and my parents and burned down our house?"

"Help me!"

She thought he sounded desperate.

"I am in pain now from my leg," he exclaimed. "My shoulder hurts, too. If I die down here, my blood will be on your hands."

"We should pray, Rachel," Pierre said.

"Yes."

"No," Jean exclaimed. "Do not pray for me. Save me!"

"Your Salvation is exactly what we are hoping for," Pierre shouted back.

Holding hands, they sat side by side on the edge of the well and prayed to God the Father for guidance in the Name of Jesus.

The thought of revenge no longer gave her pleasure. For a while she hadn't known what to do. Now that they had prayed, the answer came.

Rachel got up and stood by the well. "We are leaving now, Captain Vallae. But we will not leave you here to die. We will send someone from the village back for you. Someone who will pull you out of the well, care for your wounds and nurse you back to health until your men come for you." Rachel looked down into the well. "So this is goodbye, Captain. May God save you as He saved us."

"Help me!" the captain shouted. "Have mercy."

Mercy?

The muscles in her throat tightened. She tried to swallow, but for a moment, she couldn't.

"Are you ready?" Pierre asked.

"Yes."

Rachel heard the captain's cries for mercy and his curses from the well.

"We must hurry, Rachel, and go. The captain needs help, and his men could be here at any moment." Pierre stopped and smiled down at her. "And I am very proud of you."

"I am proud of you, too, Pierre."

And I will love you forever.

❧

Instead of going north as they had planned, they took the road back to the village. At an inn there, the innkeeper told them about an Englishman who cared for the sick.

"We call him the Bleeder." The innkeeper motioned toward the road ahead. "He lives on the road to London in a small white house with brown shutters."

Rachel and Pierre thanked the innkeeper and hurried down the road in search of the man he mentioned.

"There it is," Rachel exclaimed breathlessly, "a white house with brown shutters."

A man stood in the garden in front of the house.

"Are you the one they call the Bleeder, who cares for the sick?" Pierre asked with a heavy accent.

"I am he." The man stuck out his ample chest as if hearing his title pleased him. "What can I do for you, Frenchman?"

"We are on our way out of town. But we could not leave without finding help for a man caught in a well. He needs your assistance at once. Bring a long rope. You will find him at a farm with a bad well, not far from here."

"Oh yes, I know the house you mean."

"If you will pull the man out of the well and care for his wounds, his friends will come along soon to pay you. But in any case, we will give you all we can." Pierre counted out five coins into the man's open palm. "Please tell him his help came from the Lord. And one more thing, the man has a broken leg, a shoulder wound, and he has lost blood. Do not bleed him as you do others under your care. I am not paying for that. Merely medicate his wounds, bind them, and tie a plank of wood to his broken leg. Then bring him to an inn here in the village so he can rest. Others will find him there."

The man smiled. "I promise to do all that you asked of me."

Pierre took Rachel's arm and the two of them started down the road to London.

"Where did you get that money?" Rachel asked.

"From the priest back at the Sanctuary."

"I thought you spent the last of that some time ago."

"I saved back a little, for such a time as this."

Rachel gazed at the dying grass and trees just ahead. Fall had robbed the trees of most of their leaves, but the foliage that still remained colored the horizon in shades of yellow, gold, and rusty brown.

"Why are we traveling down this road?" she asked. "We need to go north if we expect to reach Scotland."

"You are correct, my love. We need to circle around and go north, and so we shall. When the captain's men arrive, the Bleeder might be forced to tell what he knows about us. All he can tell them is that we took the road that led to London."

"How clever you are, Pierre. Now the captain will look for us in London. Do you think his men will catch up with us?"

"Perhaps." He grabbed her hand. "We have no time to waste."

⚬❧⚬

With his legs stretched out in from of him, Jean Vallae had leaned against the rock wall for at least half an hour yelling, screaming, and sobbing. He rubbed his sore throat.

His vocal cords felt as if they had been pushed to the limit. The bleeding had stopped, but he'd lost blood. He thought his leg was broken and his body ached from all the wounds and bruises.

He was going to die of starvation and thirst at the bottom of the well, and it was all Rachel's fault. He would strangle her if he could.

She and her husband had promised to send help, but who could trust a Jew and a Huguenot? He was already as good as dead.

In agony, he looked up, hoping. He saw a blue sky and a few clouds.

He thought he heard something and strained to listen. It sounded like voices.

"Help!" he shouted. "Help me!"

He waited, but nobody came.

Did he have the strength to call out again? The voices sounded further away now. He yelled as loud as he could. His voice echoed back to him.

I am growing weaker, and my throat hurts from all the yelling.

"I am thirsty," he heard his hireling, Samuel, say. "I think I will see if there is water in the well."

They came for me. A wave of hope encouraged him. *I will be saved.*

He opened his mouth to call out. No words came. "Help," he said barely above a whisper. "I am over here."

"That woman we met on the road said the water here is bad," he heard the monk say. "We will drink when we return to the village."

Jean tried to call out. His voice produced a choked whisper.

"Help!" Jean whispered. "I am here—in the well."

"The captain is not here," he heard the monk say. "But his horse is. Let us return to the village and take his horse with us. We can look again tomorrow."

"No." Jean held his throat, hoping to force his voice to respond. "Save me! I am in the well."

They hadn't heard him. The sounds he made had been barely audible.

I am doomed. He slumped back against the side of the well and closed his eyes.

❦

Rachel and Pierre reached another village early that evening and were about to go into an inn for supper. Rachel saw a man on a brown horse at the edge of the woods. He appeared to be watching them. She turned and opened her mouth to tell Pierre what she'd seen, but before she could speak, he grabbed her hand.

"Look away from him," Pierre said. "Pretend you have not seen him and follow me."

He led her into the inn. A long narrow room filled with tables and chairs ran from the front of the building all the way to the back of it, and she saw a stairway near the counter where the inn-keeper stood.

"Are you in need of a meal and a room for the night, sir?"

Pierre shook his head. "Not just yet. We would like to sit down at one of the back tables to rest before we eat again or sleep."

"Take a seat and rest, Frenchman. We can bring your food later."

Still holding Rachel's hand, he glanced out a window. "The rider is still there," he whispered. "See the door at the far end of the room?"

"Yes."

"Walk out the back door to the garden behind the inn as if nothing unusual is happening. As soon as we are outside, start running as fast as you can. Do you understand, Rachel?"

"Of course."

They raced through the trees and kept on running. Rachel's heart pounded against her ribs, and her breath came in pants.

She thought she heard the sound of horses' hooves and started to look back.

Pierre pulled her behind a clump of trees. He put his forefinger against his mouth, warning her not to speak.

Rachel held her breath as the rider in a gray uniform stopped his brown horse within inches of them. He glanced in their direction.

"He sees us!" she whispered. "I know he does."

The man turned and rode on.

"I have seen that man somewhere," Pierre said after the man

disappeared into the woods. "And he is not one of the captain's men. He looks nothing like the others."

"Who could he be?" Rachel asked.

"I cannot say."

"Pierre, Captain Vallae said that another man has also been following us. Does this mean we have two sets of enemies now instead of only one?"

Twenty-four

Jean must have fallen asleep. Voices woke him.

"The woman said that the man is at the bottom of the well," he heard a man say. "He might be too weak to catch hold of the rope. I am going down after him."

Jean looked up as a man started down a rope. He tried to talk but his words sounded muffled. He managed to utter a weak moan.

"I see him," the man said, "and he is alive."

The man dropped to the bottom of the well and stood beside him. "They call me the Bleeder. I am going to wrap this rope around you and under your arms. They will pull you up and out of the well. Do you understand, sir?"

Jean nodded. He didn't know much English, but he'd understood everything the man had said.

"You have a bad cut here." He pointed to the gash on his leg. "And your leg looks like it is broken. Do you hurt elsewhere?"

Jean hurt everywhere, but he wanted to get out of the well as soon as possible. He shook his head.

"Good."

The man wrapped the rope around his body. Jean clinched his jaws. The rope cut into his torso and the soft flesh under his arms. The pain would increase when they pulled him to the surface, but he would endure anything if it meant leaving this damp and smelly prison.

After a painful ride to the village in the back of a cart, the Bleeder took him to an inn and placed him in bed.

The Bleeder handed Jean a piece of wood. "Put this between your teeth. I am going to make your leg straight again. It will hurt."

Jean had hoped for a chance to rest before such a painful procedure, but he put the wood in his mouth as he had been told.

His leg burned like it had been branded with a hot iron. He saw only blackness.

The pain hadn't decreased much when he woke up.

The Bleeder stood by the bed, watching him. "I tied boards to your leg. It looks straight now. Refrain from walking until I tell you. I would bleed you now to get rid of the poisons, but the man and woman who paid me made me promise that I would not bleed you."

"They hate me," Jean insisted. "They want the poison to stay in my body until I die."

"If the man and woman wanted you to die why did they pay me to pull you out of the well and make your leg straight again? They could have left you at the bottom of the well. Who would know until your bones were found someday in the future?"

Could it be that Rachel and her husband wanted to do him a kindness, knowing that he killed those they loved? It seemed unlikely. He'd never known anyone that didn't want revenge for a wrong. If Rachel and her husband repaid good for evil, they must have a motive so cunning he had not yet discovered it.

"When the woman and the man left the village, what route did they take?" Jean asked.

"I saw them take the road that leads to London Town."

Jean smiled despite his pain. So, they have gone to London.

He had many friends in London. If his hirelings returned for him, his enemies should be easy enough to find.

"Three men who say they work for you are downstairs and wish to see you," the bleeder said. "Should I send them up now? Or tell them to wait until you are feeling better?"

"Send them up. I must talk to them at once."

❧

Rachel and Pierre spent the night in another barn on the road to Scotland, but this time, they got permission from the farmer. He supplied them with a lantern to use until they left.

"The farmer and his wife are so kind," Rachel said as they lay side by side on the hay. "I wonder if they might be Christian believers." She played with a piece of fresh straw, lacing it through her fingers, as she thought about the farmer and his wife. "They fed us a wonderful supper and would have let us spend the night in the house, if we had agreed to it."

"Many people are good and kind, Rachel, but Christians show that they are believers by their love; by treating others as they would like to be treated. The farmer and his wife certainly did that.

"I would have spent the night in the house, as they graciously offered, if they hadn't had so many children. But it was a small house. Someone might have had to give up a place to sleep if we had crowded in on them."

Rachel waved the bit of straw in front of her nose and took in its fresh country odor. "I have been thinking about Captain Vallae, and I am glad we helped him—returned good for evil as the Bible says. But he is a criminal, Pierre." She turned on her side in order to face him and let the piece of straw drop. "He killed Louis, my parents, and probably Magdalena Poyer. Who knows how many other innocent lives he has taken? I think we should report him to the authorities before he kills again; for his sake as well as for the protection of others."

"I have been thinking the same thing," Pierre said in the darkness. "If only we knew someone in authority here in England so we could report his deeds." He grew quiet for a moment. "The farmer might know such a person."

"Of course he would," Rachel agreed. "What a splendid idea."

"We will tell the authorities here all we know before moving on," Pierre said. "This should put a stop to the captain's evil doings."

The next morning they paid a visit to a local squire and gave him a report.

"Thank you for coming by and telling me about these men," the squire said as if he truly appreciated it. "I will write a letter to someone in authority in London this very day. I will also pay a visit to the Bleeder you mention to see what he can tell me."

"Thank you for your efforts, sir," Pierre replied. "And if you should hear something regarding this matter, please send me a post. At least for a while, we will be living in the home of my mother, Mrs. Dupre, in the village of Luss in Scotland."

"I shall send you a letter," the squire said. "You can be sure of it."

Rachel and Pierre snaked their way across northern England toward Scotland, eating and sleeping in inns, camping on the ground or staying in barns as they had done previously. Each day, Rachel found more to like about her husband.

Fall turned to winter. A cold wind whistled down from the north. Snow blanketed the ground under their feet, and Pierre bought heavy capes and warm shoes for each of them. The last of their money had evaporated. To get the money they needed, Rachel and Pierre worked as hired hands in villages along the way. Rachel cooked and cleaned for strangers, and Pierre built fences and chicken houses.

Enormous lakes dotted the Scottish countryside and white hills, sure to turn green come spring. Still, the village of Luss on Loch Loman seemed far, far away.

At last, they reached their destination.

They stood in front of a quaint little inn with icicles hanging from the eves. Rachel read the name of the establishment in big black letters over the door. The Lion Heart.

"I am tired, Pierre, and this looks like a fine inn. Might we stay here for the night and search for your relatives in the morning?"

"Perhaps we will stay here," he said, "but first, I wish to search for my mother and little brother. This village is not large. It should not take long to find them."

Pierre opened the heavy door and motioned for Rachel to go into the inn first. He stepped up to the main desk. A short round little man with green eyes and a reddish brown beard studied them from behind the counter.

"May I help you, sir?" the innkeeper said in English.

"I am looking for a widow with a boy. She is French, and her name is Madame Dupre."

"A French woman does live in the village, but I have never met her. Please wait and I will see what my cook knows."

The bearded man returned with a rounded young woman with rosy cheeks. "This is Mary, my cook," he said, "and she knows the woman you are looking for."

Pierre smiled. "You know Madame Dupre?"

"Sure and I do. We attend the same church."

"Are she and the boy well?" Pierre asked Mary.

"Oh, yes. Very much so."

"Can you tell us where they live, Madame?"

"Follow the road in front of the inn to the left toward the loch. At the first corner, you will see a small stone house with a dog out front. They live there—and beware of the dog."

"Thank you." Pierre smiled at the cook and offered the innkeeper his hand in friendship. "You have both been helpful."

As the two men shook hands, the innkeeper asked. "Will you and the lady be spending the night here at the inn?"

"We hope to stay with Madame Dupre, but if not, we will surely stay here in this pleasant place."

They hiked on toward the cottage. Glancing back, Rachel saw a dark figure pop into the Lion Heart Inn and out of sight. He could be one of the captain's men or the man in the gray suit.

"Someone is following us," Rachel whispered. "I saw him. What should we do?"

"Keep walking," Pierre said, "that is what we should do." He pointed his forefinger at a house. "Look. That must be where my mother lives."

Rachel had to run in order to catch up with him.

"Rachel, look. Henri is standing at the window." Pierre grabbed her hand. "Hurry, we are almost there."

A black and white dog of questionable parentage stood guard at the front door of the house on the corner. The animal's bark grew louder the closer they got.

Rachel slowed to a walk. The dog's lips curled upward, baring sharp teeth. He snarled at them.

"That dog looks dangerous," Rachel said.

"Nonsense. He just does not know us yet."

"But are you not afraid the dog will bite us?"

"That dog would never bite us. That is Benoit." Pierre smiled at the dog. "Benoit, come here boy."

The dog stopped barking and wagged his tail.

"How did you know the dog's name?"

"Because Henri told me a million times that when they arrived in Scotland, he would have a dog named Beniot."

Rachel glanced back one more time to see if anyone might be following them, but in the weak light of evening, she didn't see anyone. Pierre knocked at the door.

"Who is there?" a woman said with a French accent.

"Your son, Pierre, and my new wife, Rachel."

The door burst open. Pierre and his mother embraced. They hurried inside, and Rachel gave Pierre's mother a hug. Everyone talked at once. Rachel found it impossible to focus her mind on two or perhaps three conversations going on at the same time, but the love and warmth she found in that room made her want to stay there forever.

After a moment, Pierre drifted over to the window and looked out.

"Is something wrong?" his mother asked.

"Everything will be fine." He turned and smiled.

Rachel bit her bottom lip. *Pierre is hiding something from me and his mother.*

"So, Mama," Pierre said, "how have you and Henri been since last we saw you?"

"Well enough—and please sit down. But if you will excuse me, I have stew warming." The woman took two steps and stopped. She reached for a small stack of letters in the middle of the eating table by the lighted candle. "You have two letters here for you, Pierre. One arrived some time ago." She handed the letters to Pierre. "A man brought the other one to the house less than three hours ago. Someone must have known you were coming here."

Pierre had been smiling, but the smile faded. His dark eyebrows drew together. A wrinkle appeared on his forehead. "What did the man look like, Mama?"

"He wore dark clothes, gray I believe. The dog growled when he came up to the house. I would not have been surprised if Benoit had bitten him."

"The man—" Rachel realized that she was wringing her hands again. "The man we saw at the inn must have arrived before we did."

"Apparently." Pierre opened the seal on one of the letters. Then he sat down in a chair and began reading. "This letter is from the squire we met in England," Pierre said.

"You know a squire, my son?" his mother said.

"Yes, we do." Worry-lines creased Rachel's forehead as she shifted her weight from one leg to the other. "What does the letter say?"

Pierre squinted down at the sheet of white writing paper. "I have reported the criminals you mentioned to the proper authorities in London," Pierre read, "and I also visited with the Bleeder. He said that the man with the broken leg, Jean Vallae, and his men fled the village the day after Vallae was pulled from the well. The Bleeder warned Vallae not to leave his bed, but he insisted on leaving with his men and has not been seen since."

"Then we are still in danger," Rachel concluded.

"Perhaps not so much," Pierre replied. "Jean Vallae will find it difficult to track us here. Nobody but the earl and the squire knew our destination, and I doubt they would give a criminal that information."

"This all sounds very interesting," Pierre's mother said.

"So far, you only know a small portion of what we have encountered, Mama. Now I will read the other letter." He opened the seal and smiled. "This is from Lord Wilburn's groom, Jenkins. It seems the earl sent Jenkins to follow us in case we needed help during our travels.

"And the groom followed us here, arriving before us. It seems he heard us talking and knew our destination. Jenkins must have been the man we saw in the gray suit and riding the brown horse. He plans to stay at the Lion Heart Inn until the morrow, and he wants us to meet him there in the morning before he returns to the earl's estate."

"You have befriended an English earl, my son? I am impressed."

"The earl is not like other titled men we have known, Mama. Lord Wilburn is a Christian."

"What else does the letter say?" Rachel asked.

"You may read both letters for yourself later. However, Lord Wilburn sends his regards and apologies for Carson, his friend's butler. Apparently, Carson saw us as a threat to Sir Goldberg's safety. Now he knows the truth. Lord Wilburn hopes to see Sir Goldberg very soon and will give him our regards. He also said that after reading the letter we left, he understands why we departed without saying good-bye."

His mother shook her head. "You have made a good impression on the quality, Pierre. That should serve you well." She sniffed the air. "I smell the stew cooking. Please excuse me." She went out to the kitchen.

A few minutes later, his mother returned with a big bowl of stew. "Let us eat now. We can talk at the table."

They gathered around a long rectangular table in the main room, and Pierre led them in a prayer of thanksgiving. As they ate stew and dark bread, Pierre told his mother and brother all that had happened since last they met.

"Now," Pierre's mother said. "I shall tell you all that has happened to us since we left you on that beach in Beniot."

Henri rose from his chair and glanced toward the entry door. "Mama, may I go out and sit on the front stoop? I know all this, and I would like to play with my dog."

"You may go, but keep Beniot quiet. The neighbors complain when he barks."

"Yes, Mama."

Pierre's mother turned to her son and smiled. "Now, I will tell you about what has happened to us since last we met. But I promise it will not be as exciting as the things you told me about the adventures you and Rachel had."

The front door burst open. Henri and his dog rushed inside.

"Soldiers wearing French uniforms are coming this way." Henri's dark eyes filled with excitement. "I saw them just now from the front step."

Seeing the look of pure horror on Henri's face caused Rachel's heart to pound so loudly she expected it to jump out of her chest.

Slowly, Henri's facial expression melted into a smile flavored with mischief. And the boy started laughing.

"Henri," Pierre scolded. "Are you making jokes, again?"

The boy nodded and ran out the door with the dog at his heels.

Pierre laughed and raced after him. "I shall get you for this, little brother."

Relieved, Rachel went out the door with Pierre's mother right behind her. The two brothers tumbled and rolled around in the snow in front of the cottage. Rachel laughed out loud.

At last Henri, his mother, and the dog went back inside. Rachel turned to follow them.

"Wait, wife." Pierre took her arm and guided her down the street. "I think we should stay outdoors a bit longer and inspect the full moon when it comes up."

The sun had almost reached the horizon. Still, enough light remained to make it possible to see some of the houses as they strolled down the tree-lined street, especially the little white house two doors down. It had an Alsatian look about it that Rachel liked. And when she noted the green shutters with hearts carved on them, she knew she'd found the house of her dreams.

"I would like to have a house like that one someday," she said.

"You will."

"Do you really mean that?"

"Of course. Have I ever denied you anything you ever wanted?"

She kissed him on the mouth. "I love you, Pierre Dupre, and I know I always will."

"Oh, Rachel, I have loved you for so long. I dared to hope that one day you would love me." He smiled. "God put us together. I will always believe that." His smile fell away. "But there are things I must tell you." Pierre took her hand in his and gazed into her eyes. "I fell in love with you at first sight, Rachel, and I prayed that one day you would be my wife. But after I introduced you to my family, you fell in love with my brother, Louis."

He squeezed her hand. "I always loved Louis, but for a while, I was jealous of him for taking you from me. I tried hard to hide it, but bitterness set in.

"When Louis died and I found myself married to you, I felt guilty for my good fortune. Why was he dead while I was alive? Had I caused his death in thought, word, or deed?" He shut his eyes for an instant. "I should have died in that house with my brother instead of falling asleep like I did."

"You are a good man, Pierre, and you did all you could."

"All? How can I be sure?" He shook his head. "In the hope of making things right, I tried too hard to be a good husband to you. Never letting you see the real me until that day at the cottage when I walked away with a bow and those arrows. I told myself that I needed to go hunting; that I deserved to enjoy myself. But after not finding a single animal to shoot at, I started back to you. I almost waited too long."

"Oh, Pierre." She grabbed him around the waist, pressing her head against his chest. "You did not wait too long. I would have waited for you forever."

He wrapped his arms around her. "I am not perfect, Rachel, and I kept my thoughts and feelings hidden from you for a long time."

"I kept things from you as well."

He'd been looking at her mouth. She smiled because she was looking at his. Pierre planned to kiss her. This time, she wouldn't pull away.

Rachel reached out and touched a strand of his dark, wavy hair. Her fingers moved downward and brushed his forehead, the leathery texture of his cheek, his sculptured lips; so soft, so desirable.

"I once asked you, Rachel, to tell me when you were ready to be my wife in all ways." His voice choked with emotion. "Are you ready now?"

"Yes." Rachel shut her eyes. "Oh, yes."

His lips found hers.

The kiss deepened, and she put her arms around him. More kisses followed. Breathless, they finally pulled apart. Standing there in front of the house with green shutters, they looked at each other and held hands.

A bubble of joy and longing surrounded them, encased them. Rachel hesitated to speak—perhaps break the circle of love.

However, a good wife kept the conversation moving, didn't she? And she wanted to be a good wife. Maybe she could come up with something encouraging that wouldn't change the tone of their very emotional moment and would make Pierre smile.

"I know the location of the secret place of the Most High, now," she said.

He grinned. "Do you?"

"Yes. It is the Heart of God."

"You are correct." He reached over and kissed her forehead. "Even if Jean Vallae comes here and finds us, we will live in the secret place with our children and grandchildren for as long as we both shall live."

"Yes, Pierre, for as long as we both shall live."

Epilogue

One year later, Rachel took another journey with her husband, Pierre, this time for fun. The villagers of Luss had been telling them about the view from a particular hill in the highlands of Scotland, and Pierre wanted to see it in the spring when the flowers were in bloom.

He worked on a farm at the edge of town, and they had rented the house with green shutters near his mother's home. However, they hoped to buy a farm and a house of their own one day and planned to name their future home Secret Place.

Rachel looked down at the gold ring on her finger. Pierre had promised her a wedding ring, and now she had one. She also had a present for him. Perhaps the top of a high hill would be the perfect spot to tell Pierre about the gift so dear to her heart.

They climbed all the way to the top. Rachel stood beside Pierre, looking down. The spectacular view of mountains, rivers, valleys, and patches of green land made the climb worth it.

They stood amidst spring flowers of every type and color, and Rachel thought of all the things she had been forced to do since marrying Pierre Dupre. How could she forget running down beaches, hiding in a church, pretending to be a boy and a sailor on the high seas, going into water over her head, climbing out of windows and tromping through endless miles of mud and dirt? Theirs had never been a passive lifestyle.

"I know why you brought me here." She pointed to the ground below. "You expect me to jump down and land on my feet on that tiny stretch of land, do you not? From here, it looks to be about the size of an eating table. Or would you prefer that I dive into that small lake, head first?"

He grinned. "I have no doubt that you could do all those things, my love, and do them well; but perhaps not today."

She cupped her hand behind one ear. "Pierre, I think I hear hoof beats."

He laughed and gave her a quick kiss on the lips. "Rachel, you are the love of my life."

"And you are the love of mine."

He put his arm around her waist and pulled her closer to his side.

She put her head on his shoulder. "I have a gift for your birthday tomorrow, Pierre, but you cannot open it for another six months."

His dark eyes sparkled with joy and excitement. "Is the gift what I think it is?"

"Yes. The Lord is sending us a child."

"A child! Oh Rachel, my joy is complete."

He embraced her, and then he looked at her as if asking for permission to kiss her again.

She couldn't know where his thoughts had taken him, but perhaps he remembered a time when she refused his kisses and pushed him away. What a long time ago that seemed.

Rachel reached over and kissed him, long and hard, hoping to remove his last shred of doubt. She loved him and always would, and she wanted him to know it.

They sat down on the ground. Cradled in his arms, more kisses followed.

At last he said, "What shall we name our child if it is a boy?"

"Pierre. After you, of course. But could we call him Peter? The name Peter is written in the English Bible the earl gave you."

"I know." He smiled. "And Peter it will be."

"But what if our child is a girl?" Rachel said, "What should we name her? It is your time to choose, Pierre. What name would you like?"

He leaned back and stretched out on the ground with his hands behind his head, gazing up at a blue sky. "I have not thought of a name yet, but I will." He turned his head and smiled. "What a glorious life God has planned for us."

She nodded.

He sat up and put his arm around her shoulders. "Today we named one of our children up here on this hill, and I will never forget this moment."

"Nor will I."

"How many children would you like to have, Rachel?"

"As many as God sends us."

"Amen to that," he said and kissed her again. "Amen and amen."

THE END

Coming Soon

BOOK TWO IN THE
FAITH OF OUR FATHERS SERIES

Having overcome many obstacles to finally obtain the life they have always dreamed of, Rachel and Pierre can now live in peace in Scotland—or can they? What has become of the man, Jean Vallae, who has sworn to hunt them down until death; his or theirs? Will persecution continue to plague them in their quest for a peaceful life? What of their unborn children, the dream, and their fate?

Join Rachel and Pierre in Scotland as their adventures continue in the second novel in the Faith of Our Fathers Series by Molly Noble Bull.